HALF A PIG
AND OTHER
FRONTIER STORIES

HALF A PIG AND OTHER FRONTIER STORIES

MATTHEW P. MAYO

THORNDIKE PRESS
A part of Gale, a Cengage Company

Thorndike Press® Large Print Softcover Western.
The text of this Large Print edition is unabridged.
Other aspects of the book may vary from the original edition.
Set in 16 pt. Plantin.

LIBRARY OF CONGRESS CIP DATA ON FILE.
CATALOGUING IN PUBLICATION FOR THIS BOOK
IS AVAILABLE FROM THE LIBRARY OF CONGRESS.

ISBN-13: 978-1-4328-9810-6 (softcover alk. paper)

Published in 2024 by arrangement with Matthew P. Mayo.

Printed in the USA
1 2 3 4 5   28 27 26 25 24

To my parents, for sharing their West.
And to Jennifer, for riding the range
with me all these years.

Come on in, take a seat by the fire.
But before you get too comfortable, pass
me that jug.
Ah, good. Now, where was I? Oh, yes . . .

— Maple Jack

CONTENTS

INTRODUCTION

The pleasant task of assembling this collection of stories prompted me to consider how long I have been making up characters, tossing them in hot water, and then rescuing them (or not).

As a chatty child, I told stories long before I set thick pencil to wide-line paper. And when my mother hauled out her old green Royal Royalite portable typewriter, I was off to the races and over the moon.

That clacking space- and time-travel machine took me on lunar journeys and deep-sea dives, mountaineering treks and daring rescues by balloon. And though I encountered freakish space aliens, muscle-bound jungle men, and ocean-dwelling beasties, most often I found myself mixing it up with cowboys, Indians, and mountain men.

While exploring that frontier fringe, I had occasion to travel via wagon train, steam locomotive, and stagecoach, and I befriended beasts wild and fierce, including horse, cattle, bison, and grizzly bear. And all before bedtime.

These adventures were spurred on by an abiding fondness for Hollywood's version of the Great American West, passed to me and my brother by our parents, kids themselves during the heyday of television Westerns. That those shows tended at times to play fast and loose with historical accuracy mattered little to a coonskin cap–wearing backyard bandit such as myself. They were thrilling and I was willing.

It was on those dusty trails, deep in the wild and woolly West, that I developed a fondness for history. The more I learned, the more I wanted to know, and from all perspectives — those of the explorers, to be sure, but also the stories of those who were there first, then forced to flee the endless march of rapacious newcomers.

I needed to understand the grim realities of daily life on the frontier; the brutal, unforgiving might of high mountains and low deserts in all seasons; the indifference of "Nature, red in tooth and claw," and more, more, more.

There is nothing like firsthand, on-the-ground discovery, of walking in grooves gouged in rock by wagon wheels of emigrants westbound on the Oregon Trail. Or hiking in the Northern Rockies in grizzly country, or crouching in ancient cliff dwellings in New Mexico, or inching into long-abandoned mine shafts in Arizona, ears perked for rattlesnakes and cracking timbers.

These experiences color my writing and drive me to ensure I'm accurate. Does this mean there's no room in my stories for the fantastical and the weird? For close shaves and hearty guffaws? For leg pulling, chin scratching, and sidelong winks? Not on your life.

Some of the stories in this collection are set in recognizable geography at actual locations, some are of an invented place and time, yet still in and of the West. All of them share the open range of the mind, for that is where they originated.

Long ago I lost track of that green Royal time machine, but I still embark on daily expeditions. What follows are a few of the more memorable. Are you saddled and ready? Good, let's ride.

Oh, and keep an eye out for snakes and bears and bandits and such. . . .

— *Matthew P. Mayo*
Autumn 2021

JUST ONCE

It's no shadows
as the rustlers
jingle into town.

Sweaty steeds
in a panting procession
take their places,
gleaming and chomping.

Bart and Muley
swagger through swinging doors.
Lola-Bell and her made-up mole
turn from the mirror-backed bar.

Whiskey stutters in midair
and the piano stops.
Flouncy Gigi Frené (really Katy McGuire)
gasps on the stairs.

A grimy face
works a stumpy cigar

as boots chunk
on the wood floor.

Bart sidles up for
a drink.
Muley follows.
Spurs clink; boots on brass.

Piano, poker chips, and murmur
begin again.
Giggling Gigi ascends
with Cowhand Cal.

Elbows prop backs to bar.
Muley glances and agrees
to a scanning Bart's low snarls.

Young-gun Glen
teeters to mid-room
and flips a table —
chips and insults fly.

Bart chuckles.
A red-faced Glen
draws, fans, and,
still standing,
stares . . .
wondering
if that
is all

there is
to it.

PEACHES

A stream courses low and dark beneath its crusted surface. Withered leaves rattle as a breeze worries a scrag of streamside brush. A young man leans over a thick length of branch propped beneath his arm and grunts with each hopping step.

The sight of the shack across the iced flowage surprises him. Little more than a low line of roof wedged into the hill behind, a mound of snow atop might be a chimney, he thinks. Vertical logs beneath, man height, frame a crude plank door in the center.

He doubts it has seen use in recent years. No matter. It is the most welcome thing he has seen in two days, and he indulges in hope. Thoughts of meat, a fire, blankets fill his head as he chooses his slow path across the half-frozen creek. But food first. He must eat. He cannot recall ever having such a feeling, a hunger clawing him from within like a spiny creature seeking a way out.

■ ■ ■ ■

The young woman steps into a patch of downing sun on the crusted slope above the shelter. The rising breeze has been troublesome and is now a wind that follows her, smacking her bloodied skirts against her legs and carrying with it no sign of her pursuer. But that means little.

In a lull, a faint smell stills her . . . smoke, surprising this high up when she expects to be alone.

She tops the last rise, and below sees a thin gray wisp rising from the snow, then dissipating in a gust. She grunts and approaches the shelter with interest, for she had intended to hole up there herself.

The door spasms inward and the young man, crouching before the fireplace, shouts, "Oh, no!" He falls to his backside, struggles upright, one leg bent outward.

"You are trespassing," says a young woman, perhaps a girl, aiming at him a pistol that looks as long as her arm.

"No, no! I —"

She looks around the room and sniffs, her nostrils flexing. "It still stinks of mice and smoke and sweat."

The young man stares at her. He is reminded of a dime novel he'd been taken with some months before, *Bathsheba of the Plains*. One line in particular comes to him: "She was a young, deadly thing, all freckles and pistols."

But that feels a long time ago, back in the spring of the year when he'd set off for the West, when he'd been certain of his place in the world. Now he is about to die by the hand of a flinty young woman, his future little more than a lark.

The light in the shelter is meager, but enough to glow the length of the gun, her cheek and nose and chin. Shadowed hair sticks wet against her forehead and drips melt on her brow. More snow bunches on her thin shoulders. She wears a light-pattern dress, what colors he cannot tell. The skirts are stained up high. He looks aside.

"How do you do?" He extends a shaking hand as he rises.

She looks at his hand, at his face, then cocks the gun and holds it steady on him. "I'd as soon kill you and be done with it."

"Kill me? Why?" He touches his throat. "I am defenseless. If it's your shanty you are worried about, I will leave once the storm passes. I'd rather not right now."

"It is not a shanty. It is a dugout."

21

"Fine, then. A dugout."

She turns, still holding the gun on him, and fumbles at the door.

"There is no lock," he says.

Still she jerks the handle, somehow wedges it tight.

"The fire," she says, nodding at his small, flickering effort.

"Yes, it was lucky for me there were matches in a tin on the mantel. Though there is little wood left to burn." With his boot toe, he nudges an empty tin can on the hearth. "I found that as well. I didn't know what it might be — it had no label. I pried it open. Peaches."

She stares at the wall and holds a finger to her lips. "The wind has changed."

"I expect it will do that all night," he says. "I can't make heads nor tails of the weather out here. It's not like home when a breeze off the bay washes ashore, same as the waves. Wind here will do most anything it wants, it seems."

"Stop talking." Her eyes narrow and she turns her head. "He will have smelled the smoke."

"Who?"

She looks at the young man again, not seeing him. "It would not matter. He will follow my tracks. Even a dullard can track in the snow."

"Who is he?"

She looks at the door. After some time, she whispers, "Davidson."

"Davidson?"

She regards him as if she caught him eating a handful of dirt. "I expect you were an annoying child."

She looks back to the door. "I doubted him from the first. My father, on the other hand, suspected him of some merit. Papa is kindly but prone to fits of unwarranted charity. Such was the case in his assessment of Mr. Davidson, who came to us from nowhere, seeking work."

"What has he done then, this Davidson?"

"Hush!" The girl growls the word, not looking at him. "Do you hear that?" She eyes along the front wall, the door, as if watching a speck on the horizon. She stands, the pistol held across her chest.

Through gaps in the door's planking, lines of quick-shifting yellow light leak in, disappear, move left and right, then back again.

"You are in there, girl! I seen your tracks and I smelled your smoke!" The voice from outside the door is loud and thick, as if shouted through a quilt.

The girl says nothing, but licks her lips. The young man watches her breath cloud silver in the near-dark of the cold room.

A long moment passes.

"This is no way to treat your beloved!"

The young man expects the girl to shout a reply, but she says nothing.

He pulls in a deep breath. "You had better leave me alone, mister." His voice does not sound as menacing as he had intended. "I am armed . . . and angry!"

The girl stares with wide eyes at the young man, then turns back to the door. Still, she says nothing.

A small flame licks at the last of the wood, pinches out.

"I thought I seen two sets of tracks! So, you are with another already!"

"I am armed!" the young man shouts. "Go away!" He lays a hand atop the end of the snapped branch he uses as a crutch.

"I'll go nowhere but in!" The door bucks inward once more, revealing a large man holding a lantern's bail in a wind-reddened hand. In the other, a rifle, aimed at the room. He dips his big, shaggy head to look in, and smiles. "We are not through, girl."

He shoves forward, and once inside stands full height. "Who are you?" he says to the young man. "The one who shouts that he is armed? Two thin arms is all I see!" The big man laughs. Wind blows snow at his back and he hunches, then closes the door.

Davidson wears an unbuttoned, untucked wool shirt of black-and-white checks, red longhandles beneath, and below, dark trousers bunching atop black boots.

"Back!" he shouts.

The girl steps away from him.

His bottom lip sits wet and quivery. His veined eyes are moist with anticipations that hang like bad smells in the close room. "You are of breeding age, and I am not yet through with you, girl."

"That is enough of your filthy talk, sir!" The young man, still standing, points at Davidson. The big man pays him no attention.

The young woman aims the pistol at the big man. "I am of an age and of a mind to kill you," she says. Her voice is small and it shakes.

"That's the bold girl I like. But that old relic of a pistol is not loaded." He hefts his rifle and shakes it. "This is."

He sets the lantern on the mantel. "Now, you are of an age to do as I say, nothing more. I may choose to bend you over my knee." He tugs a nearly empty bottle of rye whiskey from a trouser pocket, swigs and sighs, dribbling liquor down his haired chin.

He tosses the bottle to the floor and drags a cuff across his wet mouth.

"No matter." His eyes close as he speaks. "I will get what I want, just not as often as I want. But I will have your ranch, and though I would prefer to also have you with it, the ranch will win the day. As for you, little girl, once we are through, you will rest with your beloved papa."

He spits on the floor and his red eyes rove the dark room, then settle once more on the young man. "What are you? Worth my time or that of a bullet?"

Davidson looks down the young man's thin body. "What's this?" He steps forward, a leer forming on his wide, haired face. "I see you are a gimp." He glances at the girl, then back at the man's swollen, bent ankle wrapped in rags that had once been a shirt. "Where is your boot?"

"I lost it."

"I should say!" Davidson laughs and, with a grunt, kicks the young man's afflicted foot once, twice, his teeth gritted behind a stretched smile.

The young man screams. Even through the hot wash of pain flowering up his leg, the sound shocks him. It is a shriek no man should give voice to, yet he cannot stop.

"Shut up that yowling!" Davidson claws

the young man's collar and shoves him to the floor. His head bounces on the packed dirt and his breath snags, stuttering in his throat.

"Stay put!" The big man wags the rifle at the young man. "You will be the last thing I attend to."

Davidson steps poorly toward the girl, steadies himself, and stares at her while slipping the braces from his shoulders. His trousers drop to his knees and he shuffles forward, backing the girl to a wall. With his free hand he yanks the pistol from her and drops it to the dirt.

The young man watches, shaking, fixed by the surprise of what he sees. As the heavy-breathing man bends low and pushes himself against her, the girl looks down at the young man, her eyes wide.

The young man grabs the bed frame and shoves himself up, sucking in breath through tight teeth. He hefts his crude crutch, hops forward, and swings it hard at the side of the man's wide head. A quick, dark spray blooms outward.

Davidson stiffens and groans, the sound reminding the young man of a bullock's bellow he heard many years before as a child visiting his uncle's farm. He cannot see the girl and fears he hit her as well, but she pushes past the groaning man before he drops to his knees, facing the wall.

She yanks the rifle from the man's weak left hand, steps back, and swings it, smacking the barrel's end hard against the other side of the big man's head. A breath rushes from him and he flops forward. His forehead scuffs the log wall as he slides facedown to the floor.

"What should we do?"

"Kill him," she says, cocking the rifle.

Davidson moans and lifts his head. It wobbles and thunks once more to the floor.

"No, no!" The young man holds out trembling hands as if to push away the idea. "Don't do that. Surely there's a better way."

"Shut up," she says. "You know nothing."

"I am a baker. I don't want such trouble on my conscience."

"Then hobble on out of here, Mr. Baker, and I will deal with it myself." Her voice is low and steady and she does not look up as she sights along the barrel at Davidson's head. "I will sleep like a kitten tonight knowing this foul bastard is sucking mud and I am the one who felled him."

"Oh, Lord, young lady, this is not the way."

"Lord? You use his name as if we are at a

church supper. The Lord has nothing to do with it. This beast killed my papa and worked me over so bad I can hardly stand, and you want me to let him live? Hell no, I say. The Lord himself has a whole lot of explaining to do as it is."

Her finger flexes on the trigger for a long moment, then her shoulders sag, but she does not lower the rifle. "Pull off his boots, his socks, and his trousers. That shirt as well."

"What?"

"Do it now."

The young man regards her a moment, then, wincing, lowers himself to his good knee and commences the task. The second boot is troublesome and the man's socks are wet and ripe with an animal stink. What wool not worn through on the soles has stuck to the feet as if grown into them.

"Is this necessary?"

"Yes."

"I refuse to do any more."

"Then I will shoot you both."

The young man sighs and bends once more to his distasteful chore. When he finishes, the girl motions him back to the bed.

Eerie shadows stretch in the lantern's warm, low light. Despite the pulsing ache in his ankle, the young man fights drowsing, his eyes close and his head drops forward, then jerks upright. The girl does not move. She stands above the prone man, the rifle pointed at his head.

Eventually Davidson groans and groans, and when it seems to the young man as if the brute has expended all effort in groaning, the big man pushes himself to his knees. He touches his head and grunts.

"Stand up now."

"Huh?"

"On your feet."

It takes more groans and much effort, but Davidson gains his feet, swaying and creating new, leering shadows on the wall and ceiling.

A sudden slam of wind pushes at the door, forcing fine snow through gaps between planks.

The girl smiles. "You will take your leave now, Davidson."

"Huh?"

She points the rifle at the door. "Out. Now."

The man seems to awaken then, becomes aware of what the girl means. He shakes his head. "No," he says. The word becomes a plea, then sounds that are not words fill the air. Soon he is snotting himself and trying to drop to his knees to beg.

"Shut your foul mouth or I will shoot you deader than dead. Now leave."

"But where? I ain't got my boots!"

"Make for the ranch."

The young man knows he will not forget the sight of Davidson outside the door, staring in, standing stark against a swirl of white. His red long underwear, unbuttoned in the middle, sags open, as black and haired there as is his shaggy head, save for its two wide, white eyes. He howls as the girl slams the door and pushes against it, jamming the latch once more.

"Drag that bed here."

The door rattles.

The young man stays seated atop the sag-rope frame.

She eyes him, then picks up his crutch and wedges an end beneath a crosspiece in the center of the wooden door. She stomps the other end into the packed dirt floor.

For long minutes Davidson pounds the door, begging with desperate sounds, words lost on the wind. The girl faces the door with the rifle drawn and does not move.

The whimpering from without diminishes, reappears, pinches out, further off each time.

"This is no way to solve the matter," whispers the young man.

Some time later she replies. "I disagree. A solution solves a problem."

He looks at her. "But he is still alive."

The wind pushes a spray of snow down the cold chimney.

She smiles. "I will be surprised if he finds his way back to the ranch."

"You said he could go back there."

She shakes her head. "I suggested he might make for it. I myself might end up living in a castle in England, but it is not likely."

"What do you mean?"

"I trusted Papa. I knew his faulty judgments, yet I trusted him. He said Davidson was a solid sort, perhaps not a scholar, but steadfast and true. Those were his words." She shakes her head hard, as if in disagreement with an unseen presence. "How wrong we both were."

She opens her eyes wide and stares at the young man. "Davidson stuffed his grimy kerchief in my mouth."

She turns away, wipes at her eyes with a thin wrist.

"He was finished by the time Papa returned from chores in the stable. Then he clubbed Papa to death in the kitchen with a split of stove wood. I ran for the door, saw Papa's cap-and-ball service pistol hanging in the holster and I pulled it free. But I did not dare turn around. I felt him behind me, knew he was behind me. All the way here."

Outside, in whipping gusts, they hear the man's shouts once more, distant and thin.

"He'll be turned around by now," she says quietly.

The young man stares at the wall.

She sits before the cold fireplace, the rifle leaning against her thigh, the cap-and-ball pistol in her lap.

Some time later, the young man drapes a tatter of wool blanket on her shoulders. She does not move. He watches her breath.

The lantern gives out hours before dawn, the wind tires to an occasional whisper. Still she stares at the black ashes.

The young man does not sleep, but watches her and shivers and thinks of it all, over and over, hearing shouts that are not there.

"He was of dumber stock than I took him to be." She turns to the young man. "And that is saying something."

They stare down at Davidson, hunched in the snow as if trying to curl into a coil so tight he might warm himself somehow from within. His skin, where it shows, has purpled, and his open eyes are crusted with blown snow. A thin drift has formed along the curve of his back, but the worn red of his underwear is bare along his pooched belly and thighs and knees.

"We should bury him," says the young man. "Or at least drag him back to the dugout."

She closes her eyes, her nostrils flaring. "He was dumb and filled with ill intent. Because of that, he is dead."

"But —"

"Do as you wish. I will mourn one man today and it is not this bastard. I am going home."

He watches her slight figure walk away, her steps punching holes in the crust. Her arms, each laden with a gun, sway with the effort.

After a few moments, he shouts, "Do you have need of a baker at your ranch?"

This stops her. She turns and looks at him, the hand gripping her father's pistol held above her eyes. "I expect very few people in the world, if they are honest, have need of a baker." She regards him a moment longer, then turns away and resumes walking.

He watches her, then looks back at the

snow-crusted hump of the dead man, and beyond, the low, wind-gnawed drift atop the dugout.

When he turns back, only the girl's dark hair is visible. Then that, too, disappears, hidden by a slope in the land.

I am alone once more, he thinks. He also thinks she did not actually say she had no need of a baker.

The young man squints across the brittle, rolling sweep before him and breathes deep of the cold morning air. Hobbling forward, one step at a time, he follows her tracks.

SNAKE FARM

The kid woke to daylight and a narrow-shouldered man leaning in the shack's open door.

"See you found my old bunkhouse."

The kid blinked hard, swung his feet to the floor, and stood up from the sagged rope and chewed ticking mattress.

"I ain't caused no harm. Needed a place to sleep is all." His voice was a sore whisper. He toed a green bottle. It rolled, stopped.

They both looked at it.

"Sleeping it off then." The man pushed away from the doorframe and stepped in.

The kid saw he was old and thin, but muscled like a wiry rooster. He wore bagged overalls, his stringy arms folded inside the bib.

The old man pooched his bottom lip, nodded as if he understood. "I don't have much use for this shack no more anyhow. Truth be told, I ain't much used it, nor has anyone else, not for some time."

The kid held a trembling hand to his right eye.

"See, I made me a mistake a long time back." The old man's voice rose loud. "When I first set up on these acres here. Oh, that was nigh on forty year ago."

The kid squinted, trying to understand what the old man was on about.

"Yeah," the old man said. "Built this here shack." He stomped a curled boot on the puckered, dusty floorboards. "Smack dab on a winter den of rattlers. Whole ball of 'em under here." He stomped again, louder, raising dust. "Ever since then, folks such as yourself have had trouble sleeping in here. 'Specially, come to think on it, this here time of year. Yes sir, worrisome things have happened in this shack."

The kid looked at him. "What sort of things?"

"Oh," the old man stroked his stubbly chin whiskers. "Folks got themselves all bit up. Inside out, upside down. They was a mess. Now," the old man scratched behind an ear. "You slept off your toot here last night, so you was passed out."

The kid nodded, swallowed. His wide eyes rolled side to side. He expected to see snakes dripping like living moss from the

ceiling, sliding through the thin wall planking, wriggling their slick heads up between
the floorboard cracks.

"I . . . I was drinking some, yes sir."

"I thought so. Yes, I thought so," said the
old man, nodding and stroking his chin.
"Could be we got ourselves a problem,
then."

"What? Why?"

The old man let out a long breath. "I'll be
straight with you, son. This here's birthing
season for them. The snakes, I mean."

The kid mouthed the word *birthing*. "It
is?" His eyes strained to see into the dark
corners. He made out a plank table cob-
webbed above and below, and an old
broken-door woodstove the size of a small
pig, propped on bricks where a fourth leg
once held.

"Yes sir, this here's the time of year when
they whelp their young." The old man
leaned forward, lowered his voice. "By the
hundreds."

"No."

"Yep. And what's more, they are hungry,
curious little rascals." The old man almost
smiled. "So you will want to check yourself."
He jerked his chin at the kid. "Go on.
Clothes, them shoes, the whole works. And
that hat that fell off your head. I'd give it a

shake before you tug it on again."

"In my clothes?"

"Oh yes, most of all. But," the old man leaned closer, almost whispered, and his milky eyes narrowed. "It's the littlest ones, the young rattlers you got to watch out for. They will climb into dark places. And seeing as how you was all passed out and relaxed, sort of sagged . . ." He rasped a hand across his chin again. "How do I say this?"

The old man snapped a finger and pointed at the kid. "You was open for business all over, down back there." He pointed toward his own backside. "You see, them baby rattlers, they get curious, like to poke their pointy heads, like arrows, into every little crack and crevice. And you won't hear them, no. 'Cause they ain't got much yet in the way of rattles."

The kid swallowed, his mouth working like a banked bullpout.

The old man nodded again. "I see you know exactly what I am angling toward here. That's good because talking in riddles is not something I am particularly strong on. My way of thinking, there is far too much in life that's tricky to understand, so why not talk plain to each other? You see?"

The kid did not see, could not see a

damned thing. His eyes had teared. His breaths crawled up his throat, popping out in retches, and he pinched out a thin, high groan.

"Oh no, son, don't you do that," whispered the old man, a long, drawn look on his bristled face. "You spook one of them that's got into you and you will be callin' it quits sooner than you thought."

"What do I do?" The kid's whisper trembled.

"What?" The old man leaned forward, a knob-knuckled hand cupping his ear into a curl.

"What do I do?"

"Oh, well . . ." The old man rocked back, stuffed his hands into his overall's pockets. "You got to let it be. Sort of wait it out. Suffocate the little sons-a-bitches."

The old man furrowed his brow and stared at the kid.

The kid stared back.

Neither spoke for long moments.

"This ain't no good, son. Might be you've already waited them out. You feel anything yet?" As he said it he bent low and put an ear close to the boy's gut. "I can't hear nothing." He looked up at the kid. "You sure you don't feel anything? Down deep in there, I mean?" He poked a fingertip hard into the kid's gut.

The kid wheezed. "No!"

"Oh." The old man stood straight again, his knees popping and creaking. "Well, hell, I don't know. All I can tell you is I am late as late can be for the field." He walked to the door, one hand on the frame, then looked back in. "Might be you want to not listen to folks like me. They will cause you a world of hurt in your mind, you see. No end to the shenanigans a man's thinker can get into when it's weak and prone to worry."

He smiled, winked an eye, and stepped out the door and kept walking.

The kid watched him go, not certain of the old man's words, waiting for them to make sense.

And when they did, the kid's top lip pulled wide and thin. He snatched up his fallen hat, gave it a shake, then looked inside before he tugged it low on his aching head.

From his pocket, the kid lifted a folding knife with a false-bone handle, pried open the single blade, near worn through from excessive sharpening by the man whose house he'd spent time in some nights before.

He stepped out the doorway to the brittle grass. A swarm of bluebottles lifted up off something dead, settled again. A swishing, buzzing sound rose from beneath the sagged old shack, but the kid was gone, stomping shaky across the barnyard.

He caught up with the old man at the field's gate.

Half a Pig

"You hung yourself, boy. You know that sure as road apples are ripe year 'round."

Eamon Riggs stared at the sweaty, pocked face, but there was no sign that the boy heard him. His eyes kept that half-closed stare at nothing, as if he were bored and about to doze off. Like that his whole life, thought Riggs. It's the Mexican in him.

Riggs looked up at the ancient tree, the only one for miles. As a young man he had made it his business, from books, to know all about trees. Curious about what he didn't have, he supposed. It was a big tree, dead a long time, as long as he could recall, and wind-stripped of anything that had been its skin. Now it was just silver and hard and good for one thing. Almost as if it had grown for that one purpose.

"You have anything to say at all?" Riggs waited.

The mule on which the boy sat, hands

bound behind him, stepped in place and flicked one long ear, like a cupped leaf Riggs had read of long ago, when he had dreamed of travel south, deep into jungles.

The ear flicked again. As bored as the boy, thought Riggs. Ought to hang the damned mule, too. Just because I can.

A deerfly landed on the boy's temple. The boy didn't move.

Riggs took in a draught of air through his nose, his lower jaw canted as if he were considering how to answer a delicate question. His left hand struck out with his rawhide quirt and snapped at the beast's haunch. The mule lurched forward, digging hard, and all three men in attendance watched the boy's face finally show the light of interest, his eyes wide and pushing forward, his mouth stretched as if pulled from either side with fishhooks, his head and torso stiff and working back, then forward, like a pecking bird, black curls bouncing on his forehead.

Half-formed coughs rose and died in the boy's throat. One leg whipped wide, in arcs, and the curled boot flipped from it, landing upright ten feet away. In two minutes he stilled. An unfelt breeze spun him slowly and brown liquid like chaw juice trailed over the bare foot in veins, dripping from the dirty toes.

"You boys come back with me. I'll send Parsons and Cunningham out to cut the bastard down and bury him." Riggs paused, then moved in the saddle and regarded the pair of cowhands staring at the sparse grass. "You hear me, Dilly?"

The taller of the two men looked at his boss, nodded.

Riggs turned and heeled the black he used for close chores. "And bring that damned mule with you," he said without looking back.

The two of them sat still for a few moments, then Dilly said, "That was too much for me, Pelt," in a voice barely loud enough for the shorter man on the dun beside him to hear. "I didn't think he'd do it. Thought for sure he was out to scare the fool kid, nothing more. Didn't think he'd do it."

"What do you mean?" said Pelt Simmons, the other, younger hand. "Fella had it coming, far as I can make out. Steal half a pig and a horse to carry it on. Had it comin'." He pinched his lips tight and looked away. "Kid should of asked me. I'd of told him that. Might could have saved him."

Dilly looked at his companion. "You don't know, do you?"

"Know what?" Pelt, young and squat, sat slumped on his horse like he would someday melt into it. He was new to the Cross R and Dilly tried to ignore his hot-and-cold chatter.

Dilly looked ahead at the brown leather vest on the broad, far-off back of Riggs, and reined his buckskin to a stop by the old mule, a weal already puckering the dappled haunch. The beast's ears flicked back and it breathed hard, the man suspected from fright more than from the short run. He'd been around mules most of his life and he'd rarely seen one winded. They could work a horse to its knees and still keep the wagon rolling.

Pelt stopped beside him, his horse fidgety. "What's wrong with you, Dilly?"

Dilly looked forward again. The last of his boss's hat disappeared beyond a rise far ahead. "Man we hung back there was the boss's nephew."

Pelt shifted his chaw to a cheek. "Naw." But his eyes remained on the tall man's face. "I thought he was Mexican help."

Dilly hooked a finger around the mule's rein, and it fell in behind his horse.

Pelt caught up with Dilly. "Why?"

"Why what?"

"Why'd he hang him? I mean, his own

blood and all."

"Riggs is a hard man. He won't tolerate theft of any kind." The animals walked on. "But he pays well and is generous with time of a Sunday."

"It's 'cause he's a churchgoer, I suppose."

Dilly nodded. "Regular as a cow on sweetgrass."

Pelt sluiced a rope of juice, wiped his lips with a glove's cuff. "What made the boss so hard?"

Dilly looked up, squinting, as if watching a buzzard circle. "When I was new to this outfit, newer'n you are now, an old-timer by the name of Chick, on account of his last name ended with that sound, told me a few things about Riggs worth keepin'."

They rode in silence for some time, then Dilly said, "Riggs hates it here. Hates everything about it."

"Why does he stay?"

"Has to. Made a deathbed promise to his mother. Swore on the Bible and all."

"What did he promise?"

Dilly stopped his horse and looked at the trailing mule, then beyond, at the tree and the stilled body. He sighed. "To look after his younger sister. Family was everything to the old woman, so Chick said."

"I didn't know Riggs had a sister."

"Did. She's dead a long time now. Before I got here. The boy was hers."

Pelt twisted in his saddle and studied the tree and the body. "He looked Mexican to me."

"Part. Father, I reckon. He's dead, too."

"How?"

Dilly urged his horse into a walk. Eventually, he said, "Who, you mean."

"Riggs?"

Dilly said nothing.

"What about the boy back there?"

"You call him a boy? I reckon you two were close in age."

Pelt shrugged. "Was he fixing to run off? Seems like he'd a been better off not taking a half a pig with him. Odd thing to steal."

"He had his reasons."

"Like what?"

Dilly sighed again. "Had himself a girl, her folks. Mexican. Poor family, but they was good to him. Nice people. Not far from here. The boy let slip to me she was gonna have a baby. Had to tell someone, I suppose."

"Why didn't he just tell Riggs?"

"Bit of a hard case, like his uncle. Still, kid wasn't a bad sort."

"But he was Riggs's blood kin. Why would the boss do that? And over a pig?"

"Changed your tune, I see." Dilly looked back to the trail, then said, "I reckon Riggs weighed family with thievery and found family wanting. So he hung the boy."

The horses picked their way down the switchbacks of the big hill before the ranch came into view.

"Why'd he choose you and me, Dilly? I believe I could have lived out my days without seeing something like that. I swear."

Dilly half smiled. "Cause you're new and I ain't."

The young man nodded to himself. "I can handle it. I'm saving up for a place of my own. I'll have me a ranch, wife, kids." He looked at the older man.

"Boy," said Dilly, "if I had a gold piece for every time I heard that from a hand, I'd be richer'n Riggs."

Pelt worked more tobacco from the greasy knob he carried in his breast pocket. He packed it in his cheek. "You're older than Riggs, ain't you?"

Dilly felt heat in his cheeks. "By God, but you can be a rude pup."

"Sorry, Dilly. I only meant —"

Dilly rode ahead. "Just a kid," he said, tugging on the mule's reins.

Pelt leaned in the doorway of the barn. "So,

49

what you going to do with your Sunday?"

Dilly looked up from sorting through his possessions laid out on the dirt floor. "Spend it, I reckon. Can't save it." He bent back to his task.

"That one's older'n you are, Dilly." The voice came from the shadows to Pelt's right. Parsons emerged, swinging a canvas feedbag half-filled with oats. He winked at Pelt as he passed outside, licking the length of a quirley and slipping it between his lips.

Pelt walked over to Dilly. "Parsons. Don't know how to take him."

"Aw, don't mind him. He's a decent sort. Just thinks he's smarter than everyone else."

Pelt looked down at the man's few things. "What you doin'? Leaving?" He snorted and reached for his chaw.

Dilly didn't look up as he finished bundling his things and slipping them into his saddlebags.

"You are leaving." Pelt's jaws slowed. "But why would you leave, Dilly? You been here for a coon's age. This is your home."

"I reckon I've sucked all the goodness out of this bone, boy."

"But winter's coming."

Dilly flopped the bags onto his horse. Pelt hadn't noticed the saddled buckskin in the stall.

The tall man knotted thongs tight, snugging his blanket behind the cantle. Then he heaved a child-size, canvas-wrapped bundle up onto the blanket. He doubled knots in the hemp wrappings, then rested his hand on the bundle and looked into the dark stall.

"Time I did something, boy, instead of just sitting here growing old. Might be I'll regret it, might be it'll work out to my favor. Who can tell?"

There was a long silence, then he turned to Pelt. "Here." He forced a wad of folded bills and two gold coins into the young man's hand.

Pelt stiffened. "What's this?"

"Reckon it'll buy a half a pig, don't you?"

Pelt spit and nodded. "More than."

"I reckon we know who the pig was meant for," said Dilly. They were silent a moment, then he smiled at the young man and offered his hand. "You'll be right as rain."

Dilly gripped Pelt's hand tighter and his smile slipped. "You'd do well to figure out when it is you should leave. Find that woman, build up that spread. Somewhere aways from here. This land's less than dirt anyway." He smiled again, pumping the young man's hand once.

Dilly led the buckskin toward the big door and raised one foot to the stirrup, then heaved himself up and into the saddle. "Now look, don't you forget to pay Riggs for this half a pig." He patted the canvas-wrapped shape snugged down behind him and winked. "Or else I'll end up decorating that tree just like the boy."

Pelt shook his head fast and stared at his boots. "No, no, Dilly. I wouldn't let that happen."

"I know it, Pelt. I know it. But don't pay him more than what's fair. The folding money will do. The rest is for your ranch."

Pelt looked up. "Dilly, you know I can't —"

But the tall man was already riding away, waving a hand. "I'll need a place to stay when I'm old, boy," he called. "Fix it up nice for me. I have high taste." He touched his hat's brim and heeled the horse into a gallop.

Before long the only thing Pelt saw of his friend was a thin trail of dust rising up and over the hill. And then that, too, drifted off, leaving nothing to look at above the land but a blue sky.

A SMALL THING

I ladled more venison stew into Uncle Drift's bowl. It was peppery and the smell tickled my nose. He nudged his spoon with a big knuckle but did not tuck in. No matter how hungry he is, he waits for me. Drift Macallam ain't one to forget his manners. He also ain't one to use the word "ain't." But I am.

Thomas Dettweiler, he's the first one I heard use that word, right after Bible class, then he got clouted on the left ear by his mama. Times like those I am satisfied with my lot. No surly mother to clout me, only Uncle Drift to keep me in line. And as long as I don't shirk my tasks, as he puts it, I have little to complain about. I still complain, but that's the way it is with me.

I sat down and picked up my spoon. I should have got a mouthful in, but I made the mistake of peeking over at Uncle Drift. And he was peeking right back at me. Well, not peeking so much as looking at me. Uncle Drift, he doesn't peek. He looks. Those big, twitchy-bird eyebrows of his twitched and he didn't have to say a thing.

I set down my spoon and put my hands together. "Thank you, Lord, for this food."

Uncle Drift sat with his head bowed, didn't put his hands together, though. He never does. Finally he reached for his spoon. "That was brief, Katharine."

"Yep," I said. Because it was. I thought he'd like it, seeing as how he doesn't talk much himself.

"You spend enough time with the Dettweilers, I thought you'd stretch it out some." He tasted the stew, nodded his fondness for it as he pulled in air to cool his mouthful.

"They are a prayerful bunch," I said, knowing he would nod without looking at me.

I always make certain to serve supper hot as I can make it. Uncle Drift likes it that way. Me, I don't much care. I eat mostly to get it over with. I am forever behaving like that, rushing through a thing to get to the next thing, or else back to a book. I am fond of reading, can't seem to help it. Like picking at a scab on your knee, you just have to.

Last week Uncle Drift borrowed a hefty

book for me from his boss, Mister Lins-more. It's called *Constantine Xavier's History of the Known World.* Seems bigheaded to put your name in the title. Mostly the book confuses me, but I will give it a good going-through, then give it another, in case I missed something important on the first pass.

Sometimes Uncle Drift will say, "Having you around is like having a squirrel loose in the house." But he smiles when he says it. Every so often he will also say, "Watching you makes me tired." Which isn't the truth. Uncle Drift is always tired because he works a lot. Mostly for Mister Linsmore. The man with the books. He's the biggest rancher around. Uncle Drift's been at Linsmore's Lazy R my whole life. Or at least as long as I have been here, which is as far back as I can recall. That'd be twelve years.

I know this because today is my birthday. Well, as close as I will ever get to knowing what day I came to be in the world. Most folks are born, no choice, they just pop into a family and that's where they're stuck. But Uncle Drift, he says I am special because no one can prove I was born. Then he winks.

He says we discovered each other. That's why today is my birthday and it is the anniversary of the day he found me. But I am getting ahead of myself.

Once a month, when he is paid, Uncle Drift will come home later than usual. His cheeks are bright above his bushy, woolly-worm moustaches, and I know what he's been up to. Mostly because I got worried one time and looked all over town for him, then I found him at Ace's Bar and Livery. He was in the bar part, not the livery.

That said, Uncle Drift isn't much of a drinking man. He'll have a glass or two of beer on those days when he is paid, but the most it does is redden his cheeks and make him chatty. Well, chatty for Uncle Drift. He'll say four or five words instead of two or three.

Might be that's why I like visiting with the Dettweilers. There are about a dozen of them running around their place, all fleshy — they are a well-fed bunch — and loud and hoorah-ing and funny all at once. Their house is big and falling apart and smells like boiled shoes or, depending on the day of the week, spicy apple cake. And spending time with them is about what I imagine a circus is like and I love every minute I am there. At the end of it, I am exhausted and can't wait to get back home.

Me and Uncle Drift, we don't have what

most folks consider much. We have a tidy little home with a front room that used to be a settin' porch but now it's closed in. That's where Uncle Drift sleeps. There is a little bedroom in the back, that's where I sleep. It's off the kitchen and stays warm in winter. Out back we have a woodshed, and beside that, the outhouse, far enough away from the house proper that in summer when it gets to smelling sweet, we are spared the worst of it.

As I said, today is my birthday. It is also the first time I know of that Uncle Drift's payday is on the same day as my birthday. It doesn't much matter, but I prepared that nice venison stew I know he likes.

I was over to the Dettweilers earlier and Mrs. Dettweiler asked me why I was so smiley — I have been accused of being gloomy, but I am not, as a rule, a gloomy person. I might look it, but I am often in deep thought. I get a notion in my head and there's no end to the thinking I get up to — What would the world be like with no trees? How come a cow's hair will reach a certain length and then stop growing, but a person's hair will keep on getting longer and longer? And how long will that be? Has anyone ever found out?

Such thoughts keep me awake long into

the night. I tell Uncle Drift about them over breakfast, and he nods and his eyebrows hunch together. I know he is listening, but he never says much. Just, "Uh huh," or "Hmm." And once he said, "That's something, that is." A sort-of smile is always there on his face, but I know he's not funning me, never would. He says he takes me very seriously.

Anyway, I told Mrs. Dettweiler it was my birthday and she squealed — which if you have met her, wouldn't be a sound you'd find unusual coming from her. That was petty of me, especially considering what she did. She ran from the room, sort of ran, anyway. And came back with a very pretty snatch of calico, brown with tiny orange and yellow flowers set on it.

She put it in my hand and said, "This is for you."

Now, I don't sew all that well, enough to repair tears in Uncle Drift's clothes, though he is more of a hand at mending than I am. Every button I sew on ends up lost, lord knows where. Poor Uncle Drift, his sleeve cuffs flap loose half the time, but he doesn't say much about it. Just shakes his head and give me money for buttons and then shows me one more time how to sew them on.

I felt something inside the calico. Mrs.

Dettweiler nodded at me. By then half the kids were hugging her skirts like fuzzy chicks around a mama hen, all watching me. I unwrapped that cloth and rolled up in there was the prettiest length of blue hair ribbon.

"It's French silk, dear. I bought it for you some time ago."

"For me?"

She nodded. "I've been waiting for your special day, as I couldn't for the life of me recall which day was yours. Now it has come and so there you have it."

"You bought this for me?" I can be thick at times. I also was in danger of choking up a little.

She nodded again. "Yes, I saw it and I just knew it would look so pretty in your hair. Now turn around and let me help you with it. There should be enough for a nice bow."

You see, I have long hair, it's mostly not black, but reddish brown, and my eyes are grayish blue. That's how Uncle Drift says he knew I was no Indian child when he found me. He said true-blood Indians can't have blue eyes. I do not know why and neither does he, though I asked him a pile of times.

After the third or fourth time, he nearly smiled, then plopped on his hat, tugged up one side of his braces, and walked out back to split rounds for the stove. That was on my birthday, too, about five years ago. I was just a child then.

Every birthday he tells me the story of how he found me. Discovered me, is how he put it once — that's the word I tell him to use if he slips back into saying he found me.

Tonight, he begins the story the same way he does every year: "Now, what's important to remember is I am not really your uncle. I am not any sort of relation to you. What I am is the man who ended up with you. And I am a lucky man for it."

"And I ended up with you," I say. "And I am powerful lucky, too." I nod, but don't say anything more. Getting Uncle Drift talking can be a task, so I daren't slow the wheels. I sit on the floor and he's usually sitting in the rocker that was his mama's and he says one day will be mine. I do not like to dwell on when that day will be.

"We'll, I'll tell you, Katharine. When I come upon you that night, near dark, I was confused. Didn't seem as though what I was seeing could be possible. Why, I thought I'd come upon a little dog, lost and near starved out there on the trail. Then I leaned down out of the saddle and saw it was a child."

His eyes grew wide then, as though he were right back there at that moment a dozen years before.

I don't mind admitting that I trembled as he said it. Like I do every year. To think we were both there that cold, dark night so long ago. Us and no one else.

"I figured you'd been lost, left behind by a raving gold-seeker like in one of those stories I read in the newspaper. People are forever acting foolish where money is concerned. They get fevered up and discard everything they should hold dear. Lose a child on the trail and they're so worked up about the sniff of silver or gold they don't notice until it's too late. My word . . ."

He rubbed his big hand along his chin, it made a soft, scratchy sound. That was the first I noticed he'd not shaved this morning.

"So I stopped, made a fire, and heated up some grub. I didn't have any trouble coaxing you over. You were friendly enough . . . for a lost doggy."

That always got me to roll my eyes. I did it again, too.

"I had food to spare as I hadn't been hungry for a long while. And a good thing, too — for a little mite, you ate like a boar-grizz!"

"Did I say anything?" I knew the answer,

knew it as certain as I know my name.

"Naw," he shook his head. "You grunted plenty, though."

He grinned full-on then, something Uncle Drift doesn't do often. I like seeing that. "My word, but you were such a small thing."

Then he did something he never did before on my birthday. He stopped right in the middle of the story. He leaned forward in his rocker and put his elbows on his bony knees. Looked like a bird folding himself up. His big-knuckled fingers curled around themselves, all callous and sharp bends. They worked over each other while he decided on how to say what he was going to say next.

"Katharine," he said, looking at me.

I got a little scared, not because he said my name — he always calls me that, or "squirrel" — but because it felt like something was going to change. I didn't want anything to change, I like it just fine the way things are. I stood up. "I expect you could use some coffee. I'll fetch —"

"Katharine. Sit back down. I aim to tell you something."

I never disobey Uncle Drift. Leastwise, not to his face. Sometimes I will skip praying before I go to sleep. Who's going to know besides me and God? And I figure God's so busy I can double my efforts tomorrow night. I reckon I owe the Lord a couple dozen nights by now.

I sat down.

"But the story . . ." I said.

"Katharine, you've heard it enough so you can tell it better than me, I expect. I have something more to say to you. You see, that night when I found you out there on the trail, I was on my way somewhere."

This didn't strike me as anything worth saying. Aren't we all on our way somewhere? "Are you feeling okay, Uncle Drift?"

" 'Course I am. Just let me get down to it, will you? Like a chatty jay all the time." He tried to smile but his eyes couldn't do it.

"I was . . . oh, I don't know what I was. But I had no plan, no good thing to do." He sighed. "I have told you about my wife, Karina."

I nodded. He'd talked a little about her before. And once, when he was gone to work, I rooted around in the little trunk he keeps in the corner. I dug down through all manner of things piled atop, as if what is in there has to be covered over and hidden away.

The key has always stuck out of the front of it though, like a little brass nose. I turned it, opened the lid, and found a passel of letters, most of them written in a woman's looping hand, all addressed to "My Dearest Dover."

Took me a long time to figure out that Dover was Uncle Drift's name. I'd also like to say I didn't read those letters, but I'd be lying. I read two of them, then I saw a photograph of a handsome young man in a suit, no moustaches or big eyebrows — took me a few minutes to work out it was Uncle Drift. He stood behind a woman seated in a chair.

She was pretty, dark eyes and dark hair tucked in a bun. She wore a dress that came up around her neck, all fancy lace at the top, marked at the throat with a small brooch. Uncle Drift held a hat, a bowler, of all things, before his chest, the other hand resting on the woman's shoulder. One of her hands rested on her lap, holding a hanky, I think, the other held his hand on her shoulder.

Neither of them were smiling, but it looked to me as if they were fit to burst, as if the moment that photograph was taken they ran on out of that studio and had a whangdoodle of a time. I am learning of such things as what new-married folk get up to, but I choose to think Uncle Drift and his bride went somewhere and had themselves a fine feed. Not every day you get yourself married, after all. Nothing better than a good meal to mark an occasion.

Uncle Drift squeezed the arm of the rocker. "Katharine, I've thought a lot about this, but I reckon I didn't really need to. Truth is, that night I found you, you saved my life. I was headed for something, likely I was aiming to ride and ride until me or the horse give out."

He looked at me, eyes filling. I have never seen Uncle Drift tear up. I followed right along and did the same.

"Karina . . . she died before we could ever have a baby. A sickness brought on by a traveling family, lugged it with them. Cholera, likely."

His voice was higher than normal. That man had never looked old to me before, but with his silvery whiskers and those tears, he did right then.

"She was helping them, no thought to herself, and do you know? It worked. A couple of weeks, then they moved on, healthy enough to get to wherever was so important to them. Wasn't a day later Karina came down with the chills and stiff joints. She suffered so." He shook his head and tears slipped down his face. "She didn't last but a week. My word, we'd been married shy a year."

He was scaring me, but I didn't know what to say. Neither of us did. We sat quiet for long minutes. Then, of course, I spoke first.

"What happened next, Uncle Drift?"

He sort of smiled. "Oh, you mean when I discovered you?"

That isn't really what I'd meant, but no matter. He slipped back into the story we knew so well.

"Why, it took three days, but I drug that little squallerin' beast back here — that'd be you, by the way." He said it in a low, rumbly sort of way, like it was a secret. "I set up that room at the back for you."

"Wasn't that your old room?" I asked again, as I do each year.

He always says yes. Tonight he only nodded. "I'd not intended to come back to this town, truth be told. But with you, seemed like the thing to do. Was night when we made it back. I laid you down in that bed, covered you with that old patchwork quilt. I slept in this here rocker." He patted the arm with a big hand.

"Come morning, you were curled up on me like a squirrel, all tucked into a ball, your little head under my chin. I never . . ."

He gave me that half smile again. "And for more mornings after that than I could count, same thing. Like a little squirrel you were." Then his smile slipped away again.

Tonight of all nights, my special birthday night, something was different. I put my hand on his knee. "Uncle Drift, what's wrong?" I whispered it.

He peeked at me. I know what I said about him not being a peeker, but he did it just the same. Then he looked down again, like the Clumpett twins when they got called to the front of the schoolroom for sassing Miss Binder. Not looking up any more than they had to. It broke my heart to see him looking at me like that. I asked him again what was wrong.

He held my hand. Every so often I am reminded how big his hands are. Looking at mine between his scared me.

"I have done you a terrible wrong, Katharine."

I shook my head. "Uncle Drift, you've never done anything wrong."

He snorted. "Now that is a windy if ever I heard one."

The last of that quick smile slipped away. "You see, Katharine, I never put effort into tracking down your family."

I didn't say anything. I don't care one whit

about people who would leave their child to die in the wilderness. Uncle Drift is all the family I ever needed. I was about to say as much when he commenced talking again.

"One day came and went, then another and another." He shrugged as if I'd asked him a question he didn't know the answer to. "Before long you were jabbering like a jay, and then going to school . . ." His eyes got all squinty. "And now look at you, nearly grown."

"I am not," I said, but in truth I liked to hear it. In case you haven't met me, I am not a tall person, nor very large in any way. I guess you'd say I am small. Not long ago, I asked Uncle Drift if I would grow much more. He said I would be as big as I needed to be. That was no help.

Oh, but the evening had become confusing. Everything is changing and I want it to do that more than anything. I also want everything to stay the same forever. None of it is fair.

He had been watching me, one side of his mouth tugged up. "I gave you your name, Katharine, because it reminded me of Karina, yet different enough so I wouldn't go all sad every time I said it. But it's a good name. A big, strong name."

"But I ain't big nor so very strong, Uncle

Drift. I am just me."

"Katharine, you're about the strongest person I know. As to size, well, I know a whole lot of big folks who are a lot smaller than you, girl."

I resolved to think on that later. I expect there is something wise in it.

"Other than my last name, one that you are welcome to keep for as long as you see fit, I don't have much else to offer. What's mine is yours, always will be. But it would please me if you'd take this." He reached long fingers into the breast pocket of his flannel shirt, pulled out something that stayed hidden in his hand. He held it out, palm down, and nodded toward it. "Put out your hand, Katharine."

I did, and felt his fingers let go of something. He pulled his hand away and there in my palm was a pretty little pin I'd seen somewhere before, though at that moment I could not recollect where.

"That belonged to Karina," he said.

And then I knew where I'd seen it. It was the brooch she'd been wearing in their wedding photograph. I tried to thank him, but I am afraid I cried a little. Any words I meant to say never made it up out of my throat.

"She didn't want me to . . . send it with her, begged me to save it. Said I would have a use for it one day. And now I have. My word, but she was a smart one. I like to think if we'd had a child she would have been just like you. Yes, I believe Karina would have been a good mama to you, Katharine."

"But if she was . . . still here, you never would have discovered me." I snuffled and admired the pin.

"Well now, that is a fact, Katharine. Always two sides to the coin for you, isn't there?" He stretched out his long legs, rested his hands on his lean belly. "Now, tell me about that pretty ribbon in your hair."

My eyes widened. I'd forgotten all about it, what with supper and then our story. "Mrs. Dettweiler gave it to me. Said she'd been saving it just for me."

"Well," said Uncle Drift. "Isn't that something? They're good people, that family. The whole lot of them. They are prayerful, and I don't guess that's a bad thing. I am not much of a hand at it, haven't been in a long time." He sipped his coffee, which I am sure had gone stone cold. "I see how you and Thomas are chums."

I looked at him. I thought that was an odd thing to say, especially as I'd known Thomas my whole life. "Uncle Drift, what are you dancing around?"

He smiled, leaned back. "I swear if you don't remind me of Karina. Never could talk around a thing with her, either. She always cut right to the core of the apple."

I blushed. I like being compared with her, someone I think of as my long-dead mother. Someone who I know is watching over me, even though I never met her.

Uncle Drift cleared his throat. "Katharine, much as I like the Dettweilers and their boy, Thomas, and I do like them . . ."

I nodded. He'd said as much not a minute before.

"I think you should have what I heard are called options."

"Options," I said, not certain at all what an option was.

"That's right." He nodded, looking as uncertain as I felt. "They're sort of like different meals laid out before you. Like having your choice of stew or a beefsteak or, oh, I don't know."

"Pie?" I said. I have always been partial to pie. I can't bake a pie to save my skin, but I like it just the same.

"Sure, pie. Anyway, what I am trying to tell you is —" he sighed then continued — "I have been saving money for some time now, Katharine. Truth be told, you were here about a week when I started."

That long ago? "Why?" I said.

"That was when I knew for certain you were my little squirrel. Figured it would take a heap of money to raise you right. 'Course, it hasn't cost all that much, other than all that food you take in." He waited for me to look shocked, which I did, then he winked. "I have been saving it instead of spending it on fooferaw. Now it's time I told you why."

I didn't know what to say to that, so I kept my mouth shut, which is a trial for me.

"You see, Karina didn't come from Colorado. She traveled out here from back East as a young woman. She was sent by her church to do the Lord's work. But what she really wanted was to teach school. She was an educated woman. I met her at a social affair right here in town. I'd been living at the ranch, but whenever there was a social, why, me and the boys would draw straws to see who got to go." He winked at me. "I got lucky."

He sipped his cold coffee again. "All that come back to me when I brought you here as a little squirrel. I determined you would have as fine an education as Karina got, if I could afford to give it to you. Mr. Linsmore, he was kind enough to keep me on at the ranch, especially after he met you. Thought you were the cutest nubbin. Still does."

"He is a nice man," I said, and not just because he likes me and lets Uncle Drift bring home books for me to read.

"As I said, I've been thinking on this for too long. But what I come to is this." He held up a big hand to stop me from talking, and it's true, I was about to speak. He knows me better than I expect I do.

"Those folks Karina helped, they were headed west, for some other life. Must have thought it was better than whatever it was they were leaving behind. But they robbed me, at least that's the way I looked at it for the longest time. You see, I'd spent the better part of two years drinking and living in this little house, cursing God and doing my best to do what I thought I should be doing, but what I really wanted to do was die."

I couldn't understand what he was saying, but he kept on talking, so I held my tongue.

"I wanted so badly to die. I could not imagine life without my dear Karina. So I climbed up on that poor old horse, only thing I could afford to ride. I took a little food, and the rest of my saddlebag was filled with bottles of rye whiskey. No plan, figured I'd reach some sort of end and that would be that. I didn't care." He sat in silence.

"That's when you discovered me," I said.

"Yep." He nodded. "But when I did, I cursed God again. I wanted to hate you, so help me I did. Wanted to leave you be, in your filthy little rag of a dress, the child of travelers just like those who took my Karina from me. But you . . . you crawled on over to me like I was something worth crawling up to."

He shook his head as if he'd been told a windy. "It was as if the folks who took everything from me gave me a gift right back. I don't expect that to make much sense. Heck, I didn't parse this out as such for a few weeks myself, but somehow it all felt right, you see? So we come back here and I toed the mark, built up a new life. Not a life I ever imagined, but different. Not better or worse, just different. I am pleased with it."

That was the most I'd ever heard him speak all at once. "Why did you tell me now, Uncle Drift? This year, after all this time?"

He shrugged again, but I knew his thoughts were serious. "Been gnawing me from the inside. Most days I keep it tamped down, but seeing you today, wearing that pretty ribbon, growing into a woman all by yourself. I don't know that I have any right to be proud, but I tell you now, Katharine Macallam, I am proud of you, girl. Figured

I owed you the whole story. That way you know your ol' Uncle Drift is no better than anyone else. Not the fellow you think he is."

We sat quiet for a long moment. The small room had grown dark. For the first time in a long time, I felt like his little squirrel again. I crawled up in his lap, my head tucked under his big chin.

I fell asleep holding that pretty little brooch tight to my chest, not wanting anything to change, but knowing now it would. Everything would change.

So help me, I felt a little excited about it, too.

Scourge of the Spoils

Tico squatted in riverbank mud the color of an old miner's skin. His coarse brown hair hung from under his hat like ends of frayed rope, and the water he scooped in the bowl of his hands leaked slowly through his thick fingers.

He cut his eyes upstream, then back to the girl. Finally he drank, swallowed, made the noise that men the world over make after they've finished a needed drink, like pressure released from a worn valve.

"Shall we continue, then?" asked the girl from a horse behind him.

Tico remained squatting in the mud, his suede boots darkening as the water leached upward. "No."

The young woman said nothing, but straightened in the saddle and gritted her teeth.

Tico drank more, filled his canteen, then squelched back through the mud to where his horse, Colonel Saunderston the Third, had finished drinking. Tico checked the four glass tubes that served as reservoir level indicators, one in each of the horse's legs, the graduated numbers long since worn away. Satisfied with the water levels, he gathered the sopping reins from where they hung in the water, sluicing the excess through his fingers. Then he mounted.

The young woman forced a smile and nodded toward Colonel. "I've been meaning to ask — is that a special model? I don't recall seeing any quite —"

"Modified mount, same as that one." He nodded toward her horse.

Under the grime and welted ropes of brazing from years of repairs, Constance Gatterling saw something of the beast it once was. "The original creature must have been a beauty."

Tico stared at her as if she were speaking a foreign language. "Been a long time since it was a real horse."

"Surely you're curious."

"Gets me from here to there and back." More of the stare, then he said, "You talk too much. Let the bay drink full, then catch up with me." He heeled Colonel into a lope.

"Catch up? What? Hey!" Constance looked at the receding back of the stained buckskin shirt, an ancient holstered pistol bouncing on the man's hip with each clanking gallop. "Hey, Tico! I'm paying you to get me to the West Edge, not leave me here!"

But the horse decided for her and plunged into the river up to its knees, the cool grey water sizzling and becoming steam vapor where it touched the hot metal of its legs and sipping muzzle.

"Damn you horse, no! Tico is getting further away with each second you waste in this disgusting runnel of stinking liquid!" The flurry of words, which would have impressed her friends back home in East City, sounded childish out here in the Spoils.

The reins, looped in her hands, slipped free and slid into the water. She grabbed after them, bending low, the saddle leather creaking with her weight, her stirruped left boot inches from the river surface.

As she reached out, her fingertips trembling, clawing at the dangling rein, she noted with despair that the frilled edge of her tailored shirt's cuff, jutting from beneath the blue crushed velvet sleeve, was now grimed from constant wear. Still she strained a little further . . . then slipped from the saddle, a quick cry and her splash the only sounds until she rose, spluttering and gasping, from the rank, swirling Abandonia River.

It was the clanking, and more than that, an overriding grinding screech of steel on steel that pulled Constance from her bankside nap — her pounding heart seemed to fill her throat. The sounds, from the East, grew louder, but still she saw no sign of anything interrupting the flat, stark land.

She had not intended to fall asleep, but figured Tico would ride back, at least for his other mount, if not for her. She'd stripped off her smelly, wet garments and arranged them on the twisted branches of the stunted trees lining the river.

Perhaps Tico was only scouting ahead, and left her here because he knew this spot was relatively safe from the people of the Spoils. Constance chose to believe this, and so had waited for her hired guide's return. After all, she reasoned, she was his employer.

The grinding noise increased by the second. And then she noticed something else was wrong — the horse, what Tico had called "the bay," was gone. How could that happen? Horses, even modified mounts, didn't just vanish, did they? But it was full of water, so it could well walk off for miles, perhaps days, in any direction.

She saw no tracks, even though on both sides of the river, the solid-seeming earth gave way to softer, sandy soil as the land stretched away from the river. Constance held up a hand against the dimming light and stared southward, then west, toward the far bank.

The clanking grew louder from behind her, now joined with a grinding screech as though sand were being pressed between spinning metals.

Constance turned in time to see emerging from the sand the nose of what looked like a prewar steam-power locomotivator. It surged upward from beneath the ground, churning and chewing raw earth. Rocks, clods of dried, powdery dirt bigger than a man's head collapsed into clouds of powder. Boulders cracked like rifle shots.

It dragged itself free of its earthen tunnel, a collapsing ridge of sand, its forward set of great steel mandibles gnashing the last rocks, bouncing in its maw like unpopped corn kernels in a cast-iron pan.

She was surprised to see the rest of the machine was not black steel, but instead an old-time elixir wagon, wood, from the looks of it, like she'd seen pulled behind horses in pictorials in history tomes. She knew such transports still existed, but back East they long ago had been replaced with soft-tracked conveyances topped with polished chrome travel compartments.

The grinding, squealing sounds lessened, and great jets of steam drove at the ground from between the spoked wheels, raising swirling clouds of dust. A smell like melting metal curled its way into her nose and she fought down a sneeze.

A third of the way back, where steel met wood, a thick plank door with black strapping squawked outward and a stout little man in a long, plaid coat with once-sculpted tails, a style the likes of which Constance hadn't seen except in books, nearly fell out, surrounded by belching clouds of smoke.

He swung on the door, the hinges screaming for lubrication, and coughed as if soon he would be overcome. He stopped abruptly, pulled in a deep breath, then spat a great quantity of something that splattered in the dust, before hopping down and slapping his coat sleeves. He strode forward from out of the last of the steam, and stood still, smoke rising from a dented black bowler hat.

The little man reached up and pulled at massive goggles that came free from his face with audible pops. He lowered them to his neck, but his eyes were still covered with what looked like smaller goggles in thick brass frames. The lenses, of a dark hue, perhaps black, were surrounded with dials that looked to be for focusing. He reached up with practiced, albeit greasy, fingertips and adjusted one.

Then he stood smiling, his doughy, sweat-pocked face bubbling through a sparse beard, ginger eyebrows, and thick side whiskers. His coat continued to smoke, as if he himself were a source of heat.

"Good day to you, sir." She pointed at him. "You appear to be on fire."

His eyes never left her, though he slapped at himself a few times more. In a voice that rattled like gravel in a cup, he said, "It gets a bit . . . hot in there." He spat again, then slowly stepped closer.

Everything about him seemed of another time, as if he'd been apart somehow from normal society and fashion.

He stared at her.

"Is there a problem?" she said, a hand still visoring her eyes.

"Oh, no, no ma'am. That is to say, I'm not put out in the least by your state of . . . undress, as it were."

Constance barked an oath she reserved

for more private affairs and felt her face heat even as she turned away, groping for the stiff garments draped on the shrubs. "I'm . . . I'm so sorry."

She pulled on her clothes fast, noting the sad, wrinkled state her expensive fashions were now in. Blue velvet, silk luxlace, and camphor cotton had perhaps not been the best choices for traveling across the Spoils. At least they were drier than she expected. She continued picking and plucking her clothes from the brittle arms of the bushes, all the while keeping her brocade satchel close by, nudging it from bush to bush as she dressed.

"Why, sir, surely you must have a sense of decorum, propriety? Avert your eyes."

"I think not."

She heard the smile in his voice.

"It's been far too long since I've seen such an exquisite female form and I'll not look away. No indeed, I shan't do it."

She half turned toward him as she finished buttoning her second blouse. "Then you, sir, are a rogue."

"Mm-hmm. Among many other things, I can assure you."

"Who are you?" she finally said when she had covered enough of herself to feel bold again.

"Who am I?" The portly man spluttered, stepped aside as if to let a lady pass him on a crowded streetside, and waved an arm at his wagon. "Can you not read, my dear?"

Constance leaned to her right as she continued to button and smooth her shirt. She saw faded writing on the side of the caravan through the dissipating steam and smoke.

She shook her head as if disagreeing. "I can't make it out yet."

The man sighed, let his arms drop. He looked at his belly. "Ocularius." He looked up at her. "My name. It's Doctor Ocularius." His ample eyebrows seemed to rise higher with each syllable. "And you are . . . ?"

Constance froze in the act of primping the once-stiff collar of her inner coat. "I am Constance Gatterling. But wait . . . you said you are Doctor Ocularius?"

The man smiled and pulled the massive goggles away from his neck, stretching his chin. "Why, yes. Are you unimpressed?"

"No, it's just that . . . well, I didn't expect you to use your own name."

"Ah, so you have heard of me. Why should I not use my name? I know I'm here, they know I'm here. What good would it do to try to deceive anyone?"

"Pardon me, doctor, but isn't that what you're best at?"

"Deceit? No, dear lady, that's but a sideline. An admittedly practical, and occasionally profitable one, but nonetheless a sideline to my primary distraction."

"Which is . . ."

"Ha — I like you already. Come, let's resume this conversation over a blue flame and a decanter of refined mint wine."

She raised her eyebrows.

"Yes, dear lady, you don't think Doctor Ocularius travels the wastelands of the Spoils without the refinements of clean fire and fine libation, do you?" He smiled and disappeared inside the wagon.

In faded yellow paint arched across the side of the wagon, she read his name and the words: "Traveling Tinctures, Tonics, and Bifurcated, Multi-Purpose Nostrums for the Betterment of the Eyes, Ears, Nose, Throat, and Sundry Other Parts."

"So, Doctor, what do you call this contraption?"

"Contraption!" He peeked his head out the door. "You cut me to the core, dear girl! Why, this 'contraption,' as you call it, is more than a mere conveyance. It is more than a converted burrowing miner, more than a superior collection of hydraulic,

85

steam, and forever-gear technology." He hopped down, green bottle in hand. "It is more than a home, it is more than a workshop. Indeed, to a man once said to have promise — considering the limitations forced on me due to my unfortunate and unearned yet imposed exile — this beautiful brute," he said, patting the cooled black steel of the silent mandible, "is the incubator of my brilliance."

"Well your incubator sounded to me like it's on its last legs."

He pursed his lips, his brow puckering as he dragged an ancient gasbox from its rack underneath the wagon and rummaged in a vest pocket until he produced a small box of scratchers. Within seconds a warm, blue-flame fire hissed on the ground at their feet.

He stared at the flame. "Well, it is true she isn't suited to much more than sand travel these days — this river-valley rock nearly killed her, but this is where I found you."

"Why Doctor, I am flattered."

"Think nothing of it, dear girl. Thoughtful is my middle name."

They were quiet a moment. Dark rose around them and Constance pulled her satchel close. She thought she saw the doctor watch her, though with his eyewear, it was difficult to tell where he was looking. "Tell me about those peculiar spectacles, Doctor."

"Ah, you have a gift for stroking the peacock's feathers, my dear!" He smiled, sipped his wine, smacked his lips, and said, "In a nutshell, these odd eyepieces enable me to not be seen better."

She snorted, covered her mouth with a hand, and said, "Please, continue."

He sighed. "The technology is something I've spent my life developing. It's far more advanced than anything those dolts back East have come up with, I can assure you."

She regarded the pudgy man for a moment, then shook her head, smiling. "I think you're a talespinner, is what I think."

"Believe what you need to," said the Doc, finishing his wine. "I do." He winked and slapped his knee. "So, just what brought you out here?"

"Simple. I am a spirited young woman with a certain proclivity for the hard sciences who has just spent her formative years in the clutches of well-intentioned but fusty instructors, and I am desperate to do something tremendous with my life. Before I become one of those fusty instructors myself."

"And so," prompted Doc, pouring more

wine into their goblets.

"And so," said Constance, crossing her boots, "I aim to become the first person, a woman, no less, to cross from East to West. At least since the Long War ended, that is."

"But no one's —"

"That's why I'm doing it. If someone had, then I wouldn't be here."

"No, I suppose not. But that still doesn't explain how you came to be alone at this spot." The blue flames of the gasbox reflected in the small, dark lenses of his glasses.

"I hired a tracker who came recommended . . . in a roundabout way. And then he abandoned me here, at the river."

The doctor snorted. "Let me guess. His name was Tico?"

She sat up straight. "How did you know?"

"And you paid him half up front?"

She nodded. "How do you know?"

"Everybody knows of Tico. He's no guide. He's more like . . . a sort of an anti-bounty hunter."

"How's that?"

"He loses people."

Constance couldn't think of a reply. She felt an urge to stretch her legs. It had been a long day. She stood — and a strange dizziness pulled at her from all sides. She swayed, dropped to one knee, then fell prone by the gasbox. She tried to rise and could not figure out how to do it.

Doctor Ocularius stared at her, not quite smiling, not moving to help her. "What's wrong, my dear?"

"The wine — what did you do?"

He spread his arms wide. "The wine, the night air, the gas, the Spoils, me — something isn't agreeing with you." He laughed then, an abrasive chuckle built into a head-thrown-back guffaw that rocked his slab of a belly.

He rose from his seat and with a grunt, snatched the loop handles of her satchel and dragged it back to where he was sitting.

"Why?"

As he untwisted the clasp and parted the bag like the mouth of a fish, he said, "I know Tico. And I know he always gets half up front for taking people across. I figure the other half has to be here somewhere. I didn't see it on your person earlier." He winked at her over the hissing gasbox.

Another short laugh erupted from him and trailed into the darkening, still night. The last thing Constance saw before her eyes closed was the doctor rummaging in her satchel, smiling and humming as he held up various articles and marveled at them in the blue light.

"Hey."

Constance opened her eyes, shut them. She felt like mud. Aching mud. Her neck was as stiff as wood and it throbbed.

"Hey."

Something nudged her leg. She squinted her eyes open. The sun was up. A dark shape hovered over her and she raised a hand to visor her eyes. Someone in a wide-brim hat. The hat turned, looked up toward the sky, then back down. In that moment, something had glinted beneath the brim — glasses?

The shape shifted, blocked out the sun, and she didn't have to squint so hard. A faint image of Doctor Ocularius filled her mind for a moment.

"Who —" She coughed. Her voice was dry, full of holes. She tried it again as she sat up. "Who are you?"

"Nope, that's my question."

"What?"

He sighed, and said, "I'm Rollicker, Sheriff of the Spoils." He sent a rope of thick brown liquid to the ground, dragged the back of one hand across his mouth, then smoothed his ample moustaches. He squinted at her through finely wrought

90

spectacles, small lavender lenses set in brass frames.

"Are you sickly?" she said, standing and stretching her back.

"What? No, not that I'm aware of."

"That . . . goop you just spit up."

"Chaw, missy. That's all."

"That was intentional?"

His jaws chewed slowly, then he pursed his lips and sluiced another stream a few inches from her boots. "Yep."

She looked at him fully for the first time. He was a tall, thin man and wore a sweat-stained shirt of rough cloth the color of sand. His trousers were of a darker, stronger material, tucked into tall brown leather boots.

His hat was a stained affair, massive in height and width, and a dull brown leather vest ended just above a holstered pistol that seemed crude and of old-time construction, certainly older than the one Tico had worn.

She wondered if these men carried their ancient guns as an affectation, in the way the wives of Societeers back home carried their clockwork pets, yipping, purring, growling knots of gears wrapped in fur and feathers, as a way to show they'd not lost touch with their urban forebears, what they liked to call their "instinctual selves."

"You must be parched," he said as he untied thongs that held a leather-wrapped bottle to a saddle horn. He handed it to her.

"Is that a real horse?" She nodded toward the beast behind him, the same deep brown color as his spittle.

Rollicker snorted a laugh, "As opposed to what? One of those modified contraptions you're used to? By god, if those dandified clothes didn't give you away, your reaction to seeing a live, kickin' horse surely does."

She uncorked the top of the bottle, sniffed it, and did her best to keep from gagging as she swigged. "It's just that in the civilized East we have modern conveyances of all manner that are far tidier and less cruel."

He shook his head, half smiling, then said, "Tell me, missy, if it's so grand in the East, what are you doing out here alone into the Spoils?"

She turned her back on him. "Constance Gatterling. That's my name."

He gave her a nod.

"Thank you for finding me."

"Dumb luck on my part — and yours. I'm headed back to town anyway. So, what are you doing out here on the Plains of Abandonia?"

She said nothing. Despite the morning's dry heat, a shiver worked up her back. "It's

92

so bleak."

"Didn't used to be — used to be beautiful prairies, rich with wildlife, birds, grasses taller than a man's head."

"What happened?"

"Long story." He mounted the horse and gathered the reins, then offered a hand down to her.

She backed up and said, "Hmm, that vile doctor told me to be wary of you people of the Spoils."

So fast she had no time to react, the sheriff leaned further and snatched her shirtfront, balling her four layers in a grimy, calloused fist. "You saw Doc?" He shook her once. Her head wobbled in a nod. "Doc Ocularius?"

She nodded again.

Rollicker released her and said, "Take me to him and I won't leave you out here." They stared at each other a moment. His jaw muscles working hard, his eyes glinting behind the lavender lenses. Then he freed his left boot from the stirrup and extended his arm again. After a moment, she mounted up behind him and he guided the horse north.

Most of an hour passed, and she found that if she turned her head to one side and breathed, she could lessen the blended stink of horse, unwashed man, and raw Spoils air. Finally she said, "What do you hate Doctor Ocularius for?"

He answered quickly, as if he were waiting for Constance to ask. "You name it — theft, murder, trickery. Years ago, when the damnable Long War was still on, the dust from the blue stone you all so desperately need back East was making everyone who mined it go blind. Some genius decided that would be bad for business, so they sent Doctor Ocularius out here to help us all keep our sight, since he seemed to be the greatest thing since wind-up lightning.

"But they didn't figure on him bein' a greedy little weasel. He's been playing the middle against both ends ever since, keeps everybody blind, so to speak — us and the powers-that-be back East, while he drains off profits for himself."

"So you're out to get him."

"Pure and straight. All I need is one clear shot at his mangy hide."

"But why? Didn't he save everyone's sight? And that in turn kept the mineworks open, correct?"

"You know, for a little bit of a thing, you sure talk a lot."

"You're not the first to tell me that."

"Might be you wanna listen to others once

in a while instead of flapping your gums."

"For better or worse, it's my curiosity that got me here."

"Yeah, smack dab in the Spoils. If this is the plan you had for yourself, I'm not so sure your gears are lining up quite right." He tapped his forehead and grinned.

"Well, aren't you going to tell me?"

He sighed. "Tell you what?"

"Why you haven't . . . eradicated the doctor."

He was silent for a few paces, then in a lowered voice said, "I can't find him."

Behind him, she smiled. "Well, that doesn't seem so difficult. I found him in short order."

To her surprise, he nodded and kept riding. After a few minutes of silence, he spit again and said, "He fixed me up, same as the rest. Only he did a little something different with my eyes. I suppose you noticed these here spectacles."

"They are not the most masculine-looking things, I'll grant you. But at least you can see."

"Yep, I can see. But not everything."

She waited for more, but he grew silent again. After a few quiet minutes, Constance said, "What is that stench?"

The sheriff sat up straight, tilted his head

back, and pulled in a deep draught of air. "Aaahh." He half turned to her and said, "That, little missy, is the smell of fashion, and music, and theatres, and cinematographs, and cyclerigibles, and all manner of modern advance that you so enjoy in the East." The he turned fully toward her, his leather saddle creaking. "That, little missy, is the smell of Rankton."

"I should say."

He laughed wide-mouthed then, and she saw for the first time the blackened nubs of his teeth. "Capitol city of the Spoils and Jewel of Abandonia."

"How very wistful. Tell me, is it as forlorn as it smells?"

"No, Lord no . . . it's worse."

"If it's so bad, then why don't you leave, Sheriff Rollicker?"

"You know, for a smarty type, you're none too bright. There ain't no leaving the Spoils, girl. Once you're in, you're in. The only folks ever end up here are those born into it, those sent here because they have no choice." He spit, looked her right in the eye, and said, "and fools."

As the horse walked slowly into the little town, the whole of which seemed backed up to a blunted rise of blue-grey rock, everywhere she looked Constance saw remnants of what seemed a thriving mining past.

Great steel-and-wood conveyors, their canvas belts tattered and hanging, jutted at the base of a sprawling mass of shale that leaked between buildings and dissipated in the street.

Brass tubes and mammoth rusted gears poked between leaning planks of wind-chewed boards the color of thick smoke. Valves and smokestacks atop steel skeletons on steel wheels, shot through with rust and holes, lay dragged and forgotten in the middle of the street, the rotted carcasses of the machinery of promise.

Signs on some of the collapsed, gaunt buildings told of once-lively trade: Abandonia General Mercantile, Flo's Pleasure Palace, The Blue Dream Bar, and at the end of the street, faded black letters on a leaning sign close by a gaping hole in the rock mound read: J. S. Kalibrator's Blue Stone and Gasworks.

To her surprise, Constance saw smoke lifting up and out the top of the entrance rough-cut into the rock, and several men straggled in and out, carrying arc rods and flatpicks.

"We'll get you cleaned up at the jailhouse,

then set to work finding Doc. Strikes me he's never too far off."

"No need."

"Now see here, missy . . ."

She sighed. "Keep your big hat on, Sheriff Rollicker. He's here."

"What? In town? How do you know?" He looked left and right, his glasses glinting.

"Sheriff, he's right over there." She jutted her chin toward the Hard Shine Saloon. "See, there's his wagon."

Rollicker followed her pointing hand, looked right at the wagon, then to the left and right of it, shaking his head.

She opened her eyes wide and stared at him as if he were a dumb child. "You know, the one that reads: 'Doctor Ocularius and his Traveling Tinctures, Tonics, and Bifurcated Nostrums for the Betterment of the Eyes, Ears, Nose, Throat, and — ' "

"Girl, I don't see a damn thing but Horace Gorton's broke-down mule and that little drunk floozy, Minusha Cockburn, sleepin' off a toot by that post out front. What are you playin' at?"

She stared at Rollicker. "You're not kidding me, are you sheriff?"

With his little finger he pushed the glasses up the bridge of his nose and smoothed his moustaches. She guessed he was fighting the urge to shout at her again.

Then she understood and her mouth dropped open as she stared at him.

He looked away.

"So you weren't kidding. That's what you meant when you said you can't see everything. Of course! Last night I laughed at the doctor when he said his glasses helped him to not be seen. It must have been the wine that made me so very ignorant. Those spectacles of his would make —"

"Girl, you're doin' it again. Chattering away like old Judge Bulger when he gets a few snorts in him."

"Sorry."

But the sheriff squinted harder at the mule. "Doc Ocularius, huh? Right here under my very nose! Hell, I'm callin' him out right now."

"What? Wait, what does that mean?"

"Means I'm aiming to get the Doc out here, settle his hash once and for all, right here in the street."

"But how will you see him?"

"I won't," he smiled and spat at their feet. "But you will."

"What?"

"Yep, just muckle onto him when he tries to climb aboard his wagon there. I'll see you and I'll pepper whatever it is you're grabbin' onto."

"I'll not do it."

"You will, and I'll tell you why." He smiled wide. "I'm the only one here who knows how to get you back East to your fine, cushy life. All this here could be but a bad memory and a hell of a story to tell your little friends when you sit around a fancy dining table some night back in East City."

She smiled. "I'll just find Tico. He'd take me back to the border." She looked around as if expecting to see him waiting for her.

"Sure, yeah, just wave a coin in the air. He'll find you."

Her smile faded as the sheriff forced his moustaches into a big frown. "What? No money? Oh that's right, Doc Ocularius took your traveling cash. And if I'm not mistaken, he's in the Hard Shine right now, transforming it into little glasses full of libation for him and all his new friends."

As if on cue, a round of laughter bubbled out the batwing doors.

She bit the inside of her mouth. Of course she wanted out of the Spoils, but she also wanted the doctor's glasses. If she could get those, her future would be set — no dry academic career for her. She could travel, see Europaia, the Far Orient. The world would be hers.

"All right. I'll do it. But first I need a sip of that foul water."

"Attagirl." He handed her the leather-covered bottle. "Now here's what we'll do . . ."

In her mind Constance replayed her plan, meager though it was, as she swung the leather-bottle canteen by its strap handle and crossed the street to the wagon. Up close and even in such grey light as Rankton received, the doctor's old burrowing mine machine was nothing more than a bent, haggard relic — wood and steel, grimy, worn out, and faded. Like everything in this place.

If this withered, bled corpse of a country had a face, she thought, then it was certainly this toothless crone of a town. What had the sign at the end of Main Street said? "Rankton, Jewel of Abandonia"? Jewel, indeed. Get me those glasses and a ride out of here and I'll not so much as give it a second thought for the rest of my days.

"Well, little lady! Imagine my surprise at seeing you here."

Constance froze, then turned and looked up, and there stood Doctor Ocularius on the boardwalk, leaning against a faded wood post. A tiny drunk floozy snored, propped at the base of the next post, wearing nothing but one holey brown sock, a tattered underdress, and two black eyes beneath small brass spectacles with green lenses.

Doc's head wobbled enough to tell Constance he was inebriated. He held her satchel by the handles, almost bouncing it against his knees.

A short, thin man and an even smaller woman, both wearing clothing so begrimed she didn't know where skin ended and fabric began, walked right by the doctor, close enough that they brushed his arm — yet they paid him no heed.

Both wore green-lens eyewear in brass frames.

She waited for them to pass, then Constance strode to him and swung the glass-and-leather water vessel hard by the thong handle and caught the doctor just above his left ear.

His dented black hat pinwheeled upward, then dropped to the street. He grunted and sagged to a sitting position on the edge of the boardwalk, his back to the post.

She rummaged in the satchel. "My, but you made a mess of my things, Doctor. Shame on you."

Doctor Ocularius sat weaving and shaking his head.

She pulled a white shirt from the bag, held it up, sighed, and tore at a seam with her teeth, ripping the garment in two. With one half she tied his hands together behind the post.

His struggles were weak. "What are you doing? Oh, my head."

She lashed his feet together with the other half shirt. "It occurred to me, Doctor, that the bounty on you, I would imagine, is rather substantial. Not to mention what I can do with those glasses of yours." She smiled and depressed a small button on a polished copper device she'd retrieved from her bag.

It was palm-sized and when the click sounded, it split in two, and she pulled the halves apart. Between them stretched a thin, limp thread. "Why go all the way to the West Edge — if it's even possible — when you represent all I've been searching for?"

The doctor swallowed. "What . . . what is that, my dear?"

"I believe I hinted that I was a recent graduate of the Academy? I fear I may have neglected to mention some of the Chancellor's last words to us all: 'Bring me the head of Doctor Ocularius and your future is secure!' Funny thing at the time. We all laughed. But now I know exactly what he meant."

She pulled tight the device in her hands and the thin wire glowed a vivid blue. "Yes, this little notion heats water, helps with manicures, oh, and did I mention that it's also useful in slicing? You see, it cauterizes as it cuts. Makes rather a neat job of it, really."

The doctor swallowed audibly, straightened against the post. "You think you're the only one to come after me? Every time a new class graduates, it seems at least one fresh face intends to make a quick name for himself by capturing me."

She raised the wire up and held it at neck level. "Now, I'll need my money . . . and those glasses."

She lowered the device and with the back of one hand patted the worn black fabric of his vest. Then, still watching his dark lenses, she reached in a pocket and pulled out a wad of wrinkled circular paper bills. Coins, green with tarnish, spilled to the dirt at his feet.

"And the glasses," she said.

"N-no, no, I can't! They are part of me, you see. Attached to me, to my skull, in my eye sockets. They can't be removed."

"Masterful, Doctor. But I will have them,

one way or another —" She pushed the wire closer to his neck, so close that the hairs of his shaggy whiskers smoked and curled. A sound like steam hissing from a touchy valve rose from his mouth.

"I can't let you do that, missy!"

Behind her she heard the sheriff's voice, ragged like wind through shredded metal.

She turned her head. "Why ever not, Sheriff? You're going to do the same thing."

He didn't respond, but lurched into the street, his pistol drawn and aimed at her, though it wagged in time with his unsteady gait. His hat was gone and she was shocked to see the split purple welt and spatter of blood that covered the side of Rollicker's face, an unfortunate by-product of hitting him with the water bottle. He'd dropped as if shot, but she hadn't thought to take his pistol.

"Yes, but I'm a lawman and you're doing it for the wrong reasons."

She snorted. "Sheriff, my reasons are as valid as yours. Perhaps more so, considering I have a future — a brilliant career ahead of me as potentially one of the greater minds of my generation. While you are, well, you're here. A comparison can hardly be drawn."

"Badmouth me and Rankton all you want, girly." Rollicker's voice was right behind her now. "I've heard it all before. If I got to go through you to get to him, fine by me. You're both burrs under my saddle. One shot, two burrs gone." She heard the throaty click of the ancient gun's mechanism, felt the barrel of his pistol grazing her ruined blue velvet coat.

Constance's lips drew tight across her straight, white teeth. She stared at the doctor's unblinking lenses, the fine, beautiful precision work of the thick brass mechanisms surrounding them. And she also smelled the foul, bitter stink of his boozy breath.

She wanted nothing more than a long bath in clean water — and she knew there was only one way to get back to that life. With a slight grunt and a strained smile, she pushed the wire forward.

From the sagging balcony of the Hotel Abandonia across the street, Tico saw the sheriff's knuckle whiten, and he knew that trigger was but a baby's breath away from opening the ball.

"In for a penny," Tico mumbled. He took one step sideways, eyeing the scene in the street below, his boot heel clunking soft on the rotting wood, his spur singing like the whisper of a far-off breeze. Then he shot the sheriff in the back.

It all played out as he expected: The sheriff lurched forward, squeezed his pistol's trigger, the girl's pretty blue jacket burst apart, she pitched forward with her hotwire tool straight into Doc's throat . . . *ssup!*

Clean as you please, the old goat's head burned free of his body, teetered for a second on the stump, like a coin dropped on a bar top, then it flopped to the ground.

Tico led his horse from the shadows across the street and stood looking down at the unfortunate trio.

Doc was sagged against the post, belly-blasted and headless. The other two, their last was bubbling up, soaking into the dust. The sheriff's trigger finger kept curling into the dirt, reaching for the thing that was no longer there.

The girl whimpered something, her mouth moving like a clockwork toy nearly wound down.

"You talk too much, girl," said Tico, looking at her.

He rolled a quirley, patted his vest for a scratcher. "Aw hell." Then he saw the girl's gadget still gripped in her hands, the blue wire arcing small sparks against the dirt.

He stepped on her hand and lifted it free, fiddled with it a moment, and worked it back up to a full glow, hot enough to light his cigarette.

Tico heard a scuffing sound, looked up at the dozen or so drawn faces of the diggers trying not to look at him, the dark green lenses of their spectacles not quite hiding their fear. They advanced, hoping, he knew, for a chance at something of value.

He stared until they turned and dragged themselves back inside the Hard Shine to whimper about this day for years to come. From her post, the tiny, drunk floozy, Minusha Cockburn, snorted in her sleep.

Tico snatched up Doc's head by its greasy knot of hair, stared into its taught, shocked face, and worked a grimy couple of fingers on one of the dials surrounding a lens.

"Well, that's one way to get ahead." He blew smoke in the dead man's face, then dropped the head into the girl's satchel. He plucked the wad of cash from the girl's hand and stuffed it into his vest pocket.

Then Tico looped the handles of the satchel over his saddle horn, climbed atop the waiting Colonel Saunderston the Third, and spurred the clanking horse East, toward the sunrise.

LUCKY TAM

(A FOREWORD)

In early February 1952, while searching for
a source of iridium in the Gila Wilderness
in southwest New Mexico, geologist Dr.
Harvey Dinsmore IV happened upon a wad
of ragged oilcloth wedged tight among
boulders, seven feet up in a dry wash, barely
above spring flood height. With much effort
the scientist tugged it free and unfolded the
grimy cloth to reveal a weathered, leather-
covered book. In doing so, he unearthed
one of twentieth-century America's most
enduring mysteries, the legend of Lucky
Tam.

Who was Lucky Tam? As author of the
book, a diary, as it turns out, Tam helped
answer that question by titling the work
himself on the very first page: *A Tramp's
Tales (or Episodes from the Life of a Rover).*
That, however, would prove the extent of
his assistance in the matter.

Scholars are confident in claiming his true

identity has yet to be discovered, though not for lack of considerable effort spent by historians and countless curious readers — among them scores of self-proclaimed "Tamblers" — throughout the many decades since the mysterious man's journal was found in that unlikely wilderness locale.

Logic dictates the aforementioned Dr. Dinsmore may have been a huckster having a bit of fun at the public's expense. Yet Dinsmore had no history as a trickster, no personal motivation to foist an elaborate ruse on the public. Indeed, as a successful and respected research scientist, author, and lecturer, Dr. Harvey Dinsmore IV had every reason to avoid drawing such odd attentions as the journal brought him.

In an effort to mitigate the increasing deleterious effects the Lucky Tam tome had on his reputation and burgeoning career, Dr. Dinsmore donated the journal to the University of Washita at Cheyenne, Oklahoma. He hoped the gesture and the selection of a seemingly unbiased institution might reflect favorably on him, and further distance him from the suspicions of those who considered the discovery fraudulent.

Furthermore, when U of W Press decided, in 1954, to publish the first official edition of *A Tramp's Tales,* Dinsmore agreed to lend his name to the project, by way of a brief introduction, in an effort to give the book a scholarly bent. Although the book sold well, and Dr. Dinsmore publicly announced he received no remuneration from its sale or his participation in it, his involvement in its release did little to lessen the damage, at least in scholarly circles, to his career.

In later years, Dr. Dinsmore managed to prop up his reputation with various geologic discoveries that proved beneficial to the United States Government's global military pursuits.

Despite this, to his death in 1994 at age 77, in full retention of his faculties, Dr. Dinsmore proclaimed his innocence of what some wags referred to as "Dinsmore's Folly." He had been heard on many occasions to utter regret over having "lugged the damnable diary back home with me."

If we are to believe Lucky Tam's own brief biographical sketch, he was one of tens of thousands of young American men to return home from Europe and the madness of the First World War, dazed and overwhelmed, forever altered emotionally and physically by the filth of trench warfare, by the piercing whistle of artillery and the creeping poison of deadly gases, by the horrified screams of men reduced to blood and bone, mewling for their mothers as they bled into muck, by death and rot, by questions without answer lasting a lifetime.

On his return to the United States, and his hometown of "Filbert," Indiana, our hero eschews the life expected of him. Instead of settling down with his prewar sweetheart, "Lorena," and assuming his father's plumbing business, our everyman adopts the moniker "Lucky Tam" and takes to the road as a tramp with little more than "one slouch hat and the togs on my back, two good hands and a stout pair of boots, a dime-store diary with pencil enough for a short-stack of adventures."

By standards of the time, Lucky Tam lived a life of low-level hedonism — he smoked cigars and on occasion a corncob pipe, he drank when alcohol presented itself to him, he cut his own hair with a pocketknife that he kept "sharp as a crow's eye," he enjoyed whistling, and he paid for what material goods he required with that most base of currency, labor rendered by a strong mind and body.

Yet, for all this, Lucky Tam's fame comes not from being a returned warrior who tramped about and kept a diary. Indeed, he is not well known for any one deed from his extraordinary life, but rather for the fact that he, as a rover, simply disappeared. As of this writing, no trace of the man (save for his journal) has been found.

And yet, content-wise, we don't even know if Lucky Tam's diary is authentic. From a physical perspective, the journal itself has been verified by forensic analysis as authentic to the time in which the author's dated entries indicate.

In addition, there exist a number of second- and third-hand narrative accounts of people having met a man matching Tam's description and demeanor, and in the timeframe in which he mentions traveling the regions where the claimants dwelled.

Other clues indicating authenticity include common parlance of the times used by Tam in his entries, and various, albeit few, details sprinkled throughout his narratives about places and businesses he visited (the mercantile in West Knob, Wyoming, where he bartered labor for pencils and tobacco, for example).

There are also limited descriptions of the regiment with which he claimed to have been attached in the war, coupled with details of the war gleaned from his recountings of harrowing, recurring nightmares.

Unfortunately, incomplete attempts have been made to account for each of the seventy-two returning men in his regiment. Likewise, investigations as to the whereabouts of his hometown ("Filbert" is another name for a hazelnut and is not, as it turns out, a town in Indiana), his intended fiancée, and his family and its business have proven fruitless. And yet, there is the journal.

And there is the blood. Yes, blood — as yet lacking a DNA match — which time has rendered less bloodlike than crimson squeezings from a fresh wound. Nonetheless, the brown smears grimly decorating the pages of a late entry provide further intriguing clues as to the final days, hours, minutes, and seconds of Lucky Tam.

And something else: Stuck between future, unsullied pages in the diary, a ratted, bent feather nested, likely from the wing of a juvenile *Meleagris gallopavo* (or wild turkey), its quilly tip raggedly angled as if gnawed by teeth. We picture those teeth loosening in the puckered, bleeding mouth of a dying Tam.

Ever-present pencil apparently lost, he found the strength to transform the paltry feather into a utensil for scratching out his last words, rendered in his own blood, his savaged body as inkwell.

Consider this passage from May 24, 1928,

date of his last entry, nine years from his first. Given the weak voice and weaker visual presentation of the entry itself, we can assume Tam was scratching at death's door even as he scratched out these words:

"I aim to live, but how much longer? Bastid [*sic*] got me good. I don't know if it was man, beast, or other. Darkness hid it from me. I think it was starving. Its breath stank of fly-blown meat, of war. It grunted and snarled and savaged me with teeth like white knives. I expect it will be back, and I will not again be able to kick, nor shout it off. Dark is near. Anyways, I am bleeding from a mess of spots, most stopped but a few keep leaking, leaking out my last. My last . . . now think on that."

Did this vicious attack take place upriver of where his cloth-wrapped journal was discovered, wedged and waiting? (Fortunate for us if not for Dr. Dinsmore.) That would explain the dearth of clues as to Tam's remains.

Odd as it sounds, it is possible there are some still unfamiliar with the enigmatic author and his riveting diary. That makes this new edition, revised with updated footnotes and historical addendums, so much more special. The intention of this exhaustive volume was to attempt to answer the myriad questions that have surrounded Tam's journal since its discovery all those years ago. And yet we still find ourselves with more questions than answers — not that we mind.

The enduring appeal of the legend of Lucky Tam is its mystery, and people savor mysteries. We like their challenge, and we relish when conundrums foil our best efforts at solving them. Lucky Tam has proven to be among the twentieth century's penultimate pickles, the very cause of his enduring appeal to sleuths trained and homespun — anyone, in fact, who has ever yearned to chuck it all, walk away, and never look back.

That devil-may-care aura is the very reason I became attracted to the book as a young, moody sort, prone to haunting the darkest corners of musty libraries and mildewed bookshops. It was in one such shop, the Mouse and Thimble, in Beasley, Massachusetts, in 1973, that I unearthed a tattered, much-taped copy of *A Tramp's Tales.*

I read the words, I sensed the passion, and I smelled not mold and dust but the heady aroma of unfettered freedom as can only be envisaged by a youth with naught but possibility before him.

Years later, and after much roving, I found

myself as a professor of literature, specializing in nineteenth- and twentieth-century American literary vagabonds, among them Walt Whitman, Jack London, Jack Kerouac, and none other than Lucky Tam.

It is no surprise then, and no coincidence, that I ended up heading the English department at the University of Washita, a position requiring, in addition to various other duties, oversight of the U of W Press, including its limited back catalog of titles, among them . . . *A Tramp's Tales (or Episodes from the Life of a Rover).*

Yes, I have access to the original battered, leather-bound journal. And I have likely spent more time with it than the author himself.

In this revised, second edition, I have restored the handful of slight passages omitted from the first, lines in which, admittedly, little of worth or revelation occur. Nonetheless, offered to the public for the first time is this complete version of the original diary, word for word, as set down by its author, Lucky Tam.

Included also is Dr. Dinsmore's original introduction from 1954. (You'll note he now shares the dedication page with Lucky Tam, the man who made his life at times a vexation. I am uncertain how the good doctor would feel about this, but I could not help myself.)

So I leave it to you, reader, to sift wheat from chaff, to kick the can down your own mysterious dirt road, and decide if Lucky Tam was indeed a huckster bent on shamming the finders of conjured diary entries, or if he was, as is believed by many, honest and real and true.

If he was real and true (as I am of a mind to believe), and his last entry relates the cause of his demise, might not we also consider him . . . Unlucky Tam?

Even as I type this, young privileged idealists slouch across the greenswards of every campus in America wearing "Lucky Tam Lives!" T-shirts. And to them I say . . . yes. Yes he does, and will forever remain alive in the ragged, gripping pages of his journal, fabricated or no. For it represents a hope, an ideal, a life most of us yearn for yet will never live.

And so I ask again, who was Lucky Tam? We may know. Or we may never know. In the end, does it matter?

Been a Long Time

It happened so long ago I mostly have forgotten the why, let alone the how or the who. Or maybe it happened today. I don't really know. But I'll tell you what, I can't for a second forget that I'm not where I'm supposed to be.

Every minute of the day I feel I've been caught shuffling along the main street of a dusty little poke of a town with my drawers down around my boots, horses flicking their ears and swishing their tails, and me with my what's-it-worm wagging while up on the boardwalk mothers are grabbing their kids and pulling them into shops and here comes the marshal again.

Or at least that's what it's like until I wake up. And every time I wake up I'm in a louse-crawly bed by a busted-pane window overlooking the same dusty main street. And on the floor is a cracked porcelain thunder pot, crawling with flies and stinking.

I drop back to the shuck pillow and sigh. I've been here so many times before. The *here* is always this town — today's town, yesterday's town, tomorrow's town, all the same. You see, from day to day I can't recall much of anything. The only thing I really have are slugs of memories that seem solid, waiting for me to build on. But once my attention settles on 'em, they're gone again. So really, I have nothing.

I started trying to figure it out by keeping a diary. Thought I'd write in it every day, that was the idea. I must have bought it in the mercantile. Hell, I may have bought it this morning. I can't be sure. Anyway, I figured I'd licked it, finally knew what needed doing, and I'd be able to find my way home, wherever that was. So I jotted down what I know: It's high summer, mid-July 1871, Territory of Colorado, town of Lodestone.

But the next day, might have been this morning, the pages and pages I'd written about that day were gone, all those words and thoughts and pencil scratches — gone. Problem was . . . the pages were clean like there never were words there. The only thing I had was the *memory* of having spent all that time writing in the damn diary to begin with, and even that was fuzzy, as if

I'd been on a three-day spree. Which makes me wonder if I only *think* I remember writing it all down. You see how it is with me? Don't know if I'm coming, going, or if I'm anywhere at all.

I don't think people actually recognize me from previous visits, but I do think they sense something's off about me. Like the smell of a dog when he walks in and settles down by your chair. Somehow you know that rascal's been up to something. Then you find out he was seen carryin' off your neighbor's prize hen.

But it's more than a fresh blood smell, it's that feeling of wrongness rising off the little savage like a bad idea. That's what I think folks sense off me. And I can tell they feel that way even though I've been in town but a few hours. Hell, sometimes it's only a matter of minutes before I get the looks. That's when I think I might be better off alone.

Each morning I vow to saddle up and set off early for the hills to do some prospecting, some fishing in the streams, but somehow the day always gets away from me and I never quite make it out of town. I'll wake up the next morning and I'm right back in a nasty ol' shuck bed. And that's the way it's been for as long as I can remember —

which, I admit, isn't too far back.

At least the name I have sticks with me, I suppose because it's an easy thing to pull from one day to the next. It's not my real name, of course, somehow I know that much. I can't remember the real one, but this one'll do. I chose it because of the two letters someone sewed into each piece of clothing I'm wearing.

Inside the shank of each boot, in the collars of my shirt and vest, in the waist of my trousers, the beat and battered topper I wear on my head — someone embroidered a "T.S." on everything. Wasn't me who did it, because I can't sew worth a bean and these letters look like they were done by a professional.

A Chinese laundry man asked me my name once when I'd had my duds laundered in some little mining town that, come to think on it, looked a lot like this town. Couldn't have been that long ago because I still remember it. Maybe it was today, just after breakfast. Anyways, where was I? Oh yeah, the Chinaman.

He'd tapped with a fingertip on the black initials in the shirt, his finger going up and down like a little bird pecking for information. First thing I know I said, "Tim Shaw. Mr. Tim Shaw," and that's who I've been since, Tim Shaw.

I say it fast and it feels right somehow, like it means something. I have to believe that one day the meaning will come to me. So I've been dragging that name with me from day to day like an old satchel I can't open, but I know something good's inside.

Sometimes when I'm telling it to a riled-up marshal or a livery owner or a saloon floozy, I know for certain it's not my name. I get a feeling, like when you bite a fresh apple and it's crisp and the tang of it sets off a memory. Same thing happened to me earlier today at the mercantile, with a beef stew and four plump dumplings bubbling in a pot atop the potbelly stove.

"Oh, but doesn't that smell good," I said to the old lady counting out scoops of coarse meal into cloth sacks.

She stopped long enough to measure me up and down over those little nose glasses of hers. "It's my husband's dinner."

I'm afraid I took another peek into the pot. I couldn't help it, sitting as it was right there in the middle of the little store. The dumplings were even taking on that sheen, like sweat on a pretty girl's face when she's been asked to dance by every lad in town and she hasn't said no all evening. I tell you that stew was a sight.

"Oh, all right." The old lady's voice startled me.

I looked up from staring at the heavenly stew, and I felt my face go red like a struck thumb. "Ma'am?"

"The stew." She'd come out from behind the counter with a bowl, a spoon, and a ladle. "Worth two-bits to you?"

"Why, yes ma'am. But your husband . . ."

She'd already plunged the ladle in and lifted out two of the most heavenly dumplings oozing underneath with dark gravy. I even saw a nub or two of carrot poking up.

"He's always late anyhow. And I've et."

I barely heard her. By the time the warm, butter-strong scent reached my nose I had my coin purse in my palm and had pinched out more than what she'd asked. And let me tell you, it was worth it at twice the price. Ten times . . . because it helped me to remember.

While I was eating that stew I recalled something important. What the stew had to do with it, I've no idea. But I've thought on it all day, and now that it's night and I expect I'll fade off into sleep or whatever it is I do, wherever it is I go, I'll lose the memory by tomorrow. Or maybe tomorrow will be a little bit more of today. Maybe I'll have a two-day run of it this time. Or a week. And that's what keeps getting me out of bed. What if this time it all lasts? What if a memory sticks and I'm allowed to live instead of just exist?

So, what I remembered was this: A woman's arm — the wrist and hand with a dusting of lightish honey-color hair, a slice of sunlight laid across it prettier than if she'd draped a diamond bracelet on there. I could tell it was a woman's wrist because of that soft knob of bone that's visible even on a chunky girl and that ain't never the same on a man, no sir. But this girl was slender. And just above that prettiest of sights, a white sleeve ended, not tight and wrapped in lace, but looser.

I took another spoonful of stew, so hot it burned my tongue and I didn't care, didn't even stop, afraid that it might break the spell and I'd lose that sliver of a memory. It wasn't so much the picture in my mind of the hand, the wrist, the sleeve end, but the feeling behind it. You see, I knew that woman. I'm sure of it.

Not like you come to know a soiled dove for a few minutes, and not like you come to know your own mother or sister or wife, but somehow I knew who she was, just the same. I guess it was a feeling of familiarity I was so excited about because nothing has seemed so familiar for such a long time. If it did, I don't recall it anymore.

So I kept my eyes closed and stood right there in the little store and slurped on that stew like it was life-giving nectar from that first garden in the Bible. While I was giving thought to that wrist and coat cuff, I ever-so-gently nudged my mind's eyes to wander up that sleeve, not frilly nor tight on the arm like a dress might be, but more like a coat.

And before I knew it, there was a shoulder.

I held the spoon in my mouth, the vision I was having just kept going . . . and with no warning at all, I saw a face, the face of a woman, hair shortish, tucked around an ear, and spectacles, too. Big ones, the likes of which I've never seen, and rimmed in thick, clear frames.

Her hair was reddish brown, darker than the light hair on her wrist. And I could see an earring, small and glinting like it was a jewel. And her face was precious, easily the prettiest woman who has ever lived, more of the fine light hairs there on her cheek. She held still, like a painting. And then two things happened at once.

That old woman who'd served me squawked like a early-morning crow will do outside your window, and the pretty woman

126

in my mind cut her eyes in my direction and almost smiled.

"Are you having a fit? Cause if'n you are, then you can get out of here and right quick, too. I don't hold with anyone who can't keep control of himself."

I ignored the old stick of a woman for as long as I could, tried to keep the vision there before me. The pretty woman in my mind had moved, had looked right at me. That never happened before. Or at least not recently.

But what's more, I saw a flash of gold from down lower on her, like a brooch, maybe. But no, it wasn't at the throat, lovely as that was. It was lower, and to the side. A pin of some sort? No. And the white garment itself was not right, not like something a woman would wear. Nor were the spectacles. But what was it that I missed? There was something else, I just know it. The gold thing down below. I —

"That's it. I knew you was a madman the second I clapped eyes on you. Get out of my store right now! Right now before I call for the marshal . . ."

I opened my eyes, the spoon still clamped in my teeth. But the pretty woman was gone, replaced by the shouting old biddy in the store. I set the bowl of warm stew on the counter with the spoon beside it. The dumplings stared at me like the pasty cheeks of a dead child. I wasn't hungry any more. Just tired. I walked out of the shop, the old woman's voice following me until the door cut it off.

I made my way along the boardwalk for a minute, watched by a few folks. I didn't care. I had too much to think about to pay them any heed. Then I walked straight into a chunky bald man in arm garters and a striped shirt. He was sweeping his precious few feet of boardwalk.

"Hey, mister," he stared at me like I'd said "boo" in church. "Look out where you're headed."

Not even possible, friend, I thought. "Sorry," I said.

"I'll forget it — if you need a haircut or a bit of doctoring."

"What?"

The man shook his head and stepped back inside his shop. "Nothing. I was trying to drum up business. I ain't had coin enough for a drink all week."

I stared at him for a moment, the last of the haziness of the stew-dream leaving me. "Did you say you're a doctor?"

"Close as you'll find around these parts. I've even studied back East. 'Course, out here a man can't do just one thing. That's why I also cut hair, pull teeth, clean ears, and lend a hand at the 'Gazette.' "

I stepped into the empty shop after him and pulled off my hat. "I can use a haircut."

"Hell, for a dime I'll cut 'em all." He laughed way too long at his own joke. I tried to join in.

"Have a seat," he said, and waved me into the chair, talking the entire time.

I only half heard him. My mind was still on that woman in my memory. On her coat and the thing I didn't see but I know was there. I closed my eyes while he snipped and fiddled with my hair. I could have cared less what he did with it. Vain I ain't.

"Doc . . ."

The man stopped snipping for a second and cleared his throat. I guessed he felt flattered to be called that. "In your professional training, have you ever had any experience working with people who were, well . . . off their nut?" I tapped my head and squinted at him in the reflection before me.

He lowered the scissors and comb and looked at me in the mirror. "What?"

"You know — am I crazy?"

"Mister," he said, resuming my haircut. "If you're crazy, then you'd do well to keep it to yourself. People around here don't much like anything that's different."

Outside, a muleskinner's wagon raised a fresh cloud of dust as it rumbled past. The doc reached out with one leg and toed his door shut. He went back to work on my hair.

I sighed. This way I live feels normal to me because it's been going on for so long. Or has it? I guess I'm either full-bore crazy or not at all. I choose to think I'm not. Small comfort. It's as if I've been forgotten.

I bet that the woman in the memory could tell me everything I wish I knew. I didn't know much about her, but I couldn't get rid of her, either. She was lodged in my gizzard like a hunk of cheap steak that I can't swallow nor bring back up. Stuck, that's what she is, and me, too.

"There. Never have I seen such a fine tonsorial treatment." The doc stood behind me, hands resting on his girthy middle, looking at my head in the mirror the way a farmer might a prize cabbage.

I pushed up out of the chair and rummaged in my vest pocket for money. Then something in the corner, hanging from a peg, caught my eye. I tossed the coins on the little counter and snatched the thing down. It was a white coat.

"What's this?" I said, stretching out the

sleeves and admiring it as if it were the latest fashion I might like to buy.

"That's my doctorin' coat. We all got one when we graduated from the Kingsley Medical Program in Providence, Rhode Island."

"You ever known any women doctors?"

He snorted a laugh that tailed off like a sneeze. "Mister, you are off your rocker." He took the coat from me and draped it over his arm, smoothed it.

"There isn't anything there," I nodded at the coat and pointed to the side of my own chest. "On the coat, I mean."

"What would you expect to see? A badge? I'm a doctor, not a lawman."

But that was all I heard. I think he kept talking as I left. And I know he sent for the marshal, because a few minutes later a man with a star marched me down the street, prodding me with his pistol and telling me he didn't have time for troublemakers in his town. I didn't care much.

As long as the cell was empty it would give me the time I needed to think. And time was the one thing I guess I had more of than anything else. Besides, they could hold me there overnight but I wouldn't wake up there, that much I knew.

The door squawked and clanked shut

behind me and I made my way to the bunk. No one was in the cell with me. I leaned back against the log wall and concentrated on the woman in the white coat.

Then I had a thought: What if I've been doing the same thing forever? What if this is all there is or ever will be to my life? What if I'm being forced somehow to be the same person doing the same things, thinking the same thoughts, over and over, and a thousand more overs besides?

It's as if I'm caught in something that keeps spinning and can't stop. And the worst of it is that I have a strong hunch that it never will stop. Like a pup that's caught his tail and keeps on spinning with that thing in his teeth. Except even dogs will grow bored and chase a rabbit instead.

That's what bothers me the most — knowing that if I can't ever gain an edge on this thing, I won't ever grow older, and that means I won't ever die. And I guess that even writing in my little diary won't help me because whatever I write, whatever I learn, will all disappear come tomorrow, and I'll be back where I am right now.

All of that is truly bad, worse than a main-street showdown with a sore loser at five-card stud, because at least with him you stand a chance of dyin'. And wouldn't that be a blessed relief. But I don't believe I'm quite there yet. There's still some figuring left to do on this problem.

No, the worst part is that the only thing that keeps me doing this day after day after day, for what could well be thousands or by now millions of years (or is it just one day so far?) is that I still have hope. But what if hope should leave me? I guess then I could kill myself. I snapped my eyes open and sat up again, my knuckles pushing into the rough blanket. But what if I come to find out that death is not even possible?

The cell's grown darker now, the deputy is snoring lightly in the front room. Soon it will be night and I'll drift off, then wake up in a hotel in an uncomfortable shuck bed with a lumpy pillow, a thunder pot on the floor beside my flopped boots. It ain't much, but it's something, I reckon.

I stretch out full-length on the plank cot and try to relax. Before too long I think of the woman in the coat, the woman with short, red-brown hair, with big glasses, and . . . the gold name tag on her chest that reads, "Dr. Jennifer Kaplan," with "Time-Shares" in smaller letters underneath.

I almost open my eyes to . . . do what? Write it down in the diary? Has that ever done any good? I relax and watch her face, and even as she speaks I seem to recall what it is she's telling me. So much information to remember, I think to myself, right before I am once again lost in her words. Once again.

Her smile stretches wide and she says, "No sir, Mr. Barr, there's no need to worry. I can assure you everything has been repaired and tested, and it's perfectly safe now. You'll have the ideal vacation." She looks me up and down, leans closer, and says, in a whisper, "You look just like a real cowboy." She winks, the smile again, then louder, "This journey to the Old West will be the trip of a lifetime for you, Mr. Barr. You'll wish you'd never have to leave. Time-Shares guarantees it. Now just relax while we perform our last-minute checks."

Her face disappears, a steel door clunks shut, the bright ceiling lights dim. I can just make out faces staring at me through a glass window set into the wall by the door. She is there, standing beside others, a man and a woman, also in white coats.

Above the table where I'm strapped down there are metal rods pulsing with lights, others tipped with points, cables and wire coiled all about me.

Everything in here seems to be making a

sound, each piece rising to a pitch all its own, then something buzzes, lights on the wall above the window flash from red to green. She is still smiling. Then something explodes.

It sounds like a safe door being ripped off its hinges by too big a charge of dynamite. Arms of blue light reach toward me. I cannot move. Something else rips apart and I hear a woman's screams as if from far away, from behind thick glass.

She shrieks, "No, not again! You said it was fixed!"

A man shouts, "Get him out of there! Now!"

I try to scream, try to howl loud enough to tell them yes, yes, get me out of here. I try to wake the deputy snoring in his tipped-back chair in the next room.

I try, over and over, I try. . . .

BLOODLINE

CHAPTER ONE

The old man laid into me today with that bullwhip. It's something his son gave him a long time ago for the old man's birthday. I wish he'd given him a hat instead. I only ever seen him use the whip on the oxen. And once when he was drunk, he skinned strips of bark off a oak tree out back of the kitchen. There ain't a whole lot of trees by the house and now there's one less.

Mama says I should know better than to make the old man angry. She says I am a vexation to him. I take that to mean I cause him grief. If that is the case, then he is also a vexation to me, but I dare not say so.

Now that I think on it, Mama causes the old man grief, too. I guess that means we all have something in common. Besides being blood kin. The old man will not admit to that, though.

He calls me a " 'skin," but with other

words before it. He spits them at me as if they are hot coals in his mouth. Mama says that's because he's envious of me, but I am twelve years old now and I know better. He calls me that because I am part Indian.

The old man, he's known as Bull. Bull Barr. He's a big man, red in and out with anger and blood. I know, for I have tasted his knuckles on my teeth. He is also my mother's father. I am forbidden to call him grandfather. I don't call him anything, in fact. I only nod and keep my eyes from meeting his.

When he catches me looking at him, he calls me to him and clouts me on the ear, sometimes on both. I reckon I don't hear so well now, 'cause Mama or the old man are forever waving their hands at me as if to say hello in a crowd. Only there ain't no crowd here, just the old man, Mama, and me.

Used to be there was the old man's wife, Martha Anne. He talks to her when he's drinking, which is most every night. There was a boy, too, Mama's brother. His name was Richard. But they're both dead, been so since before I come along.

Late this afternoon, close to suppertime, I was in the barn when he laid into me. I never heard the whip until it whistled by my ear. First lashing caught me over the shoulder and snapped like a snakebite on my chest, then back across my wing bone. For a breath, it didn't hurt, then it blazed and crackled like a lightning strike.

I stuttered, couldn't pull air in nor push it out before the next blow landed on me, and I tell you, I howled then. I try never to make sounds when I'm working with the old man, which is most days, but a bullwhip peeling your hide apart like a poorly sewed seam will make most folks shout.

He liked hearing me because he laid in with vigor then, laughing that ragged, shouty sound he makes when he's happy and drunk, which is not always the same thing.

I hunched up and tried to run by him but he cornered me in Chaco's stall. Only thing I could do was make myself small. He shouted, " 'Skin! Foul 'skin — that's all you are, boy! Brought woe on the Barr clan!"

Same as always.

Later, while Mama dressed my back and I bit down hard as I could on a wad of flannel, she said I should not have done it, whatever it was. I nodded, but I don't know what it was I should not have done. It's always that way, though.

Every morning after I fill the wood box and before I go to the barn, she tells me the

138

same thing: "Keep your head bent, don't look him in the eyes. Do what he says, and it will be all right. You'll see." Then she winks and smiles and kisses me on top of the head. Mostly on my hat because I always wear it. Covers the scars up there.

Mama says it looks like a blind man laid train track on my head. I never saw it, reckon I never will. How many of us can see the tops of our heads, anyway? You have to assume it's there. Anyway, I don't wear the hat in the house when the old man is around.

After the whupping, she finishes working in the salve — the old man calls it goose grease, and he may be right. It stinks about as bad as their slimy leavings all over the yard — then she turns me around and looks at me. She is crying, which isn't unusual, but there is something else. Her mouth is twitchy and she leans close and whispers, like we do when we're not sure if the old man is awake, "We're leaving tonight."

I must look like I don't believe her because she shakes her head and squeezes my shoulders tighter. "This time it is different."

I about cry, mostly because her squeezing hurts my lash cuts. Also, we've trotted down this path before and it always leads back here. But as I say, this time she surprises me. I don't smell the wilty-flower smell of her medicine on her breath. I think it's whiskey, same as the old man, but unless she gets it from his bottles, I don't know where she lays hold of it. We neither of us leave the farm.

She don't say much, but nods toward our room, which is also the woodshed off the kitchen. It's comfortable but not so good in winter when the snow dusts in through the gaps. When it's cold, we sneak back into the kitchen and sleep by the stove once the old man's drunk and snoring in his bedroom.

I stuff things into a seed sack that smells like corn. Mama's hairbrush and the nice socks she knitted for us, and a carved wooden soldier that used to belong to her brother, which makes him my dead uncle, and a few other things, too. She's busy snatching up clothes.

Pretty soon the bag's full, but not heavy, and Mama looks at it, then at the door to the kitchen. I know she's wondering if the old man's asleep yet. I don't hear him snoring, but it can't be much longer. He was drunk when he started in on me with the whip and that was near two hours ago.

"We'll take the buggy," she whispers. "You rig it up, I'll fetch food and meet you in front of the barn."

She hands me my old wool coat, which used to be the old man's. It gave up the ghost a long time since, but it's what I got. "Go now." She squeezes my shoulder and I shiver as a hot snake crawls over that whip trail.

"He won't follow, Mama," I whisper, mostly to make her feel better. "Not now."

Mama looks at me like I filched too much bread and lied about it. I expect we both know I'm wrong. She's told me before he is relentless. "That's the word for him," she has said more than once, often when she's had more medicine than she ought.

"Go now."

I nod and ease open the back door. It squawks unless one of us remembers to grease it up. It's greased this time. Mama must have done it.

It takes me longer than it should, but I get Chaco out of her stall and I'm telling Ned to calm down — he's an old plow horse but he's sweet on Chaco — when I hear the old man.

It's cooled off, it being late October, but he sleeps with his window open. The barn's a ways from the house but I hear that growl he makes when he's drunk and too stubborn to give over to sleep. He'll either pass out or get up and stomp to the kitchen.

I don't know which to do first — get the horse rigged or run to the kitchen. If I do one, the other won't get done.

Then it's too late to decide because I hear him stomping. I ain't quick enough. By the time I get to the back door, I see him through the screening. He's snorting hard through his nose, snotting on himself like a hydrophoby dog. One of his big hands is snatched tight in Mama's hair, which is loose from her bun and sways like a horse's tail. He swings Mama back and forth like he's trying to shake something loose from her.

"Dare you!" he bellows.

I scratch for the rope loop handle and cannot seem to find it in the dark. When I do swing the door open, he shouts, "Gaah!" He adds a few words I never heard before, and he's called me a pile of odd ones. Then he lets go of Mama.

She spins from him like they are dancing, and I swear it's as if time has slowed. She falls into the black cookstove hard enough to shove it back and rattle the damper in the pipe.

I shout animal sounds and swing my arms wild and sloppy, wanting to lay into him good for hurting Mama. For a wink of time it feels good, like something I should have done long ago. Then he gives me a stunner with the back of his hand. I pile up against the dry sink and my head bounces. I hear wood crack and then I am dizzy, can't see right.

Mama looks at me. "Run!" she shouts, over and over, "Get out of here! Run! Go!" shaking her head and shouting and crying. But I can't. I won't leave her. I keep trying to get up, so help me I do, but it's like I am underwater and yet flying crazy like a blind bird, all at once.

"Quit that simpering!" The old man smacks her hard across the face. "Sound like your mother. Why'd it have to be my son who died?" His voice is blurry, thick like wool batting. "Should have been you! Not my boy . . . he died a hero, fighting the cursed redskins, my only solace."

Mama wipes her bleeding mouth with her sleeve. She is sitting back, her legs folded under her, one hand gripping the stove door's handle. Then she does something I never heard her do. She shouts at the old man.

"That's not true and you know it, Papa! He didn't die fighting Indians! He was drunk and fell off his horse! You don't want to hear the truth of it. You! You're the reason! You're the reason for all of it!"

"No!" he shouts so loud it shocks us all. Then he kicks.

I've never seen the old man so quick. His boot catches Mama on the side of the head, the same bloody cheek, and her head snaps to the side. She flops to the floor, her eyes wide and staring at me.

Then she changes from Mama to something not my mama. She looks at me but she ain't seeing a thing anymore. She is dead.

I am dizzied up, balanced on my knees, leaning against the dry sink. For a moment it's all quiet in the kitchen. The old man and me, we do the same thing, we stare down at Mama.

Then I crack open that silent moment like a dropped egg. Of all the sounds I make tonight, the one that claws up out of my throat is something from some animal that ain't yet been discovered, a beast birthed of death and such sadness and anger as I hope to never know again. But I expect I will.

The sounds take shape after a bit and come out as "Mama!" Over and over I shout her name as I shove myself to my feet. I hit the old man as hard as I ever hit them sacks of meal when no one's around. The whole time I growl and I shout.

He doesn't know I am hitting him until I

land a slap that clips his ear. Then he looks at me, and it's the only time I ever see him look confused and sad. It don't last long. Those wet eyes narrow up and I see the man in there I know too well, all anger and hate.

"Filthy 'skin!" he bellows in my face. "You're the cause!"

Good, I think. That's who I want to see. Then I land one more wide clout to his jaw before he knocks me cold.

CHAPTER TWO

I come to in stink and wet muck and something hot clouding in my face. Whoever's breathing on me smells like they've been feeding on fly-blown meat. It takes a few moments to come to my right mind and I almost wish I hadn't. That's when I recall everything that happened. Mama and the old man.

The lashes on my back begin to burn something awful. I'm on my side and my head thunders like a cannonade. With the whip strikes burning fire on my back and shoulders and the wet stink all over me, I don't know what to think.

Then something grunts in my face and I know. I'm in the sty. The old man, he must have dumped me in here. I have a memory,

145

fanciful, but I think not, of him looking down at me and spitting on me. Could be it was the pig's drool.

My next thought, given the stink, is that I am dead or on my way there because other than the pig, the only things that end up in the sty are kitchen scraps and the dead calves and kittens and chickens the old man throws over the log walls. The hog, the old man calls him King, is an enormous boar, biggest animal outside of Ned I ever seen. And he eats everything tossed to him.

I recall thinking that if the old man ever took the notion to butcher that pig, though he never will as he likes him more than he likes about anything else, except whiskey, that would be meat I could never eat. It would be a mix of all the dead things the old man ever dumped in there, some of them carcasses greening with age.

I hardly dare move, though piled up on my left side in the muck it hurts like the devil himself is stabbing me with a glowing poker. That boar's big face, tusks yellow in the dark of night, hangs in the air before me. His flat snout snuffles and pulses as he sniffs me.

I try not to breathe, but it hurts too much to hold it in. My breath leaks out and I reckon that's why he squeals low, like a warning. He backs up a step, then two, and stares at me. I see his tiny, wet, pig eyes watching me. I bet he ain't used to anything living being dumped in here with him, not sure what he's supposed to make of me. I don't think he's smart enough to dwell on it for too long. He'd as soon commence to gashing and tearing at me.

I figure I have little time to surprise the big boar. I'll have to scramble to get out of here, but I don't count on being so stiff and sore and dizzy in the head. Seems to take an hour for me to push up onto my knees.

I sway on all fours like an animal myself, gagging at the stink of the muck. Some of it went in my mouth. I spit and gag some more and then I hear a noise outside of the sty and I stop breathing again. The pig steps toward me, his head low and grunting.

I have to get out of here. Surprise is the only thing I figure will help me. I growl low like a dog and I stand and flail my right arm at the runny muck. It spittles up and the pig sidesteps from me, but commences to grunt, angry-sounding again.

I move toward the log wall behind me. The pig moves toward me. I growl again and slap at the muck. In that manner, I am able to get to the wall. I bump into it — it's closer than I think. Then King rushes me. I growl and flail and it doesn't do anything but rile him more.

I turn my back on him once, and my legs make a sucking sound in the muck as I lurch over to the log wall. His nose shoves at my trailing leg and then I feel teeth as his mouth closes on my leg. I jump for a higher handhold, the wall being near as tall as the old man, tugging my leg up with me, and that pig's nose rams the logs. He squeals and I am up, atop the wall.

I am a meal he will not be tucking into. I am also filthy and aching, but I am alive. So far the old man hasn't laid a big, bony hand on my shoulder and tossed me back in with King.

The sty sets a ways back behind the barn, where we keep the four cows and goats. Off that leans the chicken shack. As I walk to the barn, I notice the night has turned colder than I expected. It's October, so I should not be surprised. I see my breath and I am glad for it, for that means I have breath to see.

I walk to the water trough, grateful I filled it from the river only that morning, and dunk my head. It ain't big enough for me to crawl all the way in. Cold or not, I am mucky and stinking. I can at least get the filth off my face and out of my mouth and nose. I snot it out some, spit, trying to keep my sounds low, lest the old man be lurking.

As I wash, I wonder what to do next. I know what I want to do, what I should do. I have to do to the old man what he done to Mama. It's only right. It's my abiding thought as I wrap my fingers around the shaft of the hayfork. He might well kill me but he won't get far afterward, with that wagging from him.

If he hasn't heard me yet, he'll like as not hear my teeth rattling like stones in a tin can. I am that cold. I do my best to ignore the hot whip marks on my back and the thudding in my head. It thumps fresh with each step I take toward the kitchen.

The back door is part open and I listen but hear nothing. I am shaking as I nudge it. I know I'll see Mama laid out there, same as before, never to move again. I hold my breath and push in, no sound from the greased hinges.

She isn't there.

For a second I am certain I'd been wrong and she has gone off to doctor her cuts in quiet, like she always does after the old man beats on her. But I know otherwise. Don't mean I don't hope. I cross the room, looking in the dark toward the far end of the house but not seeing anything move.

I ease open the door to our room, the woodshed, and the weak light of the kitchen's oil lamp cuts in. There she is, on the bed, laid out as if she is sleeping. Her eyes are closed, and her hair is spread around her face like she is underwater and it's floating free. She looks stern, and the far side of her face is dark and lumped.

"Mama?" I whisper.

Her hands are crossed, laid atop her chest. I touch the back of her top hand with my grimy finger — pig muck don't wash off easy. Her hand is cold. She doesn't move, doesn't wake. I knew she wouldn't.

That means the old man dragged her in here. Least he felt bad enough to do that. Small comfort, as Mama used to say about near everything in a day's time, then she'd sigh. At least she wouldn't have to feel that way no more.

I am crying a little, my finger atop Mama's cold hand. I pull it back as if I've been bitten. Then I remember what I got to do. I grip the hayfork tighter and walk out, cross through the kitchen and the front room to the doorway of the old man's room. I hold there and listen.

I see from the moonglow through the open window that he is in there, on his back like Mama, but he is breathing. Hard and deep, I know the sound. Dead drunk, as Mama would say. One leg is bent at the knee, his boot on the floor as if he is about to shove upright and spring for the door. The arm on the same side, closest to me, is stretched out toward the floor and an empty bottle.

I walk over to him. That hand could easily snatch my trouser leg. I watch him a long time, the stink off me could wake the dead, but he doesn't move. He does keep snoring, though. His breath hitches up now and again and I think he might wake, but no. The whiskey holds him deep. I commence to trembling, grinding my teeth so tight I figure they'll powder.

I never feel so much as I do right then, more than I feel when Mama died in front of me. It's a powerful feeling of rage. I lift that fork, them three long, steel teeth aimed downward. I shake like a branch in a storm, and so help me the only thing that stays my hand is Mama's voice in my head, clear as a first snow, saying, "Promise me you'll never be like him. Don't bring yourself to his level, or you'll never be any better than that for all your days. You be a good man, you promise me, son?"

I would always nod and say, "Yes, ma'am." Then I'd say, "A good man like my father?"

She always looked startled, then she'd smile and say, "Yes, like your father."

Looking down at the old man, I do not want to be like my father then. But I do not want Mama to look down on me from on high in her seat of Glory and be disappointed. Though that thought burns in me, it takes a mighty effort to turn away from the old man. I leave his room without looking back, his stuttering, sawing breaths fading as I walk through the house.

It doesn't take me long to gather what I reckon I'll need. Much of it was already in a sack by the feet of the stove. It's a comfort knowing Mama had been the one to set it there, filling it before the old man had come in on her. I won't take the sack from our room, the one with clothes and trinkets. I will have to move fast and do not want to lug the extra weight.

She'd put in the last of the bread she baked, a full loaf and the nub off another, and a fist-size hunk of cheese wrapped in what Mama called her tea towel. We never drink tea, so I don't know why she named it such. She also put in a jar of her pickled cucumbers.

I see the carving knife in the block at the far end of the counter and I slide it out of its slot and hold it up. It is something I rarely ever touch, but it is a wide, keen blade and I grunt and slip it into the sack. I look around a last time and see the kitchen matches. Why I don't take the entire box, I do not know. I grab a handful of them and stuff them into my trouser pocket.

I visit Mama once more and tear up again looking at her. Before I lose my will and stay right there, I kiss her forehead and whisper, "Goodbye for now, Mama." I grab the pair of socks she knitted for me last Christmas. Then I leave, holding my breath until I am out past the barn once more.

Come morning, I'm certain he will check the sty and see I cheated King out of his dinner. I consider riding Chaco, or even Ned, but figure the old man would accuse me of horse theft and send the cavalry after me. This way, he might figure me a good riddance, since he never liked me anyway.

He always says I am to blame for everything foul that happened to his family. I never could understand that, as I am part of the same family. But with me gone, I figure he will finally have what he always wanted.

My breath feathers out silver against the purple night air. The moon is up, pinned high and about at half face, as if that other old man, the one up there, is frowning down

153

on what we did here tonight. I can't blame him. We are a pitiful sight, the Barr clan. Even if I am only half a Barr.

I take the hayfork with me, figuring it might make a useful walking staff. I am sore and the night is going away and I have much ground to tread. Doing it moving like an old-timer isn't going to get me far. I set off for the mountains I know are there, though I can only see them in the daylight.

But they are there, in the dark, and soon I will be, too.

CHAPTER THREE

There is one direction I have to go, the only one I ever considered venturing in all my life. It is northward, toward where I reckon my father is from. Mama always was tight-lipped about him, but I heard slips here and there. She said once that he was a man from the north. I asked her three, four times why he left, but she only said he had things he needed to attend to.

"But he's coming back to us, right Mama?"

She always smiled and nodded. "Someday we'll see him again, son."

As I walk, my whip wounds and my head paining me fierce, I pretend I am thinking about important things, trying not to think about Mama staring me down, telling me to run as she lay dying. Well, Mama, I am doing it. Not exactly running, but doing the thing you didn't do all those years. Maybe you couldn't do it, I don't know. I'll think about it some other time. Right now, I am going to find my father.

I walk steady for near an hour, and reach the farthest pasture I am familiar with. The stump fence proves an obstacle I had not thought would slow me. Sore as I am, I have to rove south along it to find a low break to climb through. Beyond that the trees thicken, but my luck holds and the moon stays bright enough that I can see trunks before I walk into them.

The walking is level and my steps make twigs crunch underfoot. I have to take care to keep the tines of the pitchfork pointed away from my face. I don't dare use the business end to plant and push off with, lest I stab my foot. Soon I feel my breathing coming harder and know I am walking upslope, not much but it heartens me, for that must mean mountains. My father and his people are mountain people, a tribe of the high places. I am certain of it.

Long have I dreamed of seeing such country. From books Mama read to me in a whisper at night tucked tight in our bed, I know that nested amongst the mountains there are rivers and valleys with big trees. In the highest places, there will be snow all year-round with blue ice capping the peaks. What makes it blue, I don't know, though I guess it has to do with the sky, the nearest blue thing up there.

I believe game is bountiful in the mountains, deer and rabbits and goats of some sort, and big birds such as eagles, too. Though I don't think my father's people tamper with eagles for food. Mama said they are a ceremonial bird.

I know bears like the high places. That gets me to thinking about the only bear I've ever seen. It's the one the old man uses in the cold months to cover himself. Calls it his war robe, then he looks at me and laughs, the sound you make before you spit on the ground. He spit on me plenty over the years, mostly at my feet. He is a powerful chewer of tobacco, is the old man. And he's a fair aim with it, too.

As to the bear, it's a skin he sleeps under. He says it is warmer than any woman he ever met and, once he killed the thing, quieter, too.

I know all about how he killed it because he told the story plenty of times when he was drunk and chatty in the barn. That was about the only time he seemed to want me around. Wouldn't brook no interruptions, though. I lost a tooth once when I was younger and asked him a question. It grew back. But he told the story of that cinnamon bear so much I felt like I was right there with him on the hunt for it.

It was before I was born, Mama's mama hadn't yet hanged herself in the haymow, and the boy, as the old man called him, that would be Richard, his son, brother to my Mama, was off fighting "your kind," as the old man always said, then he'd look at me and laugh and spit.

The old man had gone to town one day to sell the cream, butter, and eggs. Even when Mama's mama was alive, the old man never let anyone else go into town.

While he was at Allsop's Creamery, he overheard other farmers talking about a cinnamon bear that had come down out of the hills and terrorized the town. It killed three weanling piglets, somebody's yapping dog, and a sheep or two.

It rattled the door on the Schoenfeld's outhouse when Mrs. Schoenfeld was in there rattling the inside, as the old man said, then he'd laugh. Mama said he found that funny because Mrs. Schoenfeld is a large woman and prone to gassiness.

The gabbing men said they were fixing to go out after it, but when the old man commenced to unload his milk cans in the spring room, those men stopped talking.

"They were all afraid of me. More than they were of the bear!"

I'd nod and keep my mouth shut tight. I know how those men felt.

Then the old man drove the wagon home in high dudgeon. That's what Mama said her mama called it when the old man was worked up. He fetched out his shotgun and whiskey and food and saddled up old Ned, then lit out after that bear while, he said, "the men in town were deciding how many pairs of socks to pack!"

He was gone for three days, though he found the bear on the first day out. "I run it ragged," he'd say, nodding. Then he'd swig from his bottle and rub his big red nose. "I let it hunch up and recover its senses, then I'd prod on it and pepper it to get it moving again. Set it to bawling over hill and beyond like a no-good child! It'd bleed and run, bleed and run, barking and carrying on. Then I'd give it another taste!"

He always found that funny. Me, I was thinking of that shot-up bear, no water nor food nor sleep to speak of. And the old man, drunk and in high dudgeon, close behind.

That's when I stop and lean on the hay-fork. The new day's sunlight has been brightening my trail all the while I've been walking and thinking. My back is sizzling like fat on a fire, but that isn't what catches me up short. It's all this thinking about the bear.

After three days of pestering it and wound-ing it and laughing at it, he shot that bear dead and skinned it out and lugged it to town atop ol' Ned, who couldn't have been too happy with such freight.

"I brought shame on those soft-bellied men," the old man would say, then sneer and swig more on the bottle.

Mama said he was relentless. Long time ago I asked her what that meant. She said it's something that will not stop, cannot stop until it has done what it needs to do.

"What's it do after that?" I said.

She looked at me like I asked her for a slice of the moon for supper, then she shook her head. "He will never stop. It will never end."

Until now, I reckoned this whole time she'd been talking about the bear.

CHAPTER FOUR

By midday I am as tired as I've ever been and feeling more poorly with each step. I know I should have brought the goose grease with me, though how I was to spread it on my back I am unsure. My head is cracking apart from the inside and cooking on the outside.

My old green felt topper isn't of much use keeping the sun off as the rear of the brim's gone, chewed by moths before it was mine, back when the old man used it on a scarecrow in the garden. 'Bout cooks my neck. I hope I'm not coming down feverish. I'll find out.

I make it up into the hills where the trees thin and grow in clumps of six or a dozen, some of them sizable. Most are piney, with rough, red bark and bursts of needles with a cone nested in them like a jewel in an opening fist.

It is beneath one such tree, with a sweep of low branches, that I decide to rest. It grows downslope of me, so I slide off the scant path I've been following. I think it's a game trail, for I spy deer pellets once in a while. I barely know that I'm crawling beneath that tree's green skirt.

Though I'd sipped from streams all morning, I have no water with me and wish I had thought to take one of the old man's wooden canteens from the peg in the tack shed. They leak until they swell from the water inside, but they do the job in the end.

As I lose my fight with staying awake, I reason that as my father got along for twelve years without me, surely a few more days would matter little. In truth, I have no idea how long it will take me to reach him and his people. A week? Two? Back at the farm, the mountains never seemed far off. Now that I am making for them, they never seem to get closer.

Some time later, a smell comes to me. I feel I am asleep and having a poor dream, yet I open my eyes. It's going on toward full dark, but I see branches near my face. I fancy I smell the sweetness of pine pitch. I flex my nose and sniff again. It's faint, but it isn't pitch. My own stink? No, not mine.

The old man gives off a powerful reek, worse when he's been working setting posts or sawing lengths of stove wood. Might help if he bathed more than once a month. Mama always made certain I washed "tip to toes," as she said, at least once a week, more often in summer.

I hear his voice, grumbling downtrail of me.

My guts seize like stone, my eyes open wide as cups. He is following me. I expected he would be pleased I was gone and leave me be. Is he afraid I would tell someone how Mama died?

So the old man, Bull Barr, will take me back and make me do everything Mama always did. I would have to cook for him and milk the cows and fetch his bottle and sleep in the woodshed and . . . Mama.

Had he buried her before he lit out after me?

It got cold since I crawled under the tree. I see my breath, and shivers work me up and down. I stopper my mouth with my sleeve and shift forward away from the trunk to hear better. My back is wet and sticky, as if I grew into the tree while I was asleep.

His boots grind closer. They are his hobnail hunters. I hear the steel nibs on the soles biting into, then sliding off stone, shoving forward, upslope toward me. I hold my breath and near-close my eyes. My heart thumps like someone punching me steady. I feel it in my throat.

I know what he'll be wearing — his grimy longhandles, the pink ones that began life as bright red. His brown leather braces, the tall, lace-up boots, and his canvas rucksack on his back. There'll be a couple of bottles in there.

"He's a bad seed, a devil child with no soul. He is soulless, Martha Anne . . . wonder he didn't kill us all in our sleep.

162

Scalp the lot of us!" He moans and keeps walking, his voice louder, shouting. "Brought shame on our family!"

He stops again and I hear liquid slosh. "Should have fed him to the coyotes while his bones was soft. A wastrel . . ."

They are all things I've heard before, but that was back on the farm, in the barn or the pasture or the house. Now they are spoken in the hills that lead to the mountains that will lead me to my father. Now the old man is following me. I should have known better. I did know better, but I have been a fool.

His sloppy footsteps continue upslope, closer to me, then slowly past. I wait a long time and feel my face heat. I am feverish from the whipping. The wounds have gone too long without tending, but there's no time for thinking about that. There will be later.

I climb up out of the hole, on my knees, sliding and gripping the top of the feed sack closed. Something inside — I think it's the kitchen knife, clanks against something else. It's the loudest thing I ever heard.

I don't move a hair. I listen and listen. Then I feel something wet against my leg and a rank smell tickles my nose. Pickles. Mama's pickles. The jar broke.

Laughter, that raggedy shouting laugh that means nothing funny at all, a sound I've heard every day of my life, is close, not far upslope.

"You can't best the Bull, boy! Ain't nobody ever has! 'Specially not a cur of a 'skin!"

He is close, ten strides back to me? More? I don't know what to do. Stay put? Climb higher, westward along the slope? The pickles decide it for me. If I can smell them, he can, too, and he'll use the vinegar stink to find me. I slide back down to my spot on the far side of the tree trunk, hoping the near-darkness will mask me.

I claw at the earth, scooping a hole, and shove the sack in it, covering as much of the wet patch as I can with pine duff and gravel. It helps, but Mama's pickles, tasty as they are, will leave your breath rank for a spell after a meal, so I know the old man will smell them. Likely already has.

That's about all the thinking I have time for because I hear his boots grinding on rock, scuffing back toward me. They're draggy and sound as though he's walked days without rest. That's because of the liquor. It slows a body down.

I hunch tighter behind the tree trunk and hold my breath. He stops on the thin game trail upslope of me, muttering and shifting his position every few seconds. He sniffs and sniffs, shifting around, sniffs some more. He grunts and I hear glugging. Then I hear that sighing sound he always makes after he finishes a drink.

He tosses the bottle and it rolls by me. Then he grunts and pees, the stream drizzling down at me. I don't move, though I want to get away from that. Presently I feel wetness from it on my backside and along my right leg. He must have had to go for ages, for he keeps on and on.

I bite the inside of my mouth and close my eyes tight. It will end and he will go back home to the farm. *Go away,* I wish in silence, not looking nor breathing. *Go back the way you come.*

Finally, he stops and I know he is fumbling with the buttons on his trousers. Often at the farm he will not bother.

"Too easy," he says then, and trudges on upslope, back the way he was headed before I broke the pickles.

I peek out from beneath my arms, but I don't see nor hear anything. Same as before when I crawled up out of here.

I am little more than a frightened chipmunk down in my hole by the tree's roots, waiting for the coyote to sink his fangs into me and shake me to death. I am fevered, but my face feels hotter. Burning up with the shame of what I let him do to me. Today and all the days leading to it.

I know then I've not been thinking straight. I see it now. I hear Mama's words like I am hearing them for the first time, and she's right. He will never let me go. He will never stop hunting me. For now he has the one thing he always wanted, an excuse to kill me.

I am the cinnamon bear and the old man is playing with me.

CHAPTER FIVE

He'll camp soon and then I can leave this spot and climb higher into the mountains. Then I'll be safe. My father will be there and he will know how to stop the old man, how to send him back to the farm.

I have to get as far from here as I can.

I wait for much of an hour in case he's nearby. I don't think he can stay awake, as he's been drinking. While I wait, I roll down the top of the feed sack and pull out what I can without making the broken glass clink. Every time I make a noise I seize, but nothing moves near me in the night.

Pieces of the busted jar lift out easy enough, but the pickles, thin sliced with onions, make a soppy mess. I am tempted to eat some of them, but I can't see and I'm fearful I'll eat glass with them. I picture splinters sliding down my throat and into my belly and all the havoc they could cause down there. I feel rough enough, no need to add to the pile. The bread's not bad, though it got wet from the pickles, and I nibble on a corner of the cheese.

I ought to have put more thought into what I took from the kitchen. The matches in my pocket are damp from pickle juice, or the old man's pee, I don't know which, but I reckon they'll dry. The knife I wipe off on the sack, and after I wring that out, I slide everything back in, including the knife. There's nothing else in there for it to break.

Feeding myself once the bread and cheese are gone isn't something I planned for. I vow to give it good thought come the morning. Right now I have to get away from this hillside and the old man. I do not want to go back to that farm.

As I shift to crawl my way to the trail, my left boot toes something that makes a clunking sound. It's the empty whiskey bottle the old man tossed at me. Since I forgot to take a canteen, the bottle could prove useful. I pat the ground and find it, unbroken. Them bottles are tough.

The mouth of it smells rank, but I am used to whiskey stink. I hold the bottle in one hand and the sack in the other and climb on out of there.

The moon isn't nearly so friendly as last night. Once I'm out from under the branches I see nary a star above. There is a glow from behind great quilts of clouds that helps me see edges of things, trees and boulders and such.

Aside from stumbling over the old man, drunk and sleeping, I fear walking off the edge of the trail. I passed steep drop-offs earlier, so I know the terrain is growing more dangerous the higher I climb into the hills.

These, I remember, are called foothills, because they are the feet of the big mountains. I picture the mountains as large men sitting with their knees pulled up. Right now I am climbing up along the feet. By tonight I will work my way up a leg and reach a knee. That is my aim.

In a day or two, I will scale the chest, cross over to a shoulder, and perhaps I will see to the other side. That will be where my father and his people live. I have put much thought into this over time, but never more since walking out here.

Seems to me living way up in the mountains is not nearly so practical as in a valley with grasses and trees and a river cutting through the middle of it. That's what I feel sure I will find once I make it up to the shoulder and look down the other side. There I will see teepees or log huts. I am not certain. But that's where they will be. Over the mountains.

I plan to make tracks through the night and take care to leave no trail. It feels good to know where I am bound. Finally, I am leaving the old man behind. And I did not break my promise to Mama. I did not do what the old man deserves. Some other person will do such. Or perhaps it will be time itself that will whittle him down to a useless nub. But it won't be me. I will be gone.

It isn't until the sun is up that I realize that though I gained something in the night, the bottle, I also lost something. The sack with food and the knife swings from my right hand, but the pitchfork, my walking staff, is gone.

I must be more tired than I think, for I look around at the rocks and scant trees, as if it will be there, fetched on a low branch, or sticking in the trail behind me. But no, I did not drag it out from under that tree where I hid from the old man.

I picture that fork with its smooth handle laying there to rot out its days, never to be found, and it makes me sad inside. I'd used that fork every day for more years than I can recall. I walk on, running a knuckle into my eyes and snuffling.

It's not the fork so much as it is Mama being gone. I walk and cry and after a spell it feels better, like something knotted in my chest worked itself loose. It's there, but not so tight.

I fill the bottle at a clear-running stream and glug down the whole thing, then fill it again and walk on.

As I walk I'm surprised to feel so odd. My eyes are funning me, for the glare of the sun is not near as bad as I expect it should be this time of the day. I walk beneath trees, then out from under them again, shade and sun, shade and sun. And those mountains before me never seem to get closer. I am feverish. I walk faster.

Later I feel a tapping against my leg and see that walking has worked the tip of the kitchen knife through the sack. The entire blade, about as long as a man's foot, sticks out. This keeps up, I'll lose it and won't know it, so after some fiddling, I figure a way to carry it on my waist, wedged beneath my rope belt.

The wood handle on the underside of my right forearm feels good, knowing Mama used that knife every day of her life, working in the kitchen. That little feeling sets me to thinking about my family.

That's what Mama said I should always think of them as. She told me about how her brother, Richard, when he was younger than me, always wanted to get away from the farm. He'd run off twice, but he was caught, once by the old man, the other he was dragged back by the law. The old man beat him plenty both times.

This was years before I was born. Mama was younger than I am now. But she said she remembered it like it all happened yesterday. That's how she would say it. Me, I do my best to forget the day before today. Only good time was at night when Mama would read to me.

One night the old man heard us. He must have been lurking in the kitchen when we thought he'd passed out in his bed. He kicked in the door of the woodshed and said, "Give it here." He stuck out his big hand.

Mama must have known what he meant because she closed the book and hugged it to her chest. It was a book about King Arthur by a fellow named Bulfinch. She pulled her knees up under the blanket and I know she was trying to sit in front of me, to protect me. She held the book close and said, "Papa, please. It's only a little reading."

"Ain't reading that's the problem, you stupid girl! That's your sainted mama's book and you been readin' it to that heathen!" He swatted her hard, and her lip opened again. The next day the side of her face was the color of a ripe blackberry.

After he took the book and left us, she rubbed my head and said, "Don't worry, son, we'll not give up on books." Then she whispered. "I got others he don't know about." And she did, too. We were more careful, but it was never the same. And I never did find out what ol' King Arthur got up to in the end.

Anyway, her brother finally made it off the farm. Was near sixteen years old when he ran away in the night and joined up with the army. The old man lit out after him, searched for some time, but came home alone.

He didn't say anything about it, but Mama told me she overheard him telling her mama that the army sent him away, said the boy was their property now, not his. I can't imagine belonging to anyone, except that's what my life was like on the farm. I was his property. If that's so, I was property he never wanted.

Mama's brother was in the army for years and would write to his mama regular, telling her how they were clearing the land of the heathen savages.

Mama said the old man would have his wife read them letters to him over and over at the table at night, though they weren't never addressed to him. Never a mention of him in them. Then they got an official letter saying the boy was dead. Mama said that's when the old man got dark. She said he was not pleasant before that but after, he was mean, drinking more than ever.

One morning not but a week after they got the letter about the boy, Mama got up. The coffeepot was cold and the fire was out. She went out to the barn to gather eggs for breakfast, thinking her mother was feeling poorly or sad, and had stayed in bed. But when Mama got to the barn, there was her mama, in her old blue nightgown, blue as a pretty spring sky, Mama said. Her mama was dead, hanging from a rope around a beam in the barn.

She'd done it herself. Climbed up the ladder and tied it around her neck and climbed partway down again, then kicked off. I know this because I studied on it some. I figure if she'd of jumped from the mow out into the air, that fall would have pulled her head clean off her body. What a terrible thing for Mama to find when all she was looking for was eggs.

Mama said once that happened, the old man was downright god-awful. She tried to leave a pile of times, but between him threatening her, and her own crying, first for her brother, then for her mama, she couldn't never bring herself to do it.

Once the pain hardened over like a scar, and she got used to the old man drinking and breaking things and telling her she couldn't do a thing right, then begging her not to leave him or he'd die, she said she had no choice but to stay.

"Stayed too long," she told me once, a long time ago when I was a child. Then she looked at me and smiled. "But that ain't right neither." She touched my face. "If I had left, I wouldn't have had you."

I recall thinking that was an odd thing for her to say. "No, Mama," I told her. "I'd have been where you were going."

She thought that was funny. Now I see why.

I asked her about my father a whole lot. For the longest time she told me the same thing, that he was a good man who had to go away, back to his people in the north, but that he'd return for us one day. For the longest time I believed that. Then I got older and one night I asked her more questions.

She stopped her knitting and sighed, then looked at me. "He was a man who come through these parts looking for work. Papa hired him on to help lay in firewood and fence in the far pasture. He was a good man. Just so happened he was an Indian. Come from a tribe up north, I am not certain of its name, but that's what he told me. Somewhere up in the mountains."

I pestered her something awful after that, but other than telling me I reminded her of him, she didn't say much more. Wouldn't tell me his name. I wonder now if she knew it. Could be they didn't speak the same tongue.

After a while I got the idea that thinking about him made her angry or sad. I know he never came for us. Might mean he up and died, but I kept thinking there had to be more to the man than that.

I imagine he'd been caught up fighting to keep his people free. Maybe they had been rounded up and carted off to a reservation somewhere. Mama said that was happening to all the Indians. I didn't think much of the notion, because that would mean he wasn't where I needed him to be. Somewhere north of the farm, up in the mountains.

In my head that's where he has been all this time, waiting for me. Has to be, so that's where he is.

CHAPTER SIX

It's late afternoon before I stop for a rest. The old man likely woke up surly and decided I was not worth the bother. I'd bet a whole one of Mama's canned peach pies that he gave up and went back to the farm. But I misjudged him once, and since I am making for the mountains anyway, I decide to hoof it steady while I have the daylight.

I am tempted to sit beneath another piney shade tree and rest my feet, but the only one I find is in the open, along the edge of a small meadow, gone brown and hot with hopper bugs bouncing in the autumn heat. Seems a waste of effort to live your life jumping up and down like that.

I move along until the land dips low once more and I am in the midst of waist-high rabbit brush. I reckon it will keep the sun off, so I ease myself down and groan like I've seen a whole lot more years than twelve. I set down the half-full bottle and my sack beside it.

I tell myself I'll not sleep, and only sit long enough to gnaw cheese and bread, and rub my feet. But if I tug off my boots, they'll stink worse than pickle juice ever thought of smelling, so I prop my boots on a rock and lean. My back won't put up with much poking, so it takes a bit before I find the right spot. I rub my face with the top of my hat and before I know it, I'm dozing. That's when the gunshots commence.

The first smashes apart my water bottle. Glass bits whip everywhere, some chunking into my arms and legs and face. Another shot hits my food sack and kicks up a charge of dirt by my left leg. I think I scream, but the shots are so loud it's tough to tell what-all is happening.

It's like being woke by sudden thunder right over the farm, which happens some-times in summer in the valley. It slams back and forth for what feels like hours. Mama always pats my head and tells me it's God playing games with the angels. I wished they'd play checkers instead.

I roll and try to find something to hide behind. There is nothing, so I keep rolling and crawling on my hands and knees like a child playacting at being a dog. The shots stop and I hear the old man laughing.

I shout, surprising myself. "Leave me be! I don't want anything from you!"

His reply is quick, stomping on the end of my own words. "I want something from you! You owe me, boy! You took everything, left me with naught! I demand payment!"

I see the shot-up sack with what's left of the bread and cheese. Beside it stands the bottom half of the bottle, now a jagged stump of clear glass. I wonder if it's safe to nudge forward and grab that sack? That's all the food I have. I reach out and a bullet drives so close to my fingertips I think I've lost them. I yank my arm back and hold it close. All the fingers are there, but they're numb.

I hear him laughing again, then he shouts, "Ain't nobody don't pay Bull Barr!"

More bullets, so many so quick, fly at me like angry bees set on killing. They ping off rocks and zip into the dirt before me. I elbow my way backward, gravel working under my shirt, but I don't pay it mind. All I want is to get out of there.

After a spell, he commences with the bullets again. I gain my feet and run, keeping my head low. The old man must be up a tree or on a patch of high ground because he sends bullets my way, winging them at me from behind. They buzz close by, nicking trees or cracking off rocks to my right, so I run left, which is westward, good enough to get away from the old man.

After a spell the bullets stop, but I don't. My legs feel like logs, my fingers throb, and my back crawls with fire, but I don't dare stop. I have to get away from him this time. I cannot expect he'll leave me be. Mama was right.

It isn't until later I realize not only did I lose my water bottle and my food sack with Mama's tea towel, but my hat's back there, too. I have the knife, though, wedged under my rope belt and banging against my hip as I cut west along the valley floor at the base of the mountains.

At least there's trees. And as low as the land is, there must be water. If I keep the mountains to my right, I know where I am. I figure on hugging the trees until dark, then cutting northward once more. I make it high enough, I can get to where I need to be before he finds me again.

CHAPTER SEVEN

Dark catches me some hours later. I welcome it as I don't think I can lift another leg. I am that tired.

I hear a crushing, whacking sound and wonder if it's rock sliding off the stone face of the mountain across the way. I'm not certain what made me think that, but I'm wrong.

It's not rock sliding, but the old man, crashing through branches and shouting and laughing. I stop and look back and catch sight of a light, swinging wide, then disappearing, like an eye blinking. He must have brung the little blue chore lantern from the nail in the barn.

The night is clear and cold. I don't think he needs the lantern, as the moon's waxing and brighter than the night before. A chill breeze carries toward me and I pick out words from his shouts — " 'skin!" and "Martha Anne."

He's talking to his dead wife about me and I'm so tired all I want to do is sit down and wait for him and tell him I'll go back to the farm and work off whatever debt he says I owe.

Then I shake my head and blink hard. "No," I growl to myself. "No!"

Mama said he's relentless, so I got to be, too. I got to keep on and find my father. Then he will say, "Go back alone to your farm, old man! Leave my boy be."

I get walking again, warmed by these thoughts, swinging a leg forward, then the other. Soon, I leave the old man behind once more. I know it will not last, so I keep on, each step giving me more freedom.

I walk and walk, and it comes to me that the old man is asleep by now. I hope so, as I need rest as well. My back is paining me something fierce, my head is boiling hot again, and my teeth have gone back to chattering like river rocks.

What would Mama do? She'd smear goose grease on my back, make a poultice of comfrey and mustard for my chest, and set me up in bed. Now and again I'd take ill and couldn't hardly move. Mama said it's because I was a boy working like a man. Said the body needed time to catch up to such things. I don't know about all that, but I do know the old man didn't like it when I wasn't in the barn before him.

He'd stomp back to the house and break something in the kitchen. You'd think after all those years there wouldn't be much left to shatter into pieces, but he somehow found it.

I think about that and shiver more and tug my old coat tight about my throat. I am grateful to have it, even if it is more hole than coat in places, such as the elbows, which Mama was forever mending. "You are devilish on elbows. I never saw the like," she'd say.

I smile, and then I remember her face there in the kitchen, and I vow not to think about Mama just now.

The night is cool, and soon I'll smell snow on the breeze. Not yet, but soon. I have to get to my father and his people before that.

I keep moving and a minute later I hear water ahead, to my right. I follow the sound and splash into it before I know I am doing so. I back to the edge and get down on my hands and knees and drink deep.

Between the cool sips and my wet boots and the water I scoop over my face, I feel perked and decide to follow that river tight, keeping it close to my right. Noisy as it is, it might serve to keep my sounds hidden from the old man. Of course, that could work both ways. Come tomorrow, I'll wade across and climb north. I believe that will put me near a cleft in the mountains I saw before sunset.

Right now, I have a bigger problem than all that. I am as hungry as two dogs, and it's getting worse with each step.

I am used to feeling like I ain't had enough to eat. Seems it's always that way at the table, though Mama made certain I had bread or cheese or an apple once the old man was snoring his way through the night at the other end of the house.

But the feeling in my gut right now is the worst it's ever been. It's as if I've always been starving. I take to chewing on a nub of tree bark, then on a pine cone, but it's pitchy and gums up my teeth. It doesn't stop me from keeping an eye open for apples and late berries, though.

At least on the farm I had food, especially when the old man wasn't in earshot. Mama would fix me a bowl of hominy or slice up an apple from the keeper barrel and drip honey on it.

I take stock of my goods. I have two pairs of socks, one I use as mittens and one on my feet. Then I have the knife, and the matches in my pocket, though the heads got wet and have mostly flaked off. But a fire isn't something I have time for right now.

I stumble on a root and that jerks me back to myself on the trail. I sure wish I could make a fire tonight. It's cold enough I can't go another step. Hopefully the old man will huddle up somewhere with his jacket pulled tight about his ears.

There's a patch of rabbit brush and I figure I might find some warmth down low. I see a darker spot and kick at it. Looks like a gap, so I jam my way in, crawling and patting the ground with the socks on my hands. It's bony and hard-packed. I scooch back out and crawl on my knees some feet away where I thought I'd trod on something soft. I was right.

I snatch up a handful and hold it to my face. It's dried grasses, but it smells good. I pick as much as I can and gather it in my arms like I'm hugging it. It tickles my face and itches, but I don't care. It'll keep me warm where the fire failed me.

No, that's not right. The fire didn't fail me, I failed in building it. Turns out my matches are worthless and can't raise a whiff of smoke. It shows me how easy life at the farm was. I never gave much thought as I went about making a fire in the woodstove or eating a hunk of bread and a slice of cheese. Out here in the forest, it all comes hard. I have to give up on thoughts like that because they make me think of food.

The dry grass is the best thing I can find to keep me warm. There isn't much of it, but I stuff what I've gathered into the hole in the brush and when I crawl in this time, I notice the smell. It's musky like a billy goat, and makes my nose wrinkle, but it's too late to find a different spot.

I shove the wad of grass in as far as I can, six feet or so, then I burrow in with my head tucked down like a turtle in my old wool coat. The smell gets worse. It's an animal stink, wet and rank.

I should get out of here, but I am too cold. I don't get any sleep at all, so I sit with the grass pulled up around my chest and face like the worst blanket ever made. I start to fall asleep when a low noise wakes me. It's close, six or eight feet away. I hear it again and I know it for what it is — a growl. Then I hear more growls.

A long fingernail of ice drags up my backbone and my hair prickles all over my head. The smell, whatever is in this hole, gets a whole lot worse, too. By now I have a good idea of what it is. I hear growls all around me, and then howls.

They are range dogs, as I've heard the old man call them. Coyotes. I've seen what they do to chickens and rabbits, and even a skunk. And once, they fed on an old cow we had who was calving in the pasture.

I found her, thrashing and bawling, her back end all raw meat and chewed away. She couldn't get up, couldn't do nothing but look at me with big eyes and bawl, snot stringing out her nose and mouth. It was terrible. And no sign of her baby calf, neither.

I ran back to the farm and told the old man. He cursed me a blue streak and fetched his rifle. He shot that old cow in the head and we butchered her on the spot. We lugged the meat home in the work wagon behind Ned.

Then the old man beat me until he got tired. Said I was to blame.

Mama once told me if you hear coyotes outside your door, you are to stay in your house because they have a mystical eye that will enchant you. It's nothing they can control, but a power they're born with. Sort of like how I have skin that ain't like the old man's.

But she said their eyes will trap you if you look at them. Then they will eat you. One alone, a man might be able to fight him off, but a whole pack surrounds whatever it is they plan on eating and they dart in and tear at it, their black, wet noses all hunched up and their teeth wet and white, nipping and slashing. Before long their prey dies of a mess of bleeding bites and cuts it didn't know it had in the first place.

Tonight, the moon is not particularly bright, so I wonder how I'll see their eyes in the dark. The clouds will part at the worst moment, and I will see them staring me down, teeth bared and noses hunched, their hackles bristled. That's when they'll lunge.

My thinking goes on and on like this and I don't know what to do. I'm in the den of the range dogs, sitting right where they sleep or eat or mess, I don't know which. They are outside the brush, all around me. Their growls give sign to more of them, because I hear others, howling far off, yapping like they're trying to outdo each other, one talking over another.

Mama says that's a sign of low manners and that I should always let somebody else finish whatever it is they are saying before I commence to speak. Must be she learned that from her mama, because the old man don't care who's doing the talking. If it ain't him, he'll start right up saying whatever it is he wants to.

As it was only ever Mama and me, we stopped talking and listened to what he was saying. It was always the same thing, though. How Mama couldn't cook anything like her mother and how I was less than useless. All things we heard every day anyway.

Serves me right for holing up near dark. If I'd stopped sooner, I would have seen what was in that hole in the brush, scat or bones. But tired as I am, once the growling and howling commence, I wake like I've been dunked in an icy pond. Funny thing what fear will do to a fellow.

I am going to have to fight my way out of here. I keep telling myself not to look the range dogs in the eyes, lest they put a spell on me and eat me where I stand.

I shove up to my knees and my right hand brushes something that makes me feel almighty good, considering the situation. It's the handle of Mama's kitchen knife wedged in my rope belt. I grip it through the sock covering my hand and slide it free.

I'll wave it like a big tooth, and slash right back at them when they try the same on me with their teeth. Might be I only have the one and they have mouths full, but this tooth is long and steel and sharp. I wish for a second I had the hayfork with its three steel tines. They'd be better teeth, but the knife is what I have, and that's no complaint.

For the moment my own teeth stop chattering. The howls, from what sounds like a dozen animals, are all around me, closing in and louder than a minute ago. I know if I stop to think, I will wither and miss my chance. That always ends with a beating by the old man.

This time I say no and I grit my teeth and shove my way back to the entrance of the hole quick as I can. If I come upon one of them beasts, I'll jam into it hard, knock it back some, gain enough time to get to my feet.

The thing with the fur I ram myself into is

more surprised by me than I am of it. It's in mid howl and I slam right into it. I whip an arm up, and though it's dark, I see the animals clearly. They are all as skinny as I feel, and light colored enough that I see them hopping like they're dancing away from me.

Soon as I get out of there, I gain my feet and howl louder than any of these demons. I scare myself with the sounds I make, as I ain't never been one for shouting. Most noise I got up to was calling in the cows from the pasture or yelling at the goats once in a while when they were doing something I was sure to get blamed for.

I whip the knife side to side like I'm clearing tall grass with a hand sickle. It tastes fur at least twice, judging from the whimpers I hear. I almost feel bad, like I'm putting the hurt on a yard dog. Then I remember coyotes are wily creatures and will curse you with their eyes, then kill you with their teeth. The whole pack of them will set on me, so I aim to set on them first.

I keep up my wild slashing and run, waving the knife back and forth in front of me, partly so I won't run smack into a tree and knock myself cold. I don't want to wake up with a pack of angry, bleeding coyotes eating on me. I think I scare them so bad they don't know what to do. I also think there aren't as many of them as I guessed.

No matter, my legs keep moving and my arm keeps swinging that knife and I don't hear much behind me. Whimpers and squabbling sounds, and I get to thinking they are eating each other. As long as it ain't me.

Soon as daylight shows itself, I stop loping and listen and look behind me for sign of beasts closing in. None. I also see no cuts nor bites on myself. I do see something dark spattered on my trouser legs and the same on the knife's blade. Coyote blood, has to be.

For a second or two there is a flame in me that wants that blood to be the old man's. I almost smile at the thought, then I shake my head and say, "I'm sorry, Mama." I slide the knife back into my rope belt and I commence to lope once more, because it's keeping me warm.

CHAPTER EIGHT

By the time full light comes, I look around and I get panicky. I am down in low country, can't see the mountains. Where had I run to in the night? I covered a fair bit of ground, but what if it was back toward the farm? A hard fist of fear and anger spins back and forth in my gut. I can't go back there. I won't go back there.

For a cool night last night, the day turns off hot. Hot as homemade sin, as Mama would say when she burned her arm on the stove door baking bread. I miss her something fierce. In time it might not be so bad, but all that is a long ways off. Right now I am hot and tired and sore from my hair to my crusty toes. I am also thirsty. That's why about midday, I hear something that makes me smile.

At first I think that low sound is a breeze passing through high-up leaves. But it keeps on, not tapering nor breaking up like wind will do. I sniff, close my eyes, and sniff again. Might be there's water up ahead. I sure could use it. And then, before I expect to, I come upon a full-bore gravel-bank river.

All I think about is how good that water is going to feel in my throat. "I could drink you dry, Mr. River. Dry. And I'd be thirsty yet." My voice is a raw whisper. Hearing myself is odd.

I wonder if I sound something like my father. I know once in a while Mama will say something that sounds like the old man, the way she'll round off a word like "barn" or snap "fool" at me for dropping a split of

191

stove wood on the kitchen floor. Difference is she'll nearly cry and hug me and ask my forgiveness right off, whereas the old man will keep right on, then follow it with a clout to the ear.

I am feverish and dried out, but I reckon I could be worse off. I make for a grassy patch, more brown and nubby than green, but it looks softer than the rocks. I have a mind to drink, then bathe myself.

Since it is early enough in the day, by the sun it's midday, I consider washing my togs and stretching them on the boulders to dry. Between the sun baking them from above and the hot rocks cooking them from below, they should be dry pretty quick. I'll look in the river or on the bank for something to eat while they dry.

I shuck my coat, then my shirt, peeling it off my shoulders. The left one, in particular, is tricky, as the cloth has worked itself into the cut. I begin to tug it free, but it won't give in easy, so I stop and stuff the sleeve of my coat into my mouth and bite down hard.

The river's loud enough that it muffles my shouts. The whip marks are bleeding again, and when I look over my shoulder, I see they are red and angry like a slapped face. They are also oozing a yellow goop like what comes out of your nose when you have a winter sickness.

If I were tended by Mama, the goose grease would be an inch thick, and the bandages would be fresh every morning. But I am not, and I am feverish, and this river's looking mighty tempting. I strip off the rest of my clothes, one piece at a time, beginning with my boots.

The bottoms are near worn through, and the wadded newspaper mama put inside is about gone as well. I see my toenails have made hard work of the end of my right sock. The left is fine, which is curious. So far I have saved my extra pair of socks, except for wearing them on my hands. But I see that will have to change.

Finally, I have a pile of boots, socks, trousers, my rope belt and knife, the shirt, and my coat. Soon I am standing on bare rocks, wearing nothing more than my raggy undershorts.

I keep them in case some prospector and his family from back East should wander by. I have heard of stranger things happening in the hills. Or at least that's what my mind tells me. I pull my boots back on and clump down to the water's edge, then I step out of them and walk in.

Hot as I am, the chill of that water ripples through me. It's delicious, like the first lick of that vanilla ice cream Mama made two summers back, when the old man had gone to town. We got through a bowl each before he come back early.

Mama offered him a bowl of it and he smashed it on the floor, then took that old ice cream crank out to the dooryard and blew it to pieces with his shotgun. Never said a word, then commenced to drinking in the shade.

That nippy river won't let me mull sour thoughts of the old man for long. It's all I can do to hold onto my own breath. My chest works like a bellows and as I walk gingerly along, the water slowly rises up to my knees. I hold my right hand up under my rib cage and rub there where I know my lungs are hidden, hoping to calm them some. My breath slows as I grow used to the chill.

I chance a look down at myself. I am shocked, I don't mind saying it. I've never been much for carrying extra weight, but missing regular meals these past days shows on my body. I see bone points stretching skin where I'd not suspected I had much in the way of bones.

The river's loud, making splashing noises around big rocks, and does the same around my legs. It's tricky walking because the bottom is all rocks.

None of them are much smaller than my head, cobbles as the old man calls them. They wobble as I step on them. I lose my footing not paying attention and upend myself. I strike my back low down on a rock below the surface and wheeze my way to a sitting position.

When I stop sputtering and look back to shore, I see I've made it about halfway across the river. Before I fell in, the water was up to my knees. About six feet upstream of me is a boulder as big as a buggy, without the horse. I crawl and float over to it and see a sandy-bottom pool on the downstream side of it.

I rest there, my hands on the bottom, below my backside, and let the water come up around my head, under my chin. I close my eyes and enjoy the easier water, not quite so hard on my body, pounding downstream as it is. The big boulder gives me shade, and I sleep a little, napping like a cat will do in the sun.

After a fashion, I hear something other than the river bubbling by. It's a steady *crack crack crack.* I open my eyes and sit up enough so the water won't go in my mouth. The sun is bright and it takes me a moment to recall where I am and what I am up to.

The cracking sound keeps on. I look to my left, toward the riverbank from where I came. There, hunkered beside my clothes, is the old man. He's looking at me and grinning, whacking a rock as big as his hand against another on the ground between his boots. His rifle lays across his legs.

"You awake, 'skin?" His voice reaches me, though he has to work at it some.

I hold my hand up to my eyes and squint over at him. I don't say anything.

"Good!" he shouts and gives one of his snorting laughs. He drops the rock, then, mostly looking at me, except for glances now and again at what he is doing, he fluffs through my pile of clothes. I see my boots are up there next to him, too.

He says something, then I see his shoulders moving, so I know he is laughing. He pulls out his pipe from his left breast pocket, holds it betwixt his teeth, and lights a match. He looks at me and smiles behind the pipe. He almost touches the match to his pipe but then loses his smile and shakes his head slow-like, back and forth.

The old man moves the match down and lights something, twigs or grass, most likely, beneath the pile of my clothes. I feel my gut harden into a knot. I don't move. I keep my hand over my eyes, my eyes on him. Gray

196

smoke boils up as my clothes give way to orange flames that jerk and quiver with the riverside breezes.

He stokes the fire and once the blaze is going well, he adds small hunks of wood from a pile beside him. Then he lifts one of my boots and turns it over and over as if he found something of magical use in a cave somewhere. He shakes his head and sets the boot on the fire. It burns up pretty quick. Second one does the same.

He holds his pipe in his teeth, but it only wags with words he's saying, more to himself than to me. "Martha Anne," I bet he's saying. "Martha Anne, that 'skin is no good."

Once it all burns up beyond use, he stands, cradling the rifle across his belly, and stares across the water at me. Quick as a finger snap he hefts that rifle to his shoulder and points it at me. Jacks a shell and all.

I splash and thrash and get myself around the far side of the boulder.

I hear him snort and after a few moments I peek around the sunny side of that rock. He has the rifle cradled again and is laughing. It's the only time I ever seen him laugh that much. Almost looks like he's enjoying himself. Then I recall who it is I am seeing and I know that can't be the case. The old man never enjoys anything that much.

"We are coming to it now, boy!" he shouts and cracks off a shot.

I jerk back behind the rock.

"Nah . . . too easy," he shouts, then shakes his head. He turns away and walks up the riverbank, same way I came. I notice he has the kitchen knife wedged in his belt. That means he left me with nothing.

Then I think of two things. One is that I am wrong, because he actually has left me with something — my life. He could have shot me easy before I splashed my way around that rock. And the second thing I think is this: Mama was right. The old man will never stop. I should have known.

Thought I'd outsmarted him, but what makes me think I am smarter than that cinnamon bear? To live as it had, it had to have been a clever animal. But it still got itself killed by the old man.

One night some years back, me and Mama were in bed and I was telling her how the old man said the bear was big and scary. A "genuine man-killer," he'd said.

She looked at me and whispered. "It wasn't that big, you know."

"What wasn't?"

"That bear he shot."

I didn't know what to think of that, but Mama, she kept right on whispering. "I saw it when he brung the carcass home. It wasn't full grown yet, and did not look well. All thin and ganted up."

I thought on that, knowing Mama wouldn't lie to me. I'd not seen the bearskin but a few times in my life, as I was not allowed in that room. I do recall it didn't take up much of the top of the bed and its light-brown hair was tufty and patchy.

I think once more that he's pestering me, same as he did to that bear. Poking and prodding me until I have less and less of myself left. He didn't let that bear sleep, didn't let it eat, nor rest up out of the sun. Kept dogging it, poking it where he wanted it to go. Then he shot that bear full of holes.

I realize I've been walking along the river, not deeper into the mountains. Like he wanted me to. Could be it's the same river that flows from the east to down below the farm.

How many days would it take for him to drive me all that way? Or would he kill me first and drape me over his shoulder and lug me home, to shame my dead mother like he shamed those men in town with that bear?

CHAPTER NINE

After a while, I stand, shivering, all the flavor of the hot afternoon gone. As I walk to the riverbank, I hug myself and prod among the smoking ashes. There isn't but a curl of boot left to me, of no use at all. I look up, but I know I won't see him. He's waiting me out, waiting for me to move along the river.

We are coming to some sort of end. He's going to shoot me and that will be that. I am the cinnamon bear, all but run out, near-pestered until I am done in.

I try to be happy I'm alive, but it's not easy, naked save for my underpants, and them not anything worth gazing on. They are ragged and grimy, cut-down winter long underwears that once belonged to the old man himself. Shouldn't matter, but a fellow without clothes is just another animal in the woods. I reckon that's me now.

I look at the river once more. What I am going to do I have no idea. The old man would rather die than give up a fight. He will not stop until I am dead.

But I ain't dead. Not yet. Tired as I am, I want to get up over those mountains and find my father. There has to be a way. "First off," I say to the bone-dry slope before me. "You got to get back across this river, away from where he wants you to walk."

So I do that, moving northward once more. I wait to hear a gunshot. If I do hear it, it'll be too late to run, as the bullet will be doing its job on me.

The further I walk without hearing his rifle crack the hot afternoon air, the more I wonder. The old man says I owe him, and I thought for sure it was my life he wanted as payment, but could be he's changing his tune and wants to drag me back. To that, I say no.

How I will do that, I don't know. But crossing the river means I have bested him at one thing, at least. He's been herding me like a stray calf, driving me back toward the farm. But no more.

I set foot on the far bank for the first time. I should have crossed before I stripped down. If I had, I'd have my boots and clothes and knife. I am a fool, a fool, a fool.

I hear no laughs and no rifle shots nip at my heels. I should run, but I am barefooted and sore and tired. I see rocks that lead up toward trees. Beyond that there's another stretch of gray rock, then above that, ledges of red rock that stick out.

My feet pain me so that I have to set down often and rest them. It's slow going and I'm not making much progress, so I shuck off my underwear and tear it in half. It don't take much effort. I wrap each of my feet and peel strips to tie them about my ankles. A couple of test steps and I see it's not much of an improvement, but it is something.

The rest of the afternoon passes like that, me stepping and stopping, knowing I should move faster but not able to. By the time dark finds me I have left behind trees of size and figure I best look for cover under the stunty pines. The low brush scares me off since I tangled with the coyotes.

I don't blame them for being ornery. They didn't invite me into their home. I don't think I landed any death blows, but I sure sliced up one or two. If I come across others, I am now out of luck. No knife, no clothes, only me and my half-Indian skin.

It was already browner than the old man's and Mama's, but now I've taken on a hot glow like a fierce sunset and my whip welts throb as I walk. I select a little knot of pines that look to share the same root and set down beneath them. Heat from my burned skin and cold from the coming night air fight over me. The cold starts to win. I'm so dog-tired I rest my arms on my knees and my head on my arms and I close my eyes and try not to think. It doesn't work.

A small stone ain't much comfort, but I suck on one and pretend it's a flavorful hunk of beef. It doesn't work. I nibble on a pine branch, then on twigs from a short bush, but they don't work, neither. All they do is make me want real food.

I can't have it and I can't stop thinking about it. Mostly Mama's hot biscuits and chicken with gravy. And beef stew with them gummy dumplings bubbling on top. Or pie. Mama makes the best pie. Made the best pie.

I will never again taste Mama's pie crust, nor any other dish she made. Of all the reasons to hate the old man, it's thoughts of Mama's cooking that fill me up with so much hate I feel my heart thump faster. Tired as I am I can't find sleep for the longest time. So I sit tight beneath the little pines and I think of Mama.

CHAPTER TEN

It's slow climbing to get up these hills, as they are rockier than I thought from a distance, but they'll lead me to the knees of the mountains. That's where I can lose him. I need a place to hole up and wait him out, a cave or some such.

I've been thinking about the cinnamon bear most of the morning, wondering if he lived in a cave, and I come to something. I believe I have outlasted that bear. The old man said he dogged it for three days and I am in my fourth since I walked off the farm.

I climb higher, switchbacking and sliding now and again on drifts of loose dirt. The slope levels off and the gray rocks grow bigger up here. As it's more open, the sun warms everything, including me, and I fight the thought that I should have stayed along the river. My tongue wants for water and feels like it's filling my mouth. I lick my lips but they're dry, and when I swallow, I wish I hadn't.

I am not certain what makes me look toward a particular rock downslope of me, but I do, and I see a big rattler sunning himself. He doesn't give a care about me and I feel the same about him. I do wonder how many others there are around me, though. I carry a rock for a time as a weapon, but it's too heavy, so I let it drop again. It clunks and rolls. I look upslope for other snakes and that's when I see it.

The first sign of people, other than me and the old man, since I left the farm. It's a rusty jut of steel. Then I see it's two rails, like a small train was here once, long ago. Though what a train would be doing up here I have no notion.

I stand, swaying, staring at those bars of steel poking out of the dry gravel. One sticks straight out of the bottom of the slope, the other is curved upward. I lick my lips and look around. I don't want to meet up with whatever can bend such a thick rail.

I cough, and it feels like I been punched in the back between my wing bones. I'm about done in. I am tired and cold and sore. My feet bled right through the wraps of undershorts. Heck, that happened in the first minutes of tying them on.

Crazy thoughts pass through my mind, like using tree bark for shoes. Or rocks. I wonder if I find a couple of flat rocks and strap them on me somehow. It's a fool's thinking, but that's what I am at this point.

I don't want this anymore. I don't want to be naked and cold and hungry and thirsty and tired. I want to stop all this. But the old man won't listen to me, and he sure won't leave me alone.

He's running me down, killing me. I got nothing else to give but that one thing Mama said was the most valuable thing we all have. Surprised me when she said it ain't a gun nor land nor a bearskin blanket, but our life.

That's all I got now and since I keep going, trying to get away from him, I reckon that means my life is worth keeping. But a creature can only take so much prodding and being chased before it turns on whatever's chasing it and defends itself.

If this is the way it's going to be, then this old place is as good as any to end it. I know it can only end one way. He has a gun and clothes and food and water, and I have nothing but my last, most valuable thing. But I will try.

I poke around here most of the morning. It's midday and I can't help but think of those noon meals Mama used to make. The old man, he could eat a heap of food.

I learned to only eat what Mama put on my plate before I set down at the table. I can't get enough, though, especially the last year or so. I'm always hungry. Mama said it's 'cause I'm growing. The old man ain't growing no more, I said, so why does he put away so much of it?

"To feed his mean," Mama had whispered and winked, while I was helping her clear off the table.

I eyeball this place. I guess it's an old mine, what with the tracks, and a caved-in entrance that's filled with more rocks than I can shift in a month of steady workdays. I wonder if it was for gold or silver? I'd rather have gold as it's worth more cash money.

As I poke about the spot, I think of buttered beans and corn and pork roast and thick bread drizzled with molasses. That's when I find the hole.

I step right where I ought not to and my foot doesn't stop where the ground should be. It keeps going, and I almost fall in. I should have. I'd land on my head and it'd be all over with.

But I don't fall in. I slide to the edge and claw myself back out, facedown on the dirt. My boy parts drag something fierce on the pit's rim. That's a tender spot to be scraping along gravel like that. I'm afraid to look down at myself, sure I'm all bloody and raw. I peek and it's a little redder than before, but nothing worse.

Funny how we can be worn to a nub and thinking we can't go on another step, then we get scared by something, and quick as that we're worked up. It don't last long, though. Once I know I'm safe, I lay on the gravel and feel my heart *bump-bump-bumping* and my breath fetching up and the hot sun draining me out once more.

My right foot is lower than the rest of me along the slumpy edge of that hole and I know when I have my breath again, I want to look in there. Can't help it, I got to know such things. That's when the thought comes to me — what if the old man fell in there? Would it slow him down enough that I could get away? There's no way he'd be as dumb as me, though, and let himself fall in. He's rested and older and smarter . . . but is he?

I edge to the rim. It's a hole like most others, as wide at the mouth as a man's arms stretched outward. It looks to narrow some, but I can't see all the way down. I shift to one side, blocking the sunlight, and there's the bottom, a fair bit down. Looks to me like a dry well, a deep hole with nothing to show for it but a hole.

Gets me thinking how a man could dig such a hole alone. I reckon it would take two men to do such a thing. Two men who felt sure there was gold down there. Why dig a hole straight down? Could be the mine entrance at the base of the rock face caved in and they thought they'd get at their gold another way?

I shrug and sit up. I don't care much, as I have no need for gold. I do have a need to stay alive, and the longer I stay out in the hot sun and do nothing, the more dead I will become.

The hole is about ten paces before the old mine entrance, and the mountain above is all rock. There's lumps of dirt hanging off it like crumbs on the old man's face when he eats while he's drunk. Neither me nor Mama ever told him he had smears of egg or breadcrumbs in his whiskers. I wanted to laugh at him, but I knew how that would end.

I have no notion of how long it will take the old man to find me. He will in the end, though, so I set to my task. The whole time I do it, I feel like I am going against Mama somehow, and it feels wrong, sour in my mouth. But I go at it all the same.

What gives me the idea is the bunch of dried-out bushes clogged at the top of the hole. The way they're wedged, they could be sitting on solid ground.

Since I can't get any further north because I'm out of strength, I decide this idea is the best one I have. But these dry plants won't do, so I search for something more to lay over the hole.

Along the west edge of the mine site, past a big pile of blasted, raw-edge, gray and pink rocks, sits a jumble of planks, what's left of the miner's shack. Hard to believe somebody lived in it. Then again, Mama and I lived in the woodshed, and that wasn't no fun in winter when the snow and wind whistled through the cracks. I hope the miner at least had a friend up here in these high rocks.

I make a deal with myself as I select boards. I will take whatever punishment comes of it. What I mean is this: If the boards I lay across don't break under him or if he don't walk across them, then I will give over to whatever the old man figures on dealing me. If they collapse under him, I will see what comes of it.

Near as I can tell the hole is four or five man-heights deep. That is to say it would take four or five of the old man standing on his own shoulders — now ain't that a picture — to reach the top. Might be there's handholds along the sides, or a ladder down there. I don't know. That's another part of the deal I make with myself.

If he can climb out of there, I will take whatever he chooses to do to me once he catches me, which he will do. By then he'll be more riled than a wet cat.

CHAPTER ELEVEN

It's near dark and colder by the second. Colder than last night under the little pines. At least I had those. Here, I have nothing but a tumble of rocks and sun-puckered boards from the wrecked shack.

I lean them against rocks and make myself a hidey spot at the base of the old mine entrance. Can't hardly tell it's there from outside, and now that it's dark I expect the old man will have a devil of a time seeing me. It's not like I have a campfire to light the way for him.

It might all mean nothing anyway if he's been spying on me, which he likely has. All afternoon I eyed downslope, but didn't see anything looking like him moving up on me.

I sit with my knees pulled up and try not to rub the whip scabs on my back against the rock. I figure if I can't eat and I can't drink, I can at least sleep. Takes a while, but I get there.

Morning comes early, as I'm on a slope that sort of faces the sunrise. A soft, orange light creeps in on me and I wake right up. I remember where I am and I don't move right off. Not that I can anyway. My legs are seized up, so while I try to stretch and limber them, I peek out between the boards. There in the purple morning shadows, I see the old man leaning against a rock across the way.

"I hear you moving in there, 'skin." He puffs on his pipe and shifts his rifle to his other arm. "Best come on out and take your medicine." He coughs, a wet sound, and I know he is unwell, likely the ague has gripped him. He is prone to it in the autumn.

Mama always made him poultices for his chest and he always threw them on the floor. He'd wrap up in blankets and sit before the cookstove with the door open and drink whiskey. What will he do now?

He has me this time, as I have backed myself into a corner. Behind me sits a mountain of rock, to my sides more of the same, and before me stands the old man with his rifle.

I lick my split, shredded lips and shove out from under the boards. A couple of them slide down and clunk against each other. The sound is loud in this cold, rocky place. I lean forward onto my knees, then stand and face him.

I know what he sees. And I know for a moment he is shocked. His red, wet eyes widen. He licks his lips and rubs his mouth with the back of his left hand like he always does. Then he shakes his head and looks like he's smelling something off. "Look at you, a filthy, naked, savage 'skin, nothin' more."

This is the first time, maybe since I was a baby under his roof, that he has seen me naked. That's what I am now, a naked animal. My feet are bleeding again, I can feel them. My hair, which I expect Mama was going to cut short soon, as she does each season, is dusty and shaggy like a hummock of sheep grass at the end of summer. I am more bone-stretched skin than boy.

As I walked these last days, I took to holding my right hand cupped in that hollow in the center of my chest, where the bones rise up like in a grand cathedral, Notre Dame is the one I'm thinking of. Mama showed me an illustration of it in her book about Europe.

He shakes a finger at me. "I knew you reminded me of someone. I see it now. You look like your father. Yeah, he was a filthy Indian, no better'n an animal. Should have known. One day — One day! — I go to town for supplies and he and that trollop of a daughter of mine couple like beasts!"

He shakes his head and raises a tired hand in my direction, then lets it fall. "And here is what I get for my troubles. A creature the likes of which the world should not have to look upon."

He's talking of me, of course. And looking at me again, full on, something he's rarely done for more than a blink or two at a time. But he's not blinking now, he's staring at me. Shaking his head and staring.

For long moments we look on each other,

me leaning against the boulder, my naked-
ness only covered by dirt and dust from
these mountains that are not what I pictured
they'd be.

For a man who looked my whole life as if
he was made of tree and rock, boulders on
boulders, with hands like stout oak
branches, the old man doesn't look all that
big anymore. He looks sickly and small, sort
of caved in on himself, curling inward like a
clawed hand closing up.

A breeze pesters around a rock upslope of
us, coaxing a soft, whistling sound. It stops
and the dust settles. The old man looks
away, then back to me. "Okay, best get to
it." He sighs. "You owe me and now it's time
for you to pay. I am sick of this foolishness
and I am out of whiskey. Now come on, get
walking." He jerks his chin at me. "Get on
down here."

I stare at him and it comes to me that the
story of the bear as he always told it was
not true. Or at least he'd not told all of it.
He never said what happened before he shot
the bear. Never said how it was at the end. I
think at the end that bear turned on him. It
had to.

You pester something enough and it will
turn and fight. Any man who does not want
that from a foe is no man, for though that

means he will shoot that thing he's pestering, he will shoot it in the back, not the front. That means the old man never let that young, hungry, tired cinnamon bear turn around and face him. Fight him. Instead he shot it from behind as it ran from him, scared and crying.

I don't move. For the first time, I don't do as the old man says. His saggy face shakes and his wet eyes don't leave mine. I know he's going to shoot me.

"No," I say, and shake my head.

He looks tired and mean and I see his cheek muscles working beneath his gray, scraggly beard. Then he smiles.

"I expect you're heading north, eh? Let me guess, to your father's people." He spits and coughs. "Yeah, I thought so, I can see it in your soulless eyes, you redskin bastard. Well, I'll let you in on a little secret."

He leans forward and smiles again. "You want to meet your father, you come back to the ranch. That's right. Been there all along. I found out he was dallying with my own daughter and kin, my Mary, why, I laid him low. Didn't take much, invited him in the stable for a sip of firewater. I know how you 'skins like your liquor."

He shifts the rifle to his other arm. I watch him do it.

"I smiled and patted his shoulder and told him I knew how it was and that it was okay, see? Then I give him a drink and welcomed him to stay at the ranch as long as he liked. In fact, forever. Then I smiled and hit him on the head with a peening hammer."

He coughs again and spits a green wad, then wipes his mouth with his sleeve. He looks at me. "Then I chucked him in the sty. Been there since. So you come back to the ranch, I'll introduce you to him proper. You can stay there as long as you like. Forever, see?" He laughs again, and it ends in another cough.

Nothing he says surprises me. It all makes odd sense. Like when there's a buck at the edge of a meadow, and you can't see him, but you know he's there. Then he finally steps into view.

The old man has lost his smile once more and he walks toward me, looking small and old. As if the weight of the rifle is almost too much for him to carry. He's looking at me, not where he is walking. For the first time in my life, he is doing what I want him to do.

He steps on the planking and for a moment it looks as if it will hold him up. It barely sags. But as with everything eventually, people and boards and rocks and animals, time has made it dry and brittle. With no warning, the planks crack, and he looks at me, the beginning of surprise on his face. Then he drops into the hole.

CHAPTER TWELVE

He makes a lot of noise on the way down. I think he hits the sides, bounces off rocks as he drops. It doesn't take him long to get there, then there's a quiet moment or two, long enough to draw a big breath. That's when he commences to screaming and howling.

"Both my legs are broke! I see the bone! I see the bone! Oh god, you help me, boy! Get my pack, you got to help me. Go fetch a rope or something. Help me, boy!"

I walk wide around the pit, and I do go to his pack. He left it leaning against a big rock. Inside I see a canteen and when I lift it out, I am pleased to feel it's mostly full.

There's food in there, too, some of that jerked meat he never lets me or Mama eat, and a hard crust of bread and a block of cheese he's likely been gnawing on as he walks. I sample it all, a little at a time, and sip that cool water from the canteen and listen to him carrying on.

"Make a rope, boy, use my clothes, my blanket! Hurry! It's unbearable, I tell you! I ain't got whiskey. Got to get home . . . Oh, Martha Anne, oh it hurts . . ."

There aren't any boots in the pack, but there is an old pair of socks Mama made him last Christmas. They smell foul but I tug them on over my raggy feet and pull out the blanket. It's wool and has some holes, but it's warmer than being naked. He's got other clothes in there, a shirt, drawers, but I don't worry about that just now.

I walk over to the pit and sit down, close, but not so close he can see me. He has that rifle.

"You up there, boy?" His voice trembles and I know he's crying.

"Yes," I say.

"Help me, boy!"

For the first time, I have things to say to him. So I do. "You know, I am the last of your line . . . old man. I carry your blood in my body. And now it's on my hands. We have a lot in common, old man."

"This ain't the way it should be," he says.

His voice is wet, raw.

"Boy, listen to me! All will be forgiven! I tell you true! Come home and we'll run that farm together, boy! You and me!"

I smile. I am relieved. "Good," I say. "I wanted to hear that."

"What?"

"You. Begging."

He screams then, and I imagine he shifted around some down there. Broken bones will play devil with you if you move too sudden.

"It doesn't have to be this way, boy!"

"You should have thought of that," I tell him. "A long, long time ago."

I sit quiet for a few minutes, my eyes closed, my face to the morning sun. I listen to the wind, to the old man whimpering like a dying dog.

Some time later, I lean forward and look down at him. I am careful because of the rifle.

"Too easy," I say. Then I stand and tug on his pack and walk away.

Down in the pit, the old man whimpers, sounds that soon only he can hear.

I reckon now I'll get to see what's beyond these mountains. Already I have made it farther than the cinnamon bear ever got to.

After a while, I hear a rifle shot. I stop and listen. I do not hear another. I get back to walking north once more.

And once more I am followed, this time by ghosts.

THE LAST DROP

He had not expected the choking clouds of dry grit and powdered dung that filled his nostrils, caked his eyes, and peppered his tongue and teeth. He clenched his teeth tighter and continued his hunched-over walk, one foot poised, then the next, then pause to shake his head and bellow, to mimic the bison calf he had become in order to lead this herd to the far cliff's edge, to lead the herd to its death.

Droplets of sweat stung his eyes and he squeezed them together quickly to help clear his vision. He swung around once more and stared at the lead bison. Large brown eyes, rimmed with yellow and caked with flies and red with bloodlines, stared back. They were set in a thick head as wide as the boy's outstretched arms, and nearly as tall as he stood.

The brute snorted and lowered its mighty head, then shook it slowly back and forth, back and forth. Flies and dust boiled up, then settled.

The boy sensed the bull was becoming angry — the big males were always angry. The boy knew if he did not move, he was the first thing that would be stomped and trampled and pounded into the dust of the dry earth by that big, wide, hairy head. But why? Had he not imitated the calf as he had practiced? Yes, but the beast still seemed suspicious.

A breeze pushed forward from the rear of the herd, carrying with it more dust. But it would also disguise any scents from his tribesmen that might arouse suspicion in the bison. The boy coughed and did his best to pinch off a sneeze building in his nose.

He was but twenty paces ahead of the lead bull, far enough that with the animal's poor eyesight it would still think him a bison calf and not a young warrior wearing the skin of a calf. It was his task, the most important of the day, to tease the leaders of the herd into following him, and it was working.

The lead bison walked faster, and the following herd of thirty beasts did the same, their hooves thudding in a slow, mismatched, drumming rhythm.

Ahead he saw the beginnings of the drive lane, fifty paces across at the mouth, marked

221

with cairns, rocks stacked in piles at intervals. There were also logs and great tufts of grasses twisted together, anything they could find to define the sides of the lane to either side. Most of these had been placed there by their forebears many hunts ago. Though they, too, had repaired and added to the angling lines of cairns and logs over past days.

It was in this narrowing lane he would run, leading the herd to the cliff. He must not fail, or his own tribe as well as the three others who joined them for the hunt would all know great hunger in the coming cold season. There would be no food for the growling bellies of the babies and old ones, no sinews for lashing, no pemmican, no skins for wearing, no blankets for warmth, no bone tools. . . .

The boy shook his head to dispel the treacherous doubting thoughts and squinted. Far ahead he saw what might be the edge of the cliff. It seemed to blend with the distant vista, though the morning sun's brightness and the boiling clouds of dust conspired to blur the scene.

Behind him he heard the bison begin to thunder forward, stiff-legged but gaining speed. That could only mean the other warriors, runners and hunters, were closing together, driving them from the rear of the herd.

Move! Run faster! Isn't that what Grandfather taught him? Keep ahead of the herd, not only to lead them to the cliff's edge, but to stay alive. Alive, yes, that was the word. The boy gulped hard, swallowing back a mouthful of grit and dust and powdered dung and blinked his eyes.

Urged on by the other hunters, some capering beneath wolf skins at the rear of the herd, the great shaggy beasts broke into a run. Keeping low, lest they discover his ruse and shy from him, the boy dashed ahead.

But the great shaggy beasts gained on him. He felt hot breaths from that mammoth, red-eyed bull steaming the back of his neck. The lane narrowed as they ran, and now he was uncertain where the cliff's edge lay. Yet he ran, crouched low and not daring to look back lest he lose his footing and stumble. Then they would be on him, pounding him into the earth even as they thundered forward to their own deaths.

Through sweat-filled eyes, he saw men leap from their hiding spots behind the rock cairns and logs, their arms wide and waving. They held aloft their spears, their atlatls, and clubs, and their harsh shouts echoed loud with meaning. Others closed in, chasing from the rear, prodding and shouting and howling fearful, savage cries.

They drove back into the great running mass of animals the beasts that strayed close to the edges of the drive lines lest they break from the group and scatter the herd. Such escape would ruin the drives forever, for bison have long memories. Then all would be lost and the people would starve in the coming seasons.

Unbidden, and at the wrong moment — for Grandfather told him he must not think of anything save for being a calf, and especially not when the cliff's edge loomed so close — she came into his mind. The girl.

Right now, far below, she would be there with the other women. This was a girl he had seen for two hunts now, far across the vast campsite, she of another tribe.

"Boy, are you listening to me?"

The boy had blinked hard twice and saw once more nothing but his own breath feathering white before him in the dark of the early morning. "Yes, Grandfather."

"Good, because I thought perhaps your mind was filled with thoughts of a young woman."

Too fast, the boy spun, his eyes wide and shining, to see Grandfather's smiling face staring back at him. "Do not think you are the first to feel as you do, boy."

But now it was all dust and the girl and the heavy, rasping breaths of the ragged bison running close, too close behind him, and he could not run any faster and he was petrified of stumbling even though he felt every sharp edge of rock and pricker plant through his moccasin soles as he gasped for breath, dusty, dung-smelling breath, the rank stink of the flopping, half-cured calf skin tied about his neck and chest and arms and belly. No time for the girl! And yet, she would not leave his mind alone.

It had been at last year's drive they had spoken to one another, however fleetingly. She had commented on his grandfather, a legend among the tribes. He had grunted and nodded. Fool! Even now, the boy felt his face and ears heat deeply at the memory.

He had been but a child then, not allowed to participate with the men, and had been told to assist the women with the butchering. The memory of it shamed him still. To think she had seen him in such a lowly position.

He knew she'd only been showing him a kindness she would any little boy. But not this year. This year she would see him for what he was, the lead runner, the only warrior selected for the honor.

The boy recalled the vast encampment, where the four tribes had staked their spots, the same as each year. In his mind he saw the mass of tipis, anchored at their bases with rings of stone. He saw smoke rising from the fire pits, saw camp dogs and children at play.

By the time the drive began, the women would have settled at their positions and kindled the fires and honed their fleshing tools, bone scrapers and stone knives, that would serve to render meat from bone.

What meat not eaten fresh tonight during the grand feast would be sliced thin and dried on racks for the coming winter. Some would be pounded and mashed with fat and berries to make toothsome pemmican.

The girl would be there with the other women, awaiting the bison to hurl themselves off the edge, bellowing and bleating and screaming, their big eyes white in fear and anger and, finally, in surrender as they fell from the sky at the women's feet.

And all because he had made it so.

Yes, she would be there. With her laughing eyes and serious mouth, with her long hair that shone darker than the wing of any raven yet born. She would see him high above, atop the cliff, dropping nimbly from the edge to the narrow precipice where he would prance like a goat even as the mighty bison leaders dropped and slammed and tumbled and rolled past him to the bottom, so far down, piling their wrecked bodies, all because of him! He would feed the people.

Even in his aching lungs and dulled, wooden legs and sweat-stinging eyes, the boy smiled a grim smile over tight-set teeth and thought of the glory and of the girl awaiting him. And then he jumped off the cliff's edge.

Far below, the girl held a dirt-brown hand to her eyes and stood in a long row with the other women, squinting up at the ragged edge of the cliff far above.

"There!" shouted an old one. All the women glanced briefly her way, then followed the elder's pointing finger toward a thin feather of dust. As they watched, it bloomed over the cliff, billowing and spreading like a storm cloud.

"Soon," whispered the girl's mother, and silence settled over them once more. Far behind, at the tipis, they heard a child wailing, then that, too, ceased, as if the baby had also sensed what was about to happen.

The girl shifted her weight to her other foot and licked her lips. There was one thing she wanted to see, even more than the sadly promising sight of the great black-and-brown animals tumbling from the cliff's edge. She wished to see the boy, ahead of the herd, disguised under the calf skin. It was his first time as the lead runner, teasing the bulls forward, and she had never known such worry.

She heard them now, a distant *thud thud thud* that grew louder with each moment. Soon they would see the herd. But first they must see the boy in the lead. They must watch him dart to the side and drop off the edge, onto the narrow ledge. There he must make himself small and tight, hugging the rock face lest the falling, flailing beasts collide with him and knock him far below onto the graveled slope, a false bison crushed and broken among the true bison.

The girl knew she could not bear it if the boy were killed.

It would be an honorable way to die, to be sure. There would be songs sung of him, and storytelling around the great fires. For many of his tribe, there would be much lamentation and displays of grief, but the girl did not want that. She wanted him to live because they were to be wife and husband. Though this was the first time she had thought of this, she knew it would be so. Somehow, she was certain of it.

The rumbling grew louder, drew closer, the dust cloud boiled greater, rising and blotting out the blue of the sky. The jamming, pounding, thudding of hooves, separate sounds moments before, now became one huge sound she felt in her fingertips. It pulsed in her ears, then deeper, deeper inside her until her chest filled with the sound.

With no warning, black shapes burst from the center of the great cloud of dust, just before the cliff's edge. The girl's gut tightened — they should stop! Don't they know they will die? But the bison knew only frantic fear, and they thundered onward, ever closer to the edge. Where was the boy?

The girl held her breath, shielded with both hands above her eyes as if to dispel the dust and distance. She scarcely felt her mother's arm close tight about her, her firm hand squeezing her daughter's shoulder.

The girl trembled and held her breath and watched. Where was the boy?

Could that first dark shape she saw have been him? But hadn't that shape plunged off the edge, the first of the many to do so? Surely a young warrior might survive a thirty-foot drop.

She wanted to ask her mother, wanted to

hear someone tell her yes, he was fine. But the sounds from the cliff bloomed louder and the sight, though something she'd seen many times before, today overwhelmed her.

It seemed never to end, as the big bodies of the bison flailed and tumbled, colliding with each other at the edge, then in the air, before dropping atop one another at the base of the slope.

She heard great slapping sounds at they slammed into each other. She heard bones snap, heard the beasts scream in confused terror. Dozens of them bellowing in surprise then screaming in raw fear, trembling, white-foam and blood gouting from their mouths in sudden, unendurable pain. Pain that would only be quelled by the thrusts of many spears, ending in a slow, agonized death.

"There!"

It was her mother, shouting beside her ear and pointing, her face close to the girl's. "You see? You see him?"

And suddenly the girl did see, she saw the boy just where he should be, pressed close to the cliff's face, tight to the far side of the tiny ledge onto which he had to leap at the very last of moments. She knew then he was alive and looking down at her, too, and she could not help smiling.

Her mother's reassuring, firm hand squeezed her shoulder once more. "Come, now we do our part."

The girl nodded and could not conceal the smile on her face. Nor could her mother.

With the other women, they spread out and worked their way up the slopes, proceeding with caution among the still-thrashing beasts, drawing their stone blades across the throats of those not yet dead, slitting open the great, hairy bellies to begin the day's long labors.

The work was foul. The blood steamed and thickened in the heat. Sluggish flies bulged with it, winging slow and annoying as they fed. The girl had tied her long black hair behind her head with a leather thong, but still strands slipped loose and danced in her eyes. She blew them away and tried to think of something more pleasant. Which meant thinking about anything else.

This was her first drive participating as one of the women. She'd been given her own stone knife, and the young ones in her charge waited for her to tell them what to do with the flesh she freed from the bones, how to pull hard on the great beast's blood-slick hide, peeling it back, then rolling it upon itself before setting it aside. Later it would be cleaned, scraped, stretched, dried, and softened.

There was pride in this work, and though she was tired and the day not half-through, and though the autumn sun felt nearly as hot as it had a season before, there was no river close by for lazy bathing. Now was the time for work. For this annual bison drive had been a plentiful hunt, with many bodies of the mighty beasts before them, still waiting to be butchered.

This was the time of year when her tribe's members came together with those of other tribes. The people relied on this hunt for so much. Not only for food, but their tipis were covered with bison hides and their dresses and leggings and shirts and moccasins were fashioned from the skins.

The animals' tendons, sinew, when stretched and scraped and smoothed, was the thread that bound together vessels of skin and gut used to carry water and fire. Sinew formed the seams of their clothing and secured the harnesses used on the dogs to drag goods from camp to camp.

The girl did her best to forget the sight of the skin-clad youth on the ledge of cliff above, but she could not quite forget, for he was a bison runner. Thoughts of him renewed the rare smile on her mouth.

She did not look up again, for he would

no longer be on the ledge. He would now be among the rest of the men, spearing the last of the struggling bison.

Perhaps . . . perhaps tonight at the feast, after they gave thanks to the gods for their good fortune and great bounty, the boy would dance before her, enacting his brave and successful hunt on this special day, a day when everyone helped to feed the tribes for another year.

Snows of Montana

I don't much believe in fences, yet there I was setting posts. Pap was right. You never know in life from one minute to the next just what's coming at you. Take that morning a month back. There I was on my worn-through knees in that Texas dirt, scratching around in a hole that if it got any deeper my cheek would have been grazing ground level, when I heard that far-off dog bark.

I stood, slower than I would have liked. This farming will kill a man, maybe not as fast as a bullet or a noose or a snakebite, but it will do the job just as thoroughly in the end. I raised a hand to try to keep the sun from intruding on whatever it was I hoped to see. Which, it turned out, was nothing. Yet.

I shucked my hat and wiped my sweltering head with the soaked kerchief wadded up inside the sagged crown. To my right those flopped posts were laid out like men who've given up after a long time of not wanting to, each one needing a hole and a man to dig it. And that's where it comes back to me.

I'm Ernie Palchik, Pal to my friends and a cowpuncher by trade, though before I set out on my grand adventure in early June it had been months since I rode old Plug more than twenty minutes at a stretch. When punching gigs came too few and far between, I took what I could get. I'm proud as the next man, but as my Pap always used to say, "Put you some pride in one hand and a beefsteak in the other, see which hand fills up faster."

When a man's got to eat and his coin purse is hollow and the growling animal in his gut is gnawing for a way out, then his convictions get stuffed to the bottom of his war bag. I've been down that road many a time, though that was not exactly what drove me to work for the old couple, whose name, near as I could figure, was Schnelling. They spoke German and I don't.

The day I chanced on their place the old man showed me around. I expect he was never a tall fellow but he sure had turned those big hands of his to a fair amount of work. If I read him right he built the farm himself. And a prettier place you'd be hard-pressed to find. That house was a picture — all upright boards painted white and that roof shingled, not scrap-tinned like so many little farms are, with a pretty little shade porch and three rockers on it.

I looked past the flower beds — pinks and some purples — I never knew my flowers, other than sage, but I guess that doesn't really count. And there, beyond the vegetable patch, all fenced in with white picket like you'd see in a town, was a girl pinning washing to a line. She had her hair up just like the old woman's, but this girl's was dark. I guessed her to be younger than me, but beyond being a girl by a few years. Eighteen or twenty.

The old German's clean-shaven face scowled up at me like he'd caught me dosing his coffee with cinders.

I tried a smile. "Your daughter?"

Same look. Then he held a hand out like a plate in front of him and scooped up an imaginary version of what was drifting over from the little house — the most heavenly food smells that have ever entered a man's nose.

My Pap raised me and the other six and he was a good man, but he was no cook. So when good food is on the stove, I am the first to walk toward it like I've been caught up in the mumbo-jumbo from one of them roving preachers. My eyes go wide and my nostrils flex of their own accord and it won't do but I have to eat right then and there. And I'll promise anything for a plateful of good, home-cooked food. The smells from that old woman's kitchen got me at the perfect time — perfectly wrong for me, dead-on right for the old folks and that girl.

That first night the only English out of them I heard was "Work" and "Eat." I reckoned those were two things I knew quite a bit about. There seemed no shortage of food to come out of that old woman's stove.

Soon as my plate looked half-empty, she'd come up behind me with her chunky arm brushing my head and ladle more stew and dumplings and pan-fry chicken onto my plate.

She was stern and had a mannish face under that knob of tight gray hair with two short sticks poking from it. And she had long lines coming down either side of her mouth like a talking doll I'd seen in a stage show once a few years back in El Paso.

But Lord could that old woman cook.

I was just tucking into my second glass of buttermilk — they kept a milk cow, thank God — and I noticed I'd missed scratching out all the dirt from under a couple of my fingers with my picket knife — the old lady insisted on a superior scrubbing before she'd let me into her kitchen to eat — when the girl walked through the room with a sewing basket.

Her face didn't quite match the promise of the back of her neck as I'd seen it earlier. I wouldn't go so far as to say ugly, but she was on the hard side. She had a pretty figure though. Filled out in all the right places and that dress looked to be almost painted on.

There was a line of little pearl buttons running from under her throat right down the front of her, and they all looked to be doing their job and then some in keeping things in order. It was good to see someone closer to my own age. She smiled at me so shy and it helped her face. I set the glass down and nodded. If she was their child I doubt she knew any amount of English, but I said, "Hello," and her mouth opened.

All I heard was a tapping sound and she looked away. The old man was rapping a hard old claw-finger on the oilcloth to get my attention. It worked. I heard the girl leave the room, that dressy swish you only ever hear when a woman's around.

I was about to toss my napkin on the plate and say, "Thanks for a fine meal," when the old lady set down in front of me a steaming wedge of apple pie with a thick crust browned just right. She didn't smile. He didn't change his look. His old claw hand was still resting on the table top where he'd been tapping it.

Then that pie reached up and touched my nostrils and I sat back down. I would be gone soon anyway. Let them think what they needed to. And truly, the pie was worth it. God, but that old woman could cook. I've probably said that already.

After the pie I crossed the dark yard to a spot in the barn where there was a cot with a corn-shuck mattress that had more memory-of-shuck than shuck to it. I lay there in the dark, smoking a quirley — nothing like a slow smoke after a good meal — and I thought of what brought me there.

Twelve years of bumping skins from one hot spot to another and next to nothing to show for it but my horse, Plug, and a few scraps of clothes, finally wore me down. I decided to head north. It was an itch I'd wanted to scratch since I was a kid down along the border when we got that first snow of my life. I was twelve and I'll never forget it.

A passing friend of my Pap's, some old-timer from all over, called what we got a dusting. Then he'd gone on to tell ol' wet me just how much snow places like Montana got. That decided me right there and then.

All them years later and I was finally ready to go, but I couldn't get any takers to join me. Not even my good friend, another saddle tramp name of Snapper. He'd been there and said it was nothing but green and rolling hills. 'Course he was there in the summer, but I knew I could probably handle whatever snow Montana had to offer me.

I didn't take a pack horse. I wanted the freedom of self-reliance. Also I didn't own one. I reasoned I had enough money in my pocket to get there without working too hard — if I shied away from towns. That's about where I made my big mistake. I took what I thought would be a shortcut away from all manner of civilized temptations. And that led me right off the path altogether.

I drifted off to sleep that first night at the German couple's place, thinking of a fine, big snowstorm and me holed up in a warm line shack looking out a window at more snow than I ever could have dreamed of. No one wanted a line rider's job, but I did.

But curse my thoughts, because they kept

returning to that girl whose face was not one a man would call to mind in quiet moments. Though the rest of her made a fine memory.

On the morning of the eighth day the old man ranted at me in German. I expect the gist of it had to do with that girl because he kept wagging a finger at me and pointing to his eyes and then wagging some more as if to say he saw me. And then he'd say her name, "Marta," getting redder in the face all the while. I reckoned she was kept on a snug lead all her life.

It was sad, but it wasn't any of my concern. I planned then and there to pull up stakes. They could find someone else willing to put up with their crazy ways.

That day the sun really put its shoulder to the wheel and I couldn't think of much else except how if I ever lived through this job I would never leave the back of my horse again. It was then, as I pictured me and Plug working our way through chest-deep snowdrifts and not caring a lick about it that I heard that German couple's old dog barking. I listened to it for a full minute and it almost sounded like it was getting closer.

And then I heard a snapping sound like someone sizing down branches across a knee for a campfire. Or like back bacon crackling in a pan. Or gun shots. Then I saw something low and small, the dog maybe, in the heat waving up from the ground. I walked forward, craning my head and squinting as if that might help. Then it dawned on me I wasn't hearing the dog any more.

I pulled down the last of the water from the canteen and headed for whatever it was I saw. A few hundred yards from it I knew the dark spot I'd seen was the dog. It was lying there in the stubbly grass by the side of the cart track.

I knelt down, saying, "Hey, old girl. What's the problem here?"

Her tail gave a weak wag and her front legs trembled and I saw in the dirt and grass beneath her old black and brown ribcage the earth was moist and dark. And a spot on her top side was wet, too.

Someone had shot that old dog. I patted her head and her bloody tongue lay there in the dust. She was gone. I stood and looked around me.

Because of the long, gentle roll of the land I could not see the house and barns from where I stood. Those snapping sounds had been gunfire. The dog looked to be hit once, maybe twice. But I'd heard a dozen or so snaps. What were the other shots for? I pulled in a deep breath and took off cross-fields at a slow run toward the ranch buildings. After ten or fifteen minutes I came to the top of the second rise and made out the roofs of the buildings in the distance.

Before I got there I guessed I would find an unfortunate scene. As I drew closer to the dooryard, I saw no smoke from the kitchen chimney. And then I saw the old man. He lay on his side, his black boiled-wool suit bedeviled with dust.

The shirt was still white around the neck and cuff of a hand angling upward like he was pointing, but that old claw wasn't tapping. His hat had blown off across the yard and his eyes stared up at me. The white V of his shirtfront was the deepest red I have ever seen, darker around the four bullet holes between his chin and the top of the vest.

I cut my eyes toward the house. The front door was open but I couldn't see inside. The old woman and the girl would surely be holed up in there if they protected themselves from whoever did this.

I low-walked, half crawling on my knees right up to that damned white picket fence and pushed my way through the little gate. I scrambled through as fast as I could and rolled right into the little flowerbed before the porch, keeping as low as possible. There wasn't a sound to be heard from the house.

"In for a penny," I said in a low whisper, echoing what Snap usually said right before we crossed a river with a green herd. He was from England. A more confident or amusing bunch of people I have never found. Except maybe for the Irish. But it was a German family I was more concerned with at the moment.

I sort of rolled and dragged my way across the porch, intending to make it to the right of the door, but I upended the near rocker onto myself before flopping like a landed fish against the door. It opened wide and there on the kitchen floor not two feet from me was the old lady.

I lay still and heard a bubbling sound and looked to the stove, but saw nothing cooking. I leaned over toward the old lady.

She lay chest down but her back was a mess of wounds, the dress and apron all punched in and smoked around the holes. Shot from behind. Blood pooled beneath her.

Her face was bent to the side and her eyelid fluttered like a moth wing. The bubbling noise came again. It was her breath.

I leaned close and said, "It's going to be

alright, ma'am. You'll be fine. I'm going to get you fixed up and fetch a doc." I said a lot of things and, in truth, I'm sure I would have promised to rope her the sun if it would have kept her from dying on me.

But she raised her head and fixed that eye on my face. "Marta," she said, in little more than a whisper. Then her head dropped to the floor and that eye glassed over.

I nodded. "Yes, ma'am. I'll find her."

Three for three, so far. It didn't bode well for the girl. I backed away on my knees and it was then, as I looked into the room, that I noticed the long slick of blood that led from what I took to be the formal sitting room at the back corner of the house.

I'd never been in any of the rooms but the kitchen, so I was guessing. Not that it much mattered — it was obvious the old woman had been shot in there and had dragged herself into the kitchen before losing the fight.

The place was a mess. Dishes were broken and a glass window pane was shattered. Probably by a bullet. I found spent shells on the floor. Looked to me like someone had robbed them. What I couldn't find was the girl.

I scrambled up the stairs, my little pocket knife open and ready to throw. Fat lot of good it would have done me. The blade's duller than my teeth. I only use it to saw through chaw and pick at my fingernails.

I whisper-shouted, "Marta! Marta!" but there was no response. There looked to be nothing amiss up there. Whoever had done this didn't bother to head up the stairs. I made my way back down the stairs and into the kitchen, careful not to step in the blood trail. It was a gruesome sight.

I've seen men shot before, but never a woman, even if she was old and didn't look like she'd ever been pretty in all her days. Time will do that to a person, I reckon.

On my way out of the kitchen, between the table and the porch wall, I saw a scrap of cloth and what looked like a hundred little white pebbles scattered on the floor. I bent closer.

The pebbles were the little pearl buttons I'd admired from afar on Marta's dress front. The scrap of cloth had a button still attached, hanging limp from its thread like the head on a little dolly that's been loved too much. That scrap, little flowers on a sky-blue background, was the opposite of the dark blue of the old woman's dress.

"Marta," I said aloud and stuffed the scrap into my back pocket. Then I noticed the old woman's blood slowly surrounding those buttons.

The nag still stood at the corral where the old man reined up after dropping me off that morning in the field. In the barn I found my gear unmolested and grabbed my gun belt, skinning knife, and cartridges from my war bag and gave one last look around.

"Plug?" Nothing. And that horse is quick to respond if he thinks there's the chance of extra feed in it for him. In that respect the horse and I don't differ all that much.

I unhooked the nag from the buggy traces and slashed through several other straps in my way. I cut the lines short and jumped on bareback. No time for a saddle. That girl had been taken and I knew it was up to me to find out who was behind this mess.

The trail was plain enough, right toward that great knob of rock in the distance. The same one that I should have stayed on the far side of more than a week before.

By the time I got to the base of the rocky knob the sun was drooping down dead ahead of me, lowering and growing more orange as it dipped. I rode part way around the base, enough to afford me a good long look in the direction opposite the rocks and away west, but I saw no one. As we picked our way among the rocks I found a decent spot to climb on up. It was almost a trail.

The old nag was in no condition to go anywhere but to sleep. So I slipped down off her. I swear I heard her sigh in relief. I patted her neck and let the reins trail. Whoever had the girl had probably come up this way. I'd start with the little mountain of rock and try to explore the likely hides of its upper reaches before the sun left me altogether.

I drew my Colt and climbed up the rocks as quietly as I knew how. I saw hoofprints pushed here and there into the gravel that made up stretches of the trail.

After a few minutes of cautious scrambling, I peered around a house-size boulder and saw Marta.

Her back was to me. She was kneeling on the ground with her shoulders exposed, the top half of her dress torn apart and hanging. Her dark hair hung down her back and over her shoulders. Beyond her I saw Plug's white blaze facing me. He nickered and Marta looked over her shoulder at me. Her eyes went wide and she put her hands in front of her chest.

"Are you alone?" I whispered. She stared at me for a few seconds.

She nodded.

"Are you sure? Where did they go?"

She said, "He has gone."

They were the first words I heard her speak. There was an accent but it was English I heard.

"He?"

"It was the one man."

"Are you sure?" I looked around, expecting to be jumped any second. "I mean that he's gone?" I felt a fool for not bringing my Winchester. Haste will kill me one day, I remember thinking.

She nodded and made to stand.

"Did he hurt you?" I holstered my pistol and held her by the shoulders. A trail of dried blood marked her bottom lip and chin and one side of her face was bright red as if slapped. Her eyes had the puffed look of someone who spent a good while crying.

"Are you hurt?"

She shook her head.

"Can you ride?" She looked up at me and wiped at her eyes.

"Why?"

"I need you to go back to the farm. I'm not sure if it's the best idea but I have to go after that killer. This won't stand, Marta."

Her eyes grew big again. "No! I cannot go back alone." She looked around and said, "It will be dark soon and you will be gone."

"It takes forever for the sun to set itself

proper. I can at least figure out if he's gone off yet or not."

She came at me then, her dress top hanging half down, and she hit me pretty hard with her fists on my chest and arms.

I grabbed her hands. "Whoa. Okay, okay. I'll figure something else out. Whoa, there."

She calmed and sort of leaned against me. Pretty soon she started shivering so I let her sink back to the ground and I stripped off my work shirt, which was a dirty long underwear shirt with holes and frayed edges. But it was better than her tattered dress.

I handed it to her, but instead of putting it on she just held it in front of herself and sat there. I sat next to her. Then she leaned against me, so I sort of patted her head a bit while she cried.

I don't know how long we were there like that, but I guess we both fell asleep leaning against that boulder. It had been a long day in every way possible. It was coming on dark, too, by the time I woke up. It took a few seconds before it all came back to me.

"Marta."

No response. She was laid right on my chest, hugging me tight, her head just under my chin. I could feel that she didn't have my shirt on. And of course neither did I.

"Marta, you awake?"

"Yes."

"We need to get off this rock. We need to get going."

"Why." It wasn't a question. And at that moment I didn't know what to do.

She did, though. She started in patting me on the chest and before I knew it we were what you might call in a full embrace and from there, well, I truly don't know how to explain it. Things just plain happened.

All the while I'm thinking it's the most wrong thing I've ever done. But there wasn't a thing I could do about it, neither. One minute I'm shushing her, telling her I'd help her figure it all out, next minute . . . well, I guess I've covered that.

The biggest surprise came later when I was feeling around in the near-dark for my boots and such. Her voice cut through the quiet, closer to me than I thought she was.

"You have saved me. And now that we are married we must work the farm together."

I swear an arrow to the back wouldn't have stopped me faster. I had a handful of boot in one hand and a handful of gravel in the other and I sat there in the dark with her off to my left, still too close.

In a whisper that sounded a lot like Pap and not much like Pal, I said, "Whoa, whoa

251

Nellie. What do you mean 'married'?"

I swallowed and dropped the gravel but kept the boot. "We had us a time, for sure. Things got out of hand, I'll grant you. But there's a world of hurt waiting on us back there and we need to tend to that right quick."

She didn't say anything, so I kept on talking. "Far as I know marriage is a whole lot more'n what we did here." I jammed the boot on my foot and yarned on it.

"What do you mean?" she said, not blinking one little bit.

"Well," I said, "like a piece of official paper, stamped and signed and all. That's for one."

She reached out across my legs — I noted she was still naked — and handed me that other boot. Then she gave me that smallest of smiles like that time in the kitchen.

You know the sound a stone makes in a still pool when you drop it from way up? That gulping sound like the water was waiting for that particular rock all its life and now it's satisfied? I heard that sound in my head.

We sat there, quiet for a few minutes. It didn't occur to me until a long time after that it takes an awful lot of stones to fill up a pool.

■ ■ ■ ■

Well sir, we made it back to the farm late that night, and as soon as we got there she was a tearful wreck. She wouldn't come out of her room upstairs all that night and most of the next day. And I guess I couldn't blame her.

I took care of all the necessary cleaning up. Though some of it I wished I had a little help from her or someone, I can tell you. Arranging the bodies and all. There are certain things a man is not suited for.

I can still see their faces. It's not so easy as you'd think, trying to close eyes and mouths that death has sneaked up on and left open, caught in a moment like that with nothing or no one telling them what to do any more. But I got used to it and did what I had to do. Then I went and got the dog. The old dear was still dead where I'd left her. I did my best for her as well.

Then I dug three graves and laid them out as best as I could. Then I got Marta. She brought along the family Bible and read over them in German. I didn't grasp a lick except the amen. I got that part. I said it twice, figuring I'd need it before too long.

After I filled in the graves, I walked back

to the house and made coffee. She'd not laid out food nor fired up the stove, so I tended to that. Carved some bread off an old loaf and fried up some bacon. I didn't have the strength for much else. She ate and I poured more coffee. Then I cleared my throat.

"Marta, I know it's a rough patch for you. But we need to report this to the law. A bad thing has happened here. Bad as it gets and somebody needs to know. I figure on saddling Plug and riding back to that town, what's it called, Stutz Corners? Isn't that the closest?"

She put her cup down and stared at me hard. I'd seen that look somewhere. She finally spoke. "We have too much to do to waste on such a journey. Who will feed the animals? I cannot stay here alone." She covered her head with her arms and rocked back and forth in her seat. "What if he comes back?"

I set the pot back on the stove and tried to comfort her. She calmed after a bit and I figured I'd bring it up again in a few days.

It wasn't until later that I placed where I'd seen that hard look she gave me. It was on her mother's face every time I sat down at the table.

∎ ∎ ∎ ∎

I spent my evenings in the barn and that suited me right down to the ground. I was doing my best to forget what it was I had done up there on that damned rocky knob. Truth be told, I didn't think once about Montana all that week. I was too tired.

What with milking that little scoop-face Jersey, tending the chickens, feeding the beeves, two hogs, and the young cattle, trying to figure out the crop situation, tending the garden, plus cooking, even the laundry, why, I was dog-tired all the time. I never even made it back out to setting posts, which was dandy with me.

It was about a week later — I can't be dead sure because, as I say, I was worn to half a frazzle — a lawman rode up. I was between the barn and house, a pail of warm milk in one hand, a basket of eggs in the other, and he was already in the yard. Surprised me.

"Howdy," I said, seeing the faint reflection off his badge. I felt relief. He would solve all my problems.

"Howdy," he said. He was a shortish man, on the young side of old. Big moustaches like Pap favored. I never could get such to grow so they looked decent on me. It's my ginger hair. Too fair for a full set of whiskers.

"Step on down," I said. I set the pail and the basket on the ground and walked over to meet him. He sat a black horse, big with a white blaze on his forehead. Handsome animal.

"I'm Ernie Palchik. Friends call me Pal." I offered my hand and we shook.

"Muncey. Sheriff Muncey. Olga and Otto here?"

"Who?" I said, then it occurred to me. The old folks. "If you mean the old German couple, well, there's been some mighty misfortune here, sheriff. We can have some coffee and I'll explain it all."

He didn't move, except to put his hands on his hips. Then he scowled. "I guess you'll tell me whatever it is I need to know and right here. I know the Schnellings well. Olga and Otto and their daughter, Marta. Where are they?"

His tone served to open up the sky a bit for me and, odd as it sounds, I looked at the situation for the first time from a point of view that wasn't mine. And I didn't like what I was looking at.

Then Marta stepped out into the shade of the porch.

Sheriff Muncey said, "Marta, there you

are. Mr. Peel at the bank sent me. Your father didn't meet his payment, and that's not like him at all. We guessed something was wrong." He looked at me, then back to her.

She stepped down from the porch into the sunlight. I hardly knew her. Her face was red along one side, her lip bleeding, hair a mess, and her dress front torn open. She ran out, sobbing, right past me to the sheriff.

I swore I smelled onions. Hell, I smelled a rat.

"What's been done to you, Marta?" Muncey's voice was stern. "You tell me now."

In between sobs, we got her whole story. "He . . . he keeps me here." She pointed at me. "He shot my parents. And my dog, Lela . . ."

The sheriff's jaw muscles bunched and his nostrils flexed like a bull's. He looked at me like I'd been caught with a trick deck up my sleeve.

He patted her shoulders and offered her his coat. I just stood there with my mouth wide, catching Texas flies.

"This just ain't the truth, sheriff!" I tried but he wasn't having any of it.

"He . . . he took his way with me . . . and

he told me to keep quiet or he would kill me, too."

"That's a lie, sheriff!" I shouted. "Someone did those things, but I never! She's confused. Heck, I been doing all the work here, trying to convince her to go for the law all along. She worked her womanly ways on me. I had nothing to do with it."

The sheriff was pretty quiet and so was Marta. She'd stopped crying and was hugging his coat tight. It didn't take me long to realize I should shut my trap and right quick.

Finally Muncey spoke. "Mister, I've known this girl all her life and I've never met you. What makes you think I might believe a single word you have to say?"

For once, I had no words to offer anyone.

Well, he put handcuffs on me and hooked me to the corral rail. Plug nudged me for feed. Then Muncey came out of the barn with my Winchester and a little scrap of blue cloth with a button attached. He sniffed at the Winchester and noted how it had been fired hard in the not-too-distant past and not cleaned. He held up the cloth and shook his head.

My Winchester. I'd not so much as touched it since I arrived at the little damn farm. But someone had. He stared at me a full minute, then he went to the house.

There's not much to tell about the rest of that day or the next. Muncey stuck me, still handcuffed, on that old nag, though I swore to blue heaven Plug was my horse and there'd be hell to pay if I wasn't allowed my own horse to ride. Marta stood there and shook her head no when the sheriff asked her if I was telling the truth.

So I rode to Stutz Corners with the sheriff. I tried for the first few hours to explain my situation to him. Finally he drew on me and told me to keep my mouth shut and save it for the district judge. Which is what I did. And now here I am at the federal penitentiary at Fort Barr counting on less than two full hands the days left to me before I swing.

In the end I got nothing out of my big adventure north but a full belly, a sagged bed, and a hollow heart. Whatever it was that happened at that little ranch happened more or less right under my own nose. I guess I chose not to see it. And now here I am, the clock on this life of mine ticking down.

I will say this cot ain't half as awful as the one at the farm. At least here I find I can close my eyes and think of Montana.

Me and Plug riding through snow so white it's almost blue, and pretty soon that snow's up over Plug's head and he doesn't mind one bit. He's still running through it, heading toward mountains that never get any closer but always look so majestic.

The snow keeps rising and I let go the reins and reach out to sort of swim my way through it and find it's not snow at all. It's millions of tiny pearl buttons.

Pretty soon they're over my head and I can't see a thing or feel a thing save for those buttons all around me, and they're filling my throat and my mouth, and I can't wake up.

Pay the Ferryman

A week after he pierced the hide of old Marshal Bolduc in Wichita with a lucky slug, Turk Mincher found himself continuing on in a southerly direction. He hoped the bullet had put the ornery lawdog down for good, but suspected that particular wish wasn't to be.

Something told him Bolduc could gobble a whole lot of lead and keep fogging his trail. And the further Turk traveled from where he wanted to be — cow towns and their gambling dens — the more it gnawed on him.

Why should he be dogged by that crazy do-gooder all his days, one eye on his backtrail because the old starpacker was all worked up about him killing a handful of tight-fisted poker hens who hadn't done a day's work in years — if ever?

Hell, the way Turk looked at it, he'd been defending himself every one of those times.

261

The four latest had been eager as all get-out to have him sit in on a few hands around the baize.

Could he help it if they hadn't thumbed through the stack of "wanted" dodgers lately? Could he help it that no man among them knew Turk was wanted in three territories and twice as many states for a passel of fool reasons?

That game in Wichita had come along at the right time, too. It broke a three-week dry spell since he'd last scratched up a few dollars with the pasteboards, his reputation not being what it once was. Used to be folks were inclined to stand him a round or three once they knew he was *the* Turk Mincher. But that had been some time ago.

He couldn't really say when his notoriety stopped preceding him. It had instead been tapering over time. And then one August day a couple of years back, he woke up in a hotel, sweaty and alone on a corn-shuck mattress jumping with fleas. When he'd parted the gauzy, smoke-yellowed curtains, he saw a town he didn't recognize.

At the washstand, the man who stared back from a foggy, cracked mirror wore bagged eyes, curly gray whiskers, and a look of fear in his eyes that Turk knew he had to outrun. A throbbing deep in his head, back where his frayed collar rubbed his neck, didn't stop even after he'd guzzled the last of the bottle he'd found beside the bed.

He'd left the room and headed down to find a game — the one thing he knew he could count on to set him to rights. But it hadn't. Instead, Lady Luck did what she had never done to him — she turned away. She wrapped her smooth arms around another man's neck, showed Turk her shoulder, the long plane of her lovely back, that tempting rump, all wrapped in black satin and edged in scarlet taffeta.

As he sat there stunned, Turk knew with an odd certainty she'd never again grace him with her favors. His righteous queen had turned fickle bitch.

Before he left the game, he grew careless with a simple slipped card — a maneuver he'd worked thousands of times. One of the players accused him of being a cheat, and before he could stop himself, Turk's Schofield had barked flame from under the table.

He'd dropped that accusing bastard to the floor in a twitching, bloody heap.

Within seconds Turk found himself pushing backward through the batwings, waving that smoking six-gun at the stunned patrons. It was only then that he recalled he no longer owned a horse. But there before him stood a perfectly sound horse, saddled and looking fit to ride. In for a penny, he thought, mounting up and pounding on out of that town, hard and fast.

In the two years that followed, Turk Mincher roved to hell and back on a succession of stolen mounts, drifting from one barroom game to another, with less coin in his purse earned by skill and more gained by threat or outright killing. He also gained a dedicated and dogged parasite in one ex-lawman, former US Marshal Melvin Bolduc. Try as he might, Turk couldn't shake that determined old dog.

In Wichita, the man at the table who'd first caught on to Turk's half-hearted attempts at rigging his game had watched the proceedings, frowning behind his bushy beard. The man had looked to Turk like a Bible-thumping shopkeep. So it hadn't come as much of a surprise when that hairy-faced man turned on him, slapped his own cards down, and pointed at Turk's chest with a fat sausage finger. "Sharp! Four-flusher! Cheat!" With each barked word, he thrust that cursed digit at Turk's chest as if he were driving in a nail.

Every eye was on Turk then, even the lousy fiddle player had thankfully scraped his palsied efforts to a halt.

It wasn't as if this sort of situation hadn't happened before. Still, it had taken Turk by surprise. He'd been off his feed, so to speak, with more frequency of late, so he'd not been able to slip that jack into play just when he'd needed it. What could he do but open up on them?

The way he saw it, the ever-looming specter of Bolduc's presence, closer with every sunrise, had caused him to foul his abilities. Elsewise, he'd have pulled off that pretty little trick as neat as you please, fleeced those four dunderheads, and been on his way — no blood shed by anyone.

Instead, he'd had to flip that table, drill that pointing fool square in his haired face, then give the other three a dose for good measure. His shooting aim over the past couple of years had improved even as his card game had declined. So when he nudged his way out those batwings, much the same as after that first gone-to-hell game, he was sure the four men were all gurgling their last.

The barkeep was no threat — he'd screamed and dropped behind the long bar, weeping like a scolded schoolgirl. And the fiddler was still in the corner, his blasted instrument clamped over his head like a poorly made hat.

But once outside, Turk heard pounding hooves and a guttural yelling growing louder with every second. The old lawdog, Bolduc, was ratcheting down on him in high dudgeon from the north end of town, his long, pockmarked face leering and howling in rage and his dun's hooves hammering the packed earth.

Bolduc's doubled shots peeled wood and dug furrows to both sides of Turk and the crusted gambler knew his game was over. So he turned to face his nemesis, raised the Schofield, cranked back on the hammer, and let fly a round.

It caught Bolduc somewhere in the upper half of his foul old body and pinwheeled him off the back of his horse. The big dun thundered past Turk and kept right on going toward the south end of town. Bolduc lay face down, spread wide and unmoving, his pistols nowhere in sight.

Undeserving though he knew he was, Turk considered the possibility that some form of luck had, however fleetingly, leaked back into his life. He chose to make the most of it and mounted up on the nearest horse at hand. Bolduc may well be down, but that didn't mean the bastard was out of the game.

He had spent the week since, penniless

and nearly out of gargle, cursing that undying Bolduc for everything from the loss of his income to the sorry state of his once-fine clothes. The West used to be a bigger place, mused Turk as he plodded along on the stolen horse, which had proven to be an agreeable, if moody, traveling companion. It rarely responded to questions and seemed half-mule, so sullen did it act when they stopped for a rest.

Turk was about to stop the horse once again, give himself time to think this thing through, when he saw a string of smoke in the distance, rising from down along the dark, tree-lined river in the bottomlands below. Without the hint of a breeze, the smoke curled nearly straight upward in the blue sky like a long, white feather.

Might well be the cookfire of someone encamped along the river. Maybe he could cadge some food, a little whiskey. Maybe there'd be fish, spiced and fried in a pan, perhaps some wild onions.

His stomach responded with a sound like a small bear cub just waking. With any luck, he might not have to pay for such food. He smiled, spit a thin stream of chaw juice at the gray-green grasses of the scrubby slope, and decided to investigate. The ride down there would give him plenty of time to consider his situation and decide once and for all what he needed to do about Bolduc.

"I aim to fill my belly, and yours, too, horse, and with any luck, get us a snootful. Then we'll see about smoothing our back-trail. Cover your ass, no matter which way you're headed. Because there's always some wolf looking to bite it. That's what my own Pap said a long ol' time ago."

Turk kept the horse headed in the general direction of the far-off smoke and turned in his saddle to retrieve his bottle from a saddlebag. All that thought of finding food and drink made him hungry and thirsty. He had no food left, save for a rancid hunk of pork fat, so the nearly empty bottle would have to do. He had bought it in some nameless town a ways back and had rationed it. But the sight of the smoke ahead prom-ised much. He hoped he wasn't about to be disappointed.

"About the only thing Pap ever said that was of much use. Then he clouted my head and kicked me out of the house. Eleven years old, can you believe that, horse? Who in their right mind would get shed of a kid that young? Leastways he could have farmed me out to some old farrier or wheelwright. I could have learned a trade, been of some use to society. Instead I had to make my own way, as you see, and I will admit that at times I have not been as successful as I might have been, had I had a decent start."

As he talked, he nipped off the bottle until it was empty. All the while, the horse maintained a steady course toward the location of the smoke, down by the riverside.

"What? You smell food, too, horse?" Mincher reined up. He grasped the green glass bottle by its long neck, leaned way back in the saddle, and almost let loose. Then he saw something that made him pause.

They had neared the river, and the source of the smoke appeared before him. It looked to be a house of some sort, sod roof hanging off the outer edge like a topknot of hair needing a trim. But that dwelling was on the wrong side of the river. He studied it a moment, squinting harder than ever.

Presently, his vision settled on what looked to be a raft on the same far side of the river. Sagging from it a rope swayed and bucked in the slow, brown water. The river looked a whole lot wider than it had appeared from up high atop the slope.

Turk booted the horse into a walk and they descended to the spot where the rope was lashed around a tree stump on his side of the bank. He sat the saddle, one hand on its horn, the other holding the bottle. After a fashion, he chucked the bottle into the water, where it disappeared, then rose, neck up, bobbing downstream as if waving good-bye.

"Hey! You can't throw your trash in this here river!"

Turk looked up. On the opposite bank stood a fat man in holey, dirty, pink long-handles. He rubbed his big belly, then stood with his hands on his hips, glaring at Turk.

"I guess I will if I have to. I'm trying to fill it up so I can walk my horse across without getting wet."

"Well, if a ferry ride is what you're after, you've come to the right place. I am in that very business."

"You don't say? I thought that rope and half-soaked raft were just for appearances."

The fat man didn't seem to know how to take that. He narrowed his eyes. "You want a ride or not?"

Mincher shifted in the saddle. "Well now, that all depends. What is there to do on that side of the river that I can't do on this side?"

The fat man thought a moment, then said. "Nothing. Nothing at all. Good day to you, sir." With that, he turned and offered a quick, flopping wave of his fat hand as he departed.

"Now hold your position there one moment, mister," shouted Turk. "I never said I didn't want to explore your side of the river, just that I am particular about where I do my exploring. You got any whiskey in that shack of yourn?"

The fat man paused, then turned to face Mincher. "It happens that I have a new shipment of imbibables and all manner of delicacies from the East. I am owner of this here emporium, you see." He wagged a hairy arm at the rough cabin behind him.

"You telling me that's a trading post?"

"Yes."

"Well, let us quit this lallygagging and fetch me on over there."

"First, business, sir. Do you have the fare?"

Turk sighed. "I do not know if I have the fare since you never told me how much that might be."

"True." A grimy pink hand rasped the stubble on the fat man's face for a few moments. He finally turned back to face Mincher. "It is a dollar to cross, normally. But for passengers who intend to purchase goods from my emporium, the fare is 75 cents."

Mincher, whose brief liquor-spurred happiness had begun to dull, said, "I grow tired of this. I will pay you 50 cents and you will transport me across. I will buy goods from you, if you have anything I care to purchase. That is my final offer. Take that, sir, or leave it."

The fat man rubbed his chin again. But he, too, must have begun to tire of the chatter across the river, for he shuffled to the cusp of the bank. "I accept. Ready yourself, sir. I won't be but a moment." With that, he dropped to his backside and slid down the mudslick bank, plowing up clots of gray muck with his bare feet. True to his word, it took him the work of but a few moments, hand over hand, to reach Mincher's side of the river.

The outlaw stared at him, surprised to see that the man was fatter than he had appeared from a distance.

"Shall we cross then, Mister ah . . . ?"

"Yep," said Mincher. "Let's get to it. I've got a powerful thirst."

"Very good. Lead the horse onto the raft, to the center please. It keeps us balanced. Good, good. Now, you'll note there are no sides, so we had best not make any sudden moves."

"Why?" asked Turk. "This thing going to tip me into the water?"

"No, no no, I can assure you the ferry is

most safe and stable."

"This ain't no ferry, mister. This is a raft, and a soggy looking affair, it is, too." Mincher was feeling worse by the second about this foray.

By the time they reached the middle of the river, he was groaning audibly. "If we spill," he said to the fat man. "I will shoot you in the head. Is that understood?"

The fat ferryman's smile was as broad as his fleshy face. "I am not worried."

Turk cocked his pistol and held it to the man's head. "And I am not fooling."

They finally reached the far side of the river and Mincher zigzagged his horse up the steep bank. "From the lack of tracks, I'd say you don't make much of your week's wages on dragging people there and back again."

The fat man grunted on his hands and knees back up the bank and flopped on the grass at the top, breathing hard, his hairy backside hanging out of the longhandles that were more memory of underwear than garment anymore. "I . . . manage."

Mincher tied the horse in the shade beside the remnants of a branch-built corral. He noticed no other horse. "How?" he said, looking around him. "Just how is it that you manage out here?"

The man struggled to his feet and padded toward the sagging soddy. "With great care," he said. "Come in and accept libation." He stopped in the dark doorway and held out a palm. "After you pay the ferry fee."

"I am good for it, don't you worry."

"Ah," he said. "But I do worry . . . about money, that is."

Mincher lost the last of his patience. He leaned down, his nose pushing in the sweaty, greasy end of the little fat man's nose. "I am hungry, tired, and thirsty. Not in that order. I will settle up with you when I am ready to leave. I do not want to hear another word about it."

The fat man didn't seem to scare as easily as Turk hoped he might. That sort of bluster usually worked.

And then the fat man's sweaty, stubbled cheeks rose in a smile. "I suspect you are a gambling man. Am I right?"

Turk sniffed, not disliking the assumption. "Could be you are correct."

"I thought so. Then let us make a friendly wager."

Turk straightened. "Prattle on, but not for too long. I am a short-fused man."

The ferryman nodded. "I can see that. What I have in mind is simply this: We cut the cards."

"And?"

"And high card wins."

"Wins what? A drink?" said Turk.

"That, and something to eat."

Turk tapped the gun barrel against his chin. "And the price of a ferry ride."

The fat man smiled again. "Come right on in," he said, slipping into the dark interior of the long, low house.

As his eyes adjusted, Mincher saw scraggly brown pelts hanging from pegs in the rafters. Smashed booze crocks lay pushed into piles along the edges of the dirt-floored room, and wood smoke hung thick and low in the air. A plank bar lined the back of the room, and up from behind it popped the rank fat man, his face gleaming with grease and sweat. And he had a shotgun aimed at Mincher.

"What in the hell is that, mister?"

"Why, this is Beulah. And she does not take kindly to folks who don't pay their way. Payment is expected when services are rendered. I said as much before."

"No, you didn't."

"Well, I should have. Would have if you hadn't been so chatty."

Turk ran his tongue along his teeth. "What about our wager?"

"I did not actually agree to the price of a ferry ride. Now," motioned the fat man with his double-barrel beast. "Set that six-gun on the bartop here and back away from it."

"This is a mistake, ferryman. Do you know who I am?"

The proprietor looked worried for a brief moment, then said, "No, and I guess I do not care to. I might lose my nerve. Now do as I say and I will pour you a drink of whiskey."

Mincher licked his lips before he realized he had done it. He reached for his gun.

"Slowly, now. Slowly."

Mincher moved slower, then said, "Hell with . . ." *BLAM!* ". . . this." He sidestepped as he pulled the trigger on his Schofield.

The fat man stared for a moment, blood bubbling up and filling his mouth, then drooling down his begrimed underwear, smoke rising from the ratty hole Turk's bullet put in his chest.

The shotgun clunked to the bartop and the fat man leered at Turk, eyes wide and mouth pulling another genuine smile. He held a moment, then whispered, "You lose."

It came out as little more than a wheeze, followed by the *pop* of a blood bubble. Then the ferryman's chin slammed the edge of a barrel before his girth smacked to the floor.

A choking mass of gunsmoke had filled the rank room, but soon dissipated enough to allow Mincher to rummage. If the man's portliness was any indication, he had been pretty well set up, though Mincher had no idea how that could be possible, living out in the midst of nowhere. "First things first, I need food."

There must be something worth eating in here somewhere, he thought. *Otherwise, how could the man have gotten so fat?*

Mincher flipped empty tins and wooden boxes and burlap sacks off piles and shelves and finally found what looked like a hunk of cured bacon hanging in a dark corner. He cut its rope and sniffed. It was not too green. He sliced off a handful of hunks.

With his shirt bottom, he wiped out a fry pan sitting on a stack of firewood, then set it on the smoking woodstove. Soon he had the foul bacon sizzling. Then he turned his attention to finding booze.

He cut his eyes along the little plank bartop and spied playing cards in a neat pile. He smiled and cut the deck, lifting off the top third of the stack. The ace of spades was quite visible, even in the dim light of the rank little hovel. "No ferryman, looks like I win."

Turk snorted out a laugh and tossed the

card on the counter. He leaned over the bar-top, rummaging in the dark space under the bar, and smiled as his fingers curved around the neck of a bottle. He hefted it free and it bore promising weight.

With a thumb, he nudged free the cork and sniffed, convinced that though it was not of a fine quality, the bottle of popskull was a step up from going dry.

He looked around for anything else of interest, as he now had free rein for taking anything he cared to. It was all his, such as it was. He sighed. Why couldn't he have wandered into a modern town, with whores, a cafe, and a bar or two? He could have been full of good food and drink, been drawing on a cigar, and even had a poke by now. Instead, he was stuck in this rat's nest.

Turk tried one last wooden box, pushed a wad of shredded cotton and mouse turds away with a fingertip, and saw two gold coins and a number of gold teeth. He smiled and dumped them into his hand. "Some folks will give up anything for a drink."

Mincher sighed and went back to the stove. He prodded the bacon with his knife tip. "Could be worse, I guess."

As the meat sizzled, he looked around again. Despite his little find, he couldn't help wondering if the man had a strongbox he kept his money in. Stands to reason, thought Turk, considering he'd run a business here and all. And from the looks of things he didn't have any way to get to a town to spend the money.

Soon, the bacon was mostly cooked. He prodded it a time or two more, unimpressed with the odor rising from the pan. Then barely chewing, he swallowed some of it down as fast as the heat allowed. He'd have preferred to take his time, but it tasted godawful, just shy of rotted, and he reasoned that chewing the fatty, rubbery meat would only prolong the vile experience. Still, food was food and he was as close to starving as he ever cared to be.

When he finished, he belched long and low and poured a generous helping of whiskey into a squat grimy jar. Maybe it would chase the greasy meat-stink from his mouth. The liquor tasted more foul than it smelled, as if a dog had peed in a bottle. But it was what he had, so he drank up and wondered if he might be able to mix a little water with it to take off the rank edge.

Then thoughts of water turned to thoughts of the river, and that led him to think of that ferry. What if he wanted to get back across? Alone, it would be tricky.

He snatched up his whiskey and wandered

around outside, sipping and glancing at the river, at the rope wagging in the current, at the small raft that the dead man counted as a ferry.

"Never did get to hear his story," said Mincher, sipping and wandering the trampled grounds in front of the hovel. Tree bark, stove ashes, broken bottles, the bones of animals he'd eaten, and Lord knew what else lay strewn about and trampled into a mat underfoot. The way some people live, he thought, shaking his head as he walked back inside.

Nothing had changed, the dead man was dead, the shotgun cocked and loaded on the bar, the woodsmoke hung drowsy in the air. But something was different. What had happened?

And then he saw it — the top of a dark-haired head behind the bartop. Turk drew his pistol, eyes squinted against the smoke. "Well, hell," he said, trying to sound natural as he walked the length of the room toward the woodstove, keeping the head in his sightline.

I could spin and draw, force him out, but what if he's got another shotgun under there? Mincher gritted his teeth. *Too much thinking, Turk, and not enough doing. Time to ante up.* He prodded the last of the greasy, popping bacon and cocked the pistol as he clanked the pan on the stove.

The abrupt sound covered the clicking back of the Schofield's hammer. As he cocked it, he dove to the floor, pistol thrust outward, aimed behind the bar. There indeed squatted a dark shape, this side of the dead fat man. The rank cabin was so dim he couldn't see if the man had a gun or was but short and strange.

"Come out of there, damn you!" Mincher slid a leg underneath himself and used his free hand to grab the wobbly plank bartop and pull himself up. The shape stayed put.

To hell with this, thought Mincher as he jumped forward, pistol leading the charge, and snatched at the unmoving head. It was hair, all right, and it grunted when he yarned on it, then it stood. It looked to be a woman.

He dragged her out from behind the bar, not for one second letting go of that top-knot. As he got her out into the semi-lit gloom in front of the bar, he saw she was a short, fat Indian woman with round, dark eyes. She stood before him, her face showing no emotion, save for those eyes that stared at him. Like a dog that's been beat. It won't look away, he knew, because it always wants to see where you're at. Something else he'd learned from Pap.

"Well, little miss. Didn't know your fatso fella over there was a squaw man. Got himself a right nice setup here."

It's a little rank, he thought. What with the stink of them ripe pelts and the off-meat and all, but he could see how a man might get used to this deal. And make a little cash on the ferry out yonder, to boot. Though he couldn't see much call for folks to cross there. As he pondered the situation, he eyed her up and down.

"By god, but you are a fat little thing, fit to burst like a suckling pig, you are. So was your man. Sorry about shooting him, but he got the drop on me and ain't no one does that to ol' Turk and lives to yammer about it."

She kept staring at him with those black eyes.

"You speak English? English?"

He let go of her hair and she stepped back quickly.

"I reckon we might as well get on with the proceedings. You are a woman and I am a man and about the only useful thing them two creatures do together is best done laying down. You savvy?"

He motioned to a hide pile that had obviously been used as a bed of sorts. Then he saw a number of hopping insects atop it and shook his head. "Naw, we'll head outside to the grass." He nodded toward the door and wagged the pistol in that direction.

Within a minute, he had her out of her ragged dress made of poorly scraped skins and sacking. He motioned toward a spot in the grass that looked free of painful, poking debris, and lowered himself onto her, keeping his pistol cocked and in hand as he worked. She appeared to be used to this sort of activity, so he hadn't needed to beat her to get her to pay attention.

He closed his eyes once, briefly, and said, "Mystifies me how you and him can stay so fat out here. Looks like there ain't all that much to eat."

He opened his eyes and looked beyond her head, a few feet away, and saw a jumble of round, white things. He kept working away, but reached out and parted the grass with the pistol barrel.

Human skulls, most of them jagged and broken, stared at him with their dark sockets. Their gappy, shattered teeth grinned. Wisps of thin hair stuck to the skulls in patches of curled, puckered flesh and fluttered in a slight breeze.

"Oh god!" said Turk, then looked down at the fat little Indian woman.

For the first time, she smiled, showing her own stunted, blackened teeth in a mouth opened wide. Then she lunged up at him and her right arm swung.

He jerked away, but the rock she held caught his jaw, set his ear to ringing.

He slid from her and scrambled backward to his feet, blood running into his left eye, his head spinning.

The fat, little, naked woman shoved to her knees, her enormous breasts swinging as she grunted to stand up.

"You . . . you . . ." Mincher couldn't think of a word to call her, his head rang so.

She lunged at him from where she'd been kneeling in the grass.

He was shocked, dizzied, not sure what to do. As she drew closer, he pulled the trigger on his pistol. The instant the bullet hit her, the top of her head shifted and swelled before settling back into its shape. She flopped face down in the dirt at his feet and didn't move. A long, loud gassy sound rose up from her fat body.

Turk stared at her a moment, then backed away. He was about to pull up his ragged trousers when he looked down at himself. He dripped down there with something pink and foul. Flies landed on him, lured by a rising stink.

Thin whining sounds crawled up Turk's throat. He snatched handfuls of grass and wiped himself before pulling up his trousers. He looked around, wondering if anyone else had been within sight, but saw no one.

He ran back to the broken corral, dragged the haggard horse out into the sun, and hurried down the bank to the river. Had to be a way to make that ferry work.

After much cursing and coaxing, he got the horse to stand in the rough center of the wobbly raft, glancing back up at the flyblown shack as he worked. Then he cast off the frayed rope that held the raft to the bank. He made his way past the wide-eyed horse and mimicked as best he could the overhanded tugging the fat man had employed.

In midriver, it dawned on him that the gold teeth in his pocket had come from those very skulls he'd seen in the grass. He wanted to chuck those teeth in the water, but he didn't dare let go of the guide rope.

An unbidden belch rose up his gorge and as he expelled it. It clouded his face and he smelled that rank, half-cooked bacon he'd just eaten in the shack. Hadn't even tasted like bacon.

And then it came to him — that's because it wasn't bacon, Turk.

In the middle of the river, Turk puked long and hard, disgorging everything he'd consumed into the dark brown flow. He hung over the water, saw in the dark, wavering reflection a stubble-bearded face fouled with his own vomit, dripping from his trembling lips, his red-rimmed eyes tearing as he gagged and gagged.

And as he leaned, Turk Mincher grew convinced he would never have the strength to reach the other side of the river. All he seemed able to do was stare down at a man he did not know, strings of drool connecting him to that other sad bastard staring up at him from that dark, shady river.

Below him, small black fish, no bigger than his hand, rose to the surface and took in everything he had just given up.

THE WITCH HOLE

"Mak u."

By the time I first opened my eyes, I'd already heard those words a hundred times. I wish I hadn't opened my eyes.

I do nothing but breathe and talk and think here in this pool of water. It laps up onto my chin but never really gets in my mouth. I can't move my head, only my eyes and my mouth, and it's dark enough I can't see my body.

I don't rightly know how long I've been down here, but I'll tell you, it gets odder every day. As I said, it's mostly dark but for a glow from the damn water that's a cross between spring-moss green and moonlight.

Except when he comes around. Then he brings his own sort of glow. I can see his white eyes, hear his feet on the rock floor. He crouches down like a coyote and laps at the water in my little pool, eyeing me once in a while. As he drinks, I swear that glow off him gets brighter, then he says, "Mak u."

Lordy, but I wish I hadn't opened my eyes.

I'd give anything to be back on the farm in Dacotah Territory with Pap and even Aunt Ruthie and them twin half sisters of mine, pesky as they were. But for Aunt Ruthie trying to make me a suitable husband for that odd Lorna Tinker from up the road, I expect I would still be there.

You'd never know Aunt Ruthie was my mama's sister, that different they are. 'Course, Mama's been gone for some years now. I ever forget how long, I look at the twins. They were born a year after Mama up and disappeared.

Pap don't say boo about it, but Aunt Ruthie will bring up now and again what happened to Mama. See, they went out for a picnic when me and Pap were gone for nearly a week trying to sell the furs we'd trapped all winter so we could buy spring seeds and whatnot. We got back and Aunt Ruthie was all distressed. Said Mama went in that damn cave and a bear got her.

I never seen Pap move so fast. I tried to keep up, but he had Ruthie, who was younger than I am now, by the arm and fairly dragged her along until she pointed out the spot. She howled as much as he did — though I guess for different reasons.

Didn't matter. Mama was gone, never did come back. But neither did we ever find her — or sign of a bear. Just a musty old cave. And I am certain Mama would never have gone in that cave. No sir. At least not willingly. Now I'm not saying Aunt Ruthie was lying about the bear, but I am saying that something happened to my mama, and maybe it was in that cave, and maybe it wasn't.

See, my mama knew of that cave all along. She'd told me whilst I was growing up that it was not a place I should ever set foot in. Said it was a devilish grotto that led straight to hell. I guess her threats worked on this little boy, 'cause I always found something else to occupy my time.

I don't think them threats worked on Aunt Ruthie, though, for I heard Mama telling her once that if she ever found out she'd been in that cave again, she'd send her back East, back to the cousins in Ohio.

After a year or so, Aunt Ruthie and Pap up and got married, had the twins, and life ain't never been the same. I reckon that was Aunt Ruthie's plan all along. Every once in a while she'd bring up the bear story again, almost as a way to keep Pap from forgetting, like a threat.

I didn't like hearing that business come up time and again, and one day I as much as told her so. But she gave me one of them looks and said something about how I was too much like my mother, and look what it got her. Then she went back to doting on the twins.

She spent more time on what she called their "lessons" than she did tending the house and Pap. It was always "the girls" this and "the girls" that. And "my little sprites" or "lovely nymphs." I swear, no one ever talked like that in our family. It's like Aunt Ruthie was from some other branch of the tree.

If I'd only known this would be the sad outcome of disagreeing with Aunt Ruthie so much of the time, I would have taken Pap's advice and kept my mouth shut, become a husband to Lorna Tinker, and been glad of it. But then again, like Pap said after Mama disappeared, the only things worth knowing come to us too late to be of use.

And I expect that's why I sit here festerin' in this pool of warm water what feels like miles and miles below ground, listening to that pasty little half-naked fellow say things I don't hardly understand a lick of.

It don't matter what I know or don't know, 'cause it ain't no use to me now.

I heard enough of the Lakota lingo to sort of savvy what he's saying. Least it sounds Lakota. Something like "Give it" or "Give me." Other than Indians, the only person I'd ever heard yammering strange words like that was Aunt Ruthie. But she's as white as me or Pap. The Sioux used that phrase, too, when they'd come riding up bold as brass and point at something like they wanted it.

Last time that happened was more than a year before I left. Pap and me had come in for noon meal and was at the wash stand when four Sioux thundered on in.

One was the leader, rode out front of the others. He stared a long time at us, then at the house. He bent low and tried to look in the door, which was open. He sniffed the air, too, like a dog will do, his nostrils flexing on a scent. Then he rested his eyes on the leather belt and sheath knife Pap had taken off when he'd shucked his shirt to wash.

"Mak u."

Pap sort of frowned at him. The Indian repeated what he said and pointed again at the knife, then at his own chest.

"He wants your knife, Pap. Don't give it."

291

"Son," said Pap to me. "Ain't much I can do. Them other three have rifles at hand and I don't. A knife's an easy enough thing to replace." Then he looked at me and as he reached for the knife, he said, "A life ain't."

He'd been talking more like that every year since Mama disappeared. Like he wanted everything to mean something. Anyway, that Sioux got the knife, then it wasn't long before others came around and started in with their "Mak u! Mak u!" pointing and demanding things from us. Before you knew it we were like a regular trading post.

Pap, he went along with it, said after all we were the ones who took their land, which is true. But enough's enough. And all that time, cheap and grabby as she is, by God if Aunt Ruthie didn't go along with him. I never.

I thought sure as day follows night them Sioux would try to make off with Aunt Ruthie or the twins, especially considering she made no effort, like any normal woman in the Territory, to keep her and the girls from sight when the Indians were about the place.

But the only notice they gave Aunt Ruthie and the girls was a squinty look. A couple of times one or two of them would back up their horses, like she was something they didn't want to be near. Like when you're out hunting and you get a whiff of skunk and change your course. That should have told me something right there, 'cause a Sioux ain't afraid of nothing, near as I can tell.

If Ruthie noticed, it didn't slow her down none. Kept right on lecturing them girls about herbs and how to make tinctures and whatnot. Lorna Tinker'd come down, too, most days, and they'd take long walks collecting weeds without a care in the world given to the riled-up natives. Then they'd all gabble around the table indoors, yammering over them recipes and who knows what else. Lord, but it's like women speak a different language.

There ain't no day or night down here, just time, time to think, and then think some more. I've gotten a good bit of headscratching in, as Pap would call it, and I reckon I've solved problems I didn't even know I had. Trouble is, I can't tell anyone about them.

That little white-skinned fellow must be a person, though he don't much resemble one. He's no bigger than one of the twins, but a whole lot thinner, and with stringy

hair like wet moss and that pale body looking like tendons you'd peel out of a deer
carcass. Even if I don't understand much of
his language, he chatters up a storm. I hear
him sometimes coughing up growly noises
from his throat, other times making squeaky,
whistling noises, or saying some sort of
Indian-sounding words, talking away with
himself.

Sometimes he sounds like Aunt Ruthie
did at night, when she was alone and
thought we had all gone to sleep. Chattering away like a finch at springtime. I'd hear
her voice through the log wall my sleeping
space shared with the main room of the
cabin, sounding like she was talking through
a stack of blankets.

No words I knew, but the sound of her
voice was enough, sort of mumbly and even.
I swear it wasn't in any language I ever
heard. Then I'd fall asleep anyway, worrying
about the crops, though mostly about Pap.

For some time, Pap had been looking
older and poorer than ever I could imagine.
He'd taken to bed more and more for
chilblains. His arms got stringier looking,
and even his hair changed from thick and
brown to sort of weak and grey. Odd for a
man who'd been one of the stoutest fellows
to settle in the region. Why, I seen him whup

Sioux raiders, steady as you like, one at a time, like he was plucking pasture grubs off the cow's back.

Lucky I was young enough to keep up with chores, even if no matter what I did wasn't good enough for Aunt Ruthie. I was tired most all the time, and reckoned that's how Pap felt his whole life. If that was the case, I figured I didn't want none of that.

If it weren't for Pap, I'd have gone off to see the elephant a long time before, maybe join up with a cowboyin' outfit. But he needed me. Sure as shootin' no one else was going to help him.

Them twins were primped and pampered something awful and Aunt Ruthie would just about chew coals and spit fire if you so much as looked askance at them. Heaven forbid you should ask the princesses to lend a hand filling the woodbox or working the churn. By the end of each day, me and Pap were bone-tired, falling asleep at the table over bowls of stew. But the twins and Aunt Ruthie were always rested and fine.

Then it all changed that hot autumn afternoon when Aunt Ruthie shouted for me. I was at the forge with Pap, working up a new set of pin hinges for the barn. One thing I've always liked is heating steel until it looks like the prettiest sunset you ever

295

saw, then swinging down hard on it. The spray of sparks shoots out every which way — nothing like it.

And that's about where I was. Truly enjoying myself, you know? Working with Pap and scattering sparks. Nothing like it.

So when she called to me, said I should come on in, get cleaned up, I looked to Pap to tell her she'd have to do without me. But he kept his eyes down, then shook his head. Well there it is, I thought to myself as I stomped on down the hill to the house.

I was mumbling and fuming and trying to think of a way I could sass Aunt Ruthie. Even though I was seventeen and man enough, I reckon, for most any chore she could stick me with, Pap was forever telling me to not spar with her so much. Keep the peace, he'd say. Do what she wants and treat her like you would a mother.

But that afternoon, I reckoned I'd had enough of that kind of chatter, Pap or no. Then as I come around the corner of the cabin, I lost whatever argument I might have cooked up, and any sense I had, too. For there stood Lorna Tinker.

Now, I'd see her all the time growing up. Heck, we used to play together at church functions and the like. And I saw plenty of her over the past few years, too, what with

Aunt Ruthie instructing her and the twins in what Ruthie called, "the herbal arts." But for all that, I'd never seen her looking quite like she did that day.

She wore some sort of frock that, from the way she was standing with the afternoon light behind her, why I could nearly see through. Across her chest there wasn't much in the way of cloth, and she was trussed tight, bubbling up soft and pink. And her hair, now there was something different there, too. All told, I'd never seen a girl look any prettier.

I must have gawked too long, because Aunt Ruthie come stamping up to me like she always did, but this time she just handed me a clean shirt and pointed to the wash basin. And do you know what? She was smiling. Yes sir. Smiling at me. Not at the twins, but at me. I hadn't seen that sight in a coon's age. Took me as long to recover as it did on seeing Lorna so gussied up.

"You two will be going on a picnic." That's all Ruthie said.

I reckoned that was all I needed to hear. Plumb forgot about Pap and the forge and hinges and sparks showering.

We didn't talk much as we strolled away from the farm. I thought we might take the basket full of food into the hills, and set out on that rocky knob with the one stunty tree atop. I'd only seen a snake sunning there a time or two. There might be prettier views on earth, but I'd not seen 'em. From that knoll a body could see a good fair bit of the Black Hills.

But Lorna had other ideas. Said she heard all about the low road from Aunt Ruthie. All about how gold was fairly popping out of the ground no matter where you stepped, how she wouldn't be afraid of bears if she was with me in them woods, how there would be more privacy for a pair of young folks such as ourselves.

Well, all those notions added up in my head, and soon I found myself trailing Lorna Tinker, swaying ahead of me like she'd been through there a hundred times or more. And before I knew where I was or what I was doing, she'd pulled up short at a hanging snag of roots and vines all matted together and draped over a rock face.

"What's this, Lorna?" I said.

But she didn't say a thing. She walked over to me, stood on her toes, and I felt her warm breath on my face. For some reason I closed my eyes.

Then I felt the picnic basket pull out of my hand and I heard a giggle and opened my eyes in time to see her slip in between them vines, laughing the entire time.

And that's when I knew where we were at. The cave.

"Lorna, no girl! You don't know what you're doing!" I ran to the vines, stood there without touching them, my hands held out as if I was testing heat off a stove. "Lorna!"

I heard more giggles, from deeper in. I tried to sound mad and not scared. "Lorna, you come out here right now. This ain't funny."

She giggled more and said, "Come get me."

I rolled my eyes, gritted my teeth, and parted them vines and roots. Then I took a breath and in I went, thinking of Mama the entire time.

It wasn't nearly so dark in there as you'd think. I didn't know where the light came from, but there was glow enough I could see where to put my feet. It was what you'd expect, sort of dry and dusty.

"Lorna!" I whispered her name, not daring to shout. I got a look around me then. If I'd reached up I could have touched the ceiling. It curved down wider inside than you'd guess from the outside, maybe as wide as two men laid out end to end. But how far back it went, I didn't know. She giggled again, from way back in there, and I knew I'd find out soon enough.

"Lorna, Lorna, where you at, girl? This has gone on long enough. This cave ain't for playing in. Bad things happen here —"

Her giggling stopped my talking. It was deeper in. I swallowed a hard, dry lump in my throat. It got darker the deeper in I walked. I was trailing my fingers along one wall and crouching, lest I skin my head.

Seems like I went back in there forever. Then I heard Lorna whisper, "Here I am." And by god if she wasn't right in front of me.

I reached out to grab hold of her, ready to drag her straight out of there. But my hands closed on nothing, no pretty arms nor anything else, and I pitched forward.

I didn't hit the cave floor. I kept right on going. Falling.

Today I saw something that doesn't give me much hope. That old man-creature took to sipping from the pool like he does, then waggled his hands in the water down by my legs, though I never feel it. I guess I've grown too numb, being in the water all this time.

His glow grew brighter, which had never happened before. It crawled upward, lighting the walls, like when you first open your eyes in the morning. I saw to my right hollowed nooks in the rock. And they had faces in them, like carvings.

Most of them were men. One was a woman, I think, because I saw what looked like part of a bonnet attached to her head. I believe I saw a few snouts, too. One looked mighty big, a bear maybe, and a few were doglike. I fancy one was a badger. There were lots more, I think, lost in the dark.

But here's the odd part — they were all staring at me, I swear it. And for a moment, I do believe I saw their eyes move, mouths open and close, eyebrows rise up, that sort of thing. But I guessed it was the dark playing tricks on me. Had to be. I know it sounds crazy, because they were only heads.

The glowing fellow pulled his hands from my little pond and reached out toward that wall, though he was too far away to touch it. But as I watched — and I swear I saw all them heads cut their eyes in his direction — his hands clawed at the air, as if he was waving like a tired child. Then I saw what was happening.

He was scooping at the wall, but without touching it. Bits of rock no bigger than a bean dropped to the stone floor. Even a little dust kicked up as the hole he was digging at widened and deepened.

Every once in a while he faced me without opening his eyes and let out a soft, "Mak u." His eyes fluttered like they might spring open any second.

All the while he scratched at the air with those long, white, claw fingers and said, "Mak u, mak u." I'd never seen anything like it.

When I shifted my eyes back to them heads, I saw most of them staring at me again. That's when I was certain they were alive. I know how it sounds, but I tell you I saw their wide, white eyes move. And I saw raw fear in those eyes.

Next, he turned and shuffled toward the end of the chamber. I thought he was leaving again, and I usually start singing when he leaves, to have something to do, maybe annoy him a bit.

But today he'd drunk from my pool a good long time, and the water, like it always did, gave him more of a glow as he moved around the chamber. Like when you carry an oil lamp from room to room. He bent low, a wedge of rock close by the floor half hiding him. He made a grunting noise, and it looked as though he had hold of a rope and he was yarning on it something fierce.

But do you know, there was nothing there. No rope, nothing attached to it, and still he kept grunting, crouched and hauling in something hand over hand. And then I heard it — a sliding sound, matching his dragging efforts, little by little.

At first it was a low, dark shape slowly scraping into view. Then, as it slid into the paltry green-white glow, I saw it for what it was — a man's body, inching into the chamber head first. But there was no rope attached to the man, and he appeared to be unconscious or dead.

I watched the progress and thought I saw the man's left arm move, rise up and flop back down. Probably fetched on a rock, but I chose to believe it meant he was alive.

"Hey, you there, fella. Wake up!"

The skinny little man straightened and looked at me. "Mak u, mak u."

"Yeah, yeah, mak u to you, too." I said it like I always say to him.

As if to agree with me, he pointed to the spot he'd gouged in the wall and nodded, his mouth whispering, "Mak u." And he pointed to me.

And that's when I understood more than I wanted to.

"Oh Lord, he's going to cut off my head!" I shouted it loud enough to echo around that dank chamber like a ricocheted rifle shot.

The little man grunted at his task for a minute more, then he shuffled on over to me, bringing his glow with him. He'd never done this before. He leaned in close and smiled, really smiled. And when his mouth opened wide, there was nothing in there but blackness.

He looked me over, like you'd do with an apple before you decide to pick it or not, as if he was making sure I was ready for whatever it was he had in mind. I was to soon find out.

Whatever he saw must have pleased him, because he backed off, all the while keeping on with his "mak u" mumbling. Then he closed his eyes in that twitchy sort of way and pointed his claw hands at me.

Imagine my surprise at seeing I was rising out of the water. I heard little splashing sounds as I left the pool, and I looked down, wondering what my body would look like after soaking for so long.

There was nothing to see. I was but a head swinging in the air.

I kept looking at the little pool where I'd spent so much time, but I saw nothing else in it. There damn sure was no body of mine in there. Where it went I could not tell you.

Before, I had been sort of emotionless and accepting of my foul situation, but now the horrible nature of it hit me hard. And it was bad, I tell you. As bad a feeling as that day when Aunt Ruthie slapped my face and told me that my mama was never coming back. And I'd finally understood.

I saw my face in the water, like a mirror. It was me, all right. But I didn't look like a prize winner. My patchy beard had grown in, my hair was longish and sticking up, my eyes were opened full and showed all white, my mouth wide. And that's when I realized no sound was coming from me any more, even though I was screaming like I was on fire.

I floated toward the little hollowed space in the wall he'd dug for me. He spun me around with his skinny white claw hands, one of them bunched tight like he was hefting a lantern in the dark, like he had a handful of my topknot. Only there was nothing in his hand.

As the little man spun me around again on the slow journey to my hollow in the stone wall, I saw the last thing I ever expected to see. Ever. There she was: Mama.

I kid you not — my own mama staring at me from one of them holes in the wall. Her head had been the one with the flopped bonnet I'd seen before. Her eyes followed me. And them eyes were alive, as sure as I knew I was.

Not only did her eyes follow me, wide open and pleading, her eyebrows working up and down, but her mouth was in a full scream. Mine, too. But we made no noise. Only thing I heard was "Mak u, mak u," and I wished the evil little creature man would die right there or drop me. Anything to stop the craziness.

But it didn't happen. He spun me around and set me down, far enough back in my hole that I couldn't see whoever was beside me. I guess that means they couldn't see me, neither.

I kept trying to shout, but nothing came out. He gave me that shy smile again, and then he shuffled away, his feet dragging on the stone.

I watched his glow. He walked around the end of the pond and pretended to muckle onto something again. Then without touching him, he dragged on that other fellow, who by now had set up a low, steady dribble of moans.

Closer he got to the pool, which was right below me, I saw the moaner was an old man with stringy gray hair and a sparse beard bristling off his face. He was thinner than a body had a right to be. He wore raggedy brown pants tucked into boots that were wore clean through. And his homespun shirt was more hole than cloth. His right leg, below the knee, had snapped and trailed at a poor angle. He was a raw-looking affair, all around.

I tried to shout to him, warn him, tell him to jump up and give that little animal-like medicine man what-for, and get the heck out of there. But of course, I hadn't a squeak to my name. Nor a body. There'd be no running for me. And if he didn't wake up, the same thing awaited him. From the looks of it, he wasn't waking up.

I've had a load of time to think on it, and I figure that old fellow must have taken the same fall I did — straight through the dirt floor at the back of that cave. Maybe he went in there to avoid a storm and met a bear, maybe his horse run off — who knows? Misfortune dogged him, as it did all of us.

Some way or other, each of us, big and small, animal and man, took shelter where we shouldn't. Or were led in there by something or someone, like curiosity . . . or maybe a wily, near-naked young thing put up to it by an aunt who always seemed to know more than the rest of us.

As the little white creature-man circled the room, I saw he was in fine form, glowing up a storm. He passed close to the other walls, and I saw they were full of faces, hundreds or thousands or more, all staring down.

Some of them were creatures I'd never seen nor heard of. Some of them were tiny, like mice, some were bears or horses or buffalo. Some of them were people, whites and Indians. And there were others, too, with an old-timey look to them, older than Indians. And all of them staring, mouths working open and shut, each trying to make the only sounds they knew how.

Yes sir, all of us critters hollering and not amounting to a whisper. And all of us had fed this creature — though I don't rightly know what he is, for surely he isn't an animal, isn't a man.

As he flopped the old fellow into that shallow pool, clothes and all, the man moaned a whisper, but he never woke. I knew whatever I had been through couldn't get any worse. Then that little witchy man leaned down over the old moaning man and his glow shined on the codger's face. Sure enough, all at once it all got worse.

For that old man is Pap.

Sure as the morning light won't never warm any of our faces again, there lies my Pap in the pool. And I can't do a thing but watch him wither away.

I wonder how Aunt Ruthie wore him down enough to get him to the cave. Knowing her, she carried him on in. No matter now, at least me and Mama and Pap are all together again.

I expect that when Pap does wake up, he'll see us heads staring down and wonder what has happened.

When he does finally look up at me and our eyes meet, I would like to be able to tell him that it's nothing but a bad, bad dream. That the only things worth knowing come to us too late to be of use.

But I guess he already knows that.

■ ■ ■ ■

ROAMER AND MAPLE JACK STORIES

■ ■ ■ ■

Maple Jack and the Christmas Kid

A ROAMER AND MAPLE JACK STORY

It's about the boy. I call him a boy now, but on that dark, howly winter night, way up where I live in the Beartooths of Montana Territory, when I heard that pounding and saw my cabin door rattle, and I yanked it wide . . . there stood a giant.

He was a full two heads taller than me and as broad at the shoulders as the door-frame. He wore what looked like layers of rags. Patches of red skin, like they'd been scrubbed with sand, glowed through holes in his wrappings.

I don't really know what to call that assortment of scraps he'd swaddled his head with, but it covered most of his face, save for the eyes. And they were dark, staring things. I recall thinking that they were the eyes of a man mulling over bad thoughts, intent on bad deeds.

He stared down at me and I wished my Colt Navy hadn't been in pieces on the table behind me. Of all the nights to clean my pistol. Who would have thought a snowstorm would bring out a visitor — and this high up? It's not as though I live near anything most folks would find of interest.

Even when I had the fearful mouth of my Hawken, Ol' Dragon ('cause she belches fire and smoke), stuffed up his sniffer, the stranger didn't hardly flinch. Big as he was, I guess he didn't feel the need to. Also, he was shivering something fierce. So I started in on him. "Just what are you doing skulking around my place in the middle of a blizzard?"

"Cold . . . sir."

The "sir" part pulled me up short, but I recovered. " 'Course you are. Said it's a blizzard, didn't I?"

He stood filling my doorway, holding up his big damn hands covered with holey socks as though I was actually going to shoot him.

"Got a mount?" I asked.

He nodded. I peeked around him, but all I saw was snow, snow, and more snow, driving down thick. He was covered in it. "Well, if you're not lying, you best put it in my lean-to."

"I did, sir."

I don't mind saying that bothered me not

a little. The lean-to is attached to the cabin. There's even a door into it from the cabin, so I don't have to go outside in such weather.

But I'd not heard him, nor braying from Jasper, my stump-headed mule who, evil as he may be, always lets me know if something's amiss. Just the thought of boarding whatever creature it took to cart this big fella's carcass around made me groan. Any notion I had of feeding Jasper in style all winter powdered before my eyes.

I sighed and stepped back. "Better come in, then. Seein's how you already frosted up my fire and forced your nag on me. But shake off that vile white stuff first." He did and I waved him in with the barrel of Ol' Dragon, but kept her at the ready. I didn't get to be this old by playing the fool.

I shut the door, then I give him the hard stare. It didn't seem to have much of an effect. In truth, I was not a little worried about my own self, he was that big. "You have a name, fella?"

He'd been unwrapping the welter of snow-packed rags from his head. And at first glance, I'd wished he'd left them be. For when he was finished, I see he had a head like a bastard kitten. Hard looking doesn't begin to cover it.

His hair was black and sort of bristly, forehead wide as a spade. The eyebrows were thick affairs that rose up in the middle, like two wooly worms squaring off to fight.

His eyes were brown, but one of them, his left, looked as if it had heated up, then drooped a bit, sort of slouched. And his cheek below that did the same. His nose looked to have been broken a time or two, as the bridge sported a couple of switch-backs. And beneath his nose, where a man's moustaches reside, was a rough situation. Born that way, I suspect. It looked as though part of his lip had been cinched up like curtains in a drawing room.

The teeth behind that odd lip looked firm and strong, though, which spoke well of his hygiene. I have little tolerance for a man who can't keep his teeth clean. The rest of him can go to pot for all I care, but take care of your biters and you'll never have a sick day in your life, I say.

His beard was a paltry affair, curling off his face like spidery young shoots in rough-plowed soil. I could well understand him wanting to work up a beard, though. Hell, I was in his shoes I'd grow those eyebrows long and comb 'em down over my face.

He looked at me then and I will admit I lost a hank of nerve. You would, too, you seen that glaring down at you. Did I mention he was a full two heads taller than me — and a good deal wider at the shoulder? I don't mind saying that around the middle I had him beat. My waistline has reached a considerable girth. I've heard that in some cultures, portliness is a sign of success. To that end, it appears I've achieved a fair bit in my time. At least by my own standards.

I motioned him over to one of the two low benches before the fireplace.

He settled with a sigh. For all his obvious faults, I could see he was a raw youth, maybe on the green side of twenty.

"Scorfano," he said in a low voice, more to his feet than to me, as though it pained or shamed him to say it.

"How's that?" I handed him a tin cup of coffee, hot enough that it was near to blistering even my horned hands. His big paws still sported those socks that were more hole than sock. His fingers, where they poked through, looked like pork sausages, raw and red.

"My name. It's Scorfano," he repeated.

His voice was big, just like him. And sort of rumbled and clunked, like that sound river rocks make when they knock together underwater. If you don't know what I'm on about, get yourself to a river and stick an ear in.

I sat down across from him. "That a family name?" I sipped and smoothed my moustaches. I am partial to clean, dry whiskers. And not averse to asking questions of people, particularly if they appear on my doorstep unannounced and bigger than any man has a right to be.

He pulled in a deep draught of air and when it finally came back out, that face softened and he closed his eyes. "It's Italian. It means 'ugly one.' "

That hung in the air between us like the effects of rank meat on a man's digestion. It wouldn't do to insult the young man's intelligence by telling him the name was surely a mistake. We both knew better.

Before I could think of something to say, he spoke again. Downright chatty, was this lad.

"In the two years since I left home," he said, looking at me again, "I've told no one that name."

"Well," I said, chewing a stray whisker, "apart from its meaning, the word itself ain't so bad."

"I hate it." He sipped his coffee.

I nodded and prodded the fire with my old walking stick. I'd done more poking at the fire with it than walking, and now it was no longer than my arm. "Where's home?"

He shook his head. "Everywhere, nowhere. The horse and I, we go where we go."

"Even in a blizzard?" I grunted and shook my head, but he said nothing. "Makes for lean times, I would guess."

From the haggard look of him, I suspected he was currently in the grip of one of them lean times. "Speaking of," I said, rubbing my hands together. "I haven't et yet tonight, but the venison shank on that hook over yonder has our names written all over it."

He looked at the meat, his eyes wide. I got up and shoved the Colt's parts to the back of the table. "Take them socks off and fetch the flour sack." I nodded toward the wood keg I kept my flour in. "We'll get you busy on some biscuits. That bucket beyond holds the water."

When he had the sack in hand, he peeked in as if it were a bag of serpents.

I set to carving on the meat. "Funny thing," I said, "but I've yet to be bit by a flour snake."

He didn't even smile. "I was just . . . thinking," he said.

Right then my stomach echoed in the little cabin, sounding like an abandoned grizz cub. "Well mix your thinking with your biscuit making and we'll all be better off for it."

I tended the fire, set the slabs of meat to sizzling on the griddle, dollops of bear grease skating and popping around the pan. Then I happened to look up at him.

That big, hard face was red — and it wasn't that hot in the cabin. Not a one biscuit had been made, though there was a pile of gummy flour, most of a week's supply, on the table before him.

"Whatever are you doing, boy? My old gut won't keep, I hope you know."

He poked at it a bit more with his sticky hands. "I'm not all that handy in the kitchen."

"You don't say." I shook my head as I elbowed him out of the way. I swear the youth of today couldn't pour sand out of a boot if the instructions were carved on the sole.

"So, what was it you were you thinking about?" I said as I worked at reviving the biscuit dough.

He looked at me as if I'd asked him to recite the Bible from memory.

"It ain't Latin I'm asking for, just a bit of conversation."

"Oh, yes, the thinking." He sighed, then

said, "By my calculations, it is Christmas Day. Or at least it was before dark."

That stopped me short, I'll tell you. And there are few things that will slow Maple Jack — that's me — in his tracks. Christmas, he'd said. Funny to think I'd lost all account of such things.

Why, tell me it's Christmas and I'll wallow in memories. Mostly of a warm kitchen back on the little hill farm in Vermont, my parents and six brothers and sisters, and at least one neighbor, usually Pastor Anglund (he wasn't really a pastor, just partial to misquoting scripture at odd times).

We'd all crowd around that table, groaning and swaying — the table and, after Mother's big meal, the people, too. Those were some times, I tell you. Christmas, indeed.

"How can you be so sure?" I asked him.

"Because I think my calculations are correct." He paused for a minute, as if deciding whether or not to keep talking. Then he looked at me and said, "And because Christmas Day is my birthday."

Now, I'll argue with a man from now until his toes curl from sheer exhaustion, but you can't banter with a fellow about his own birth date. You can, by God, raise a glass to him. And as I held up a warning finger and rummaged in the cupboard with my other hand, his face did something then that it hadn't done since he showed up — it smiled.

I'd like to say it changed his appearance in a grand way, but I'd be lying. It did soften it, though. I worked up a grin myself, and hoisted out my special occasion jug.

I have two jugs. One sees regular use. This wasn't that one. This holds fine sipping mash, and there was a goodly reserve of it, judging from its heft and the sloshing I heard as I set it on the table.

I splashed water in our coffee cups to work the grounds free, dumped them, then poured us each a snort and raised my cup high. "Happy birthday to you, young man. May you have many more."

It's not often I get the chance to make a speech, so after we sipped, I raised my cup again. "And happy Christmas to you."

"And to you, sir."

"About this 'sir' business," I said. "I am Maple Jack, on account of me being from Vermont as a boy. Why, I used to haul maple sap in wooden buckets with a shoulder yoke, and in weather worse than this. And if I made it to the sledge with less sap than Pap thought I should, well, let's just say that wool breeches weren't no match for Pap's switch hand."

He stared at me, sort of confused. I will admit that thoughts of the old days make me chatty. I can't help it. "Anyways." I cleared my throat. "Call me Jack and we'll get along fine."

That big fellow looked relieved. I was afraid he might actually smile again. I laid out the food and found a spare knife, and as we ate, I pestered him some more. "That name of yours . . . Scor—"

"Scorfano."

"That a name your folks give you?"

He nodded. When he spoke, it was slow, as if he was describing a dream to me. "I was born this way. They handed me to my mother and she screamed. Said I was *diavolo,* the devil."

He looked right at me then. His nostrils were wide, his jaw set hard. And damned if his eyes weren't red, too, though from tears, nothing more. But the devil? No sir. Not a Christmas baby.

He wiped at his eyes with a thick hand. "Cook raised me."

"So your folks named you, then give you away?"

He snorted as if I'd said something funny, then took a bite of meat. "I didn't get far. They made me stable boy on their estate in

Virginia."

I slowed my own chewing. "Money people, then, your folks?"

He smiled. "And I was firstborn."

I had to set my knife down at that. "Don't that mean you're entitled to something? Why, boy, you could be sitting pretty in Ol' Virginia instead of nearly dying in a blizzard up here in the Rockies."

The boy just shook his head. "I never knew any of it until that Christmas Eve, when I turned fourteen. Cook was drunk. I overheard her telling my whole story to a girl on the kitchen staff." His face got tight again. "That's when I left."

Now, I can't claim to be the sharpest knife in the rack, but neither am I a dull blade. So when he told me he'd been traveling on his own for all of two years, and that he'd left home on the very night before he was to turn fourteen, well, the mathematical calculation tallied right quick in my fuzzy old head. That big brute was no more than sixteen that very day. He looked like he'd lived harder — and certainly was bigger — than most any man I'd ever met.

Funny, the things we're handed at birth. We do what we can with them, then hope for the best. But what made the boy wander lost in winter in the Rockies, and after roaming for two years on his own?

I curdled inside thinking what might have happened if he hadn't smelled my wood smoke, nor seen what little there was to see of my cabin poking from her drift. And of all people, why tell me his sad tale? But he had, and that's what matters. As Mother used to say, "Even a blind chicken will scratch up corn once in a while."

We ate on in silence for a spell. He seemed particular about his manners, so I kept myself from licking the plate as I usually do. It seemed the right thing. Then I leaned back, sucking my teeth and thinking about a smoke on my pipe. I stared at him.

"Boy," I finally said. "If you don't have anywhere to get to, I recommend you stay on for a spell so's I can show you a few things." There was a silence, so I plowed ahead. "Like how to make yourself some buckskins."

"That's very kind of you, but I should keep going."

"Where?" I leaned forward, giving him the hard stare again. "With what on your back? And what about the nag you rode in on? No doubt it's half-starved, too."

I wagged my knife at him for emphasis. "No sir, you'd do well to calculate your losses and figure out how to grab a few gains, or life will wear you down. Maybe not as fast as it will a smaller man, but it will get you, mark my words. It's one thing to poke around looking for work, it's another thing to fend for yourself and make it a full-bore lifestyle." I leaned back and crossed my arms.

"I don't know what to say." He gave me that red-face stare again.

"Don't say nothing, except that you agree with me you need clothes that will keep your snow-burned hide from showing."

He smiled again.

I sensed headway and yammered on. "Woven cloth is useless to a traveling man, a roamer such as yourself. You'd do better with a suit of buckskins like these." I held up a fringed sleeve.

He flinched, and though he tried to disguise it by scratching at his nose, I saw his nostrils flex and twitch. I will admit to sporting an earthy aroma, especially in winter. But I'll be damned if I'm going to shuck my skins while the snow's stacking up outside. And if any stranger takes offense to my scent, he can ride on out.

"You ought to make yourself a full set." I poured us another snort. " 'Course, it might take a small herd of elk to fit you out with duds."

When he didn't respond, I looked at him. "That was a joke, by the way."

He went all red again, and smiled. That was getting to be a downright habit.

Well, we spent the night sipping and talking. I figured if he was old enough to nearly die in a snowdrift, he was old enough to sip whiskey. I for one enjoyed the conversation. It seems that listening to no one but myself for months at a stretch had left me starved for talk, and I caught myself chattering like a circus monkey. And I sensed the boy hadn't talked that much in a long, long time.

I don't want to give the impression he was a conversationalist, but he told me enough about himself that I resolved to sort of help him, teach him a bit of what I've learnt on life's trails. Seemed the thing to do, somehow.

I tell you what, that's one surefire story. Took place four years ago, more or less to the day. It's the truth, too, or near as you're likely to get from Maple Jack. Was the boy's birthday really on Christmas? Did he look that way from birth? Did his kin give him up for nothing more than being homely? No telling . . . but who am I to argue? In my book, a man is what he makes himself to be, no more, no less.

Since that night, I've grown right fond of the boy. Roamer, that's what I took to calling him, has proved to be a good man. Quiet, keeps to himself, but a good man just the same. Full of surprises, too.

To look at him, you'd never guess he'd be capable of anything more than gutting someone like a fish for whatever they might have in their coin purse. But heck, if that big boy don't pick up every little thing I show him. He's a natural.

And he can read and write and decipher, though I can't take credit for those skills. And if you put a jug in front of him, he'll recite in three, four languages. Real ones, too. And it turns out he reads books like they're going out of fashion. I never. . . .

He's been and gone, been and gone a number of times, always roaming. I mostly stay put. Leave the going to the young. That's not to say I'm an old gimp. Just that when a man reaches my age — and no, thank you kindly, I'll not mention that number — he gets to feeling nesty and finds himself inclined to stay in one place. So it's good to have a friend who will drop in for a spell. One friend is enough, though. Especially if he eats like two starved wolves and snores like a bull grizz in winter.

Well, I have a last run of lacing left on one shoulder, then the world's largest set of buckskins will be about done (he outgrew his first set). And just in time, too. Snow's stacking up and it's a howly sort of night. Somehow, I know December's winding down, and it's Christmas time again.

This pot of venison stew with dumplings bubbling on top can't compare with Mother's table, but it should make for a fine birthday feed, if I do say so myself.

Ol' Roamer better hurry, though, 'cause Maple Jack's about ready to sample the Christmas jug.

LOST VALLEY OF THE SKOOCOOM

A MAPLE JACK TALE

This here story is as real as a case of hydrophoby. Happened years ago, back when I was a young man, on a hunt with my friend, Tilquata, a Chinook warrior. It's something so strange and drop-jaw unbelievable that if it were anybody telling it other than me, Maple Jack, you might have cause to doubt. Just the same, if you get to feelin' skeptical, I'll ask you kindly to get out of my cabin. But hand me that jug first.

The notion that something was wrong come to me early on our eighth day out, whilst I was hunched up behind a fire-leaf bush. I ate too much berry paste the day before and it went right through me like a spring freshet through a mountain gorge. Only not so pretty, I can assure you. I'd nearly passed out twice and was fixing to rejoin the land of the coherent when I looked up from finishing my business, and I see a pair of eyes, not ten feet away, watching me.

You know the look I'm talking of. It's the one a mountain lion settles on right before it decides to pounce. Or the wide-open stare a grizz will give a man just as it recalls that it was a man who shot her cubs.

I couldn't maintain that pose for too long, buckskins half-shucked and wavering as I was. So, slow as you please, I slid them trousers back up to where they belonged and did my best to stand. And do you know, that whole time them eyes stayed on me, peeking through the wagging green leaves. Dark like black river rocks, those eyes were, and if they blinked, I didn't see it.

I wanted to shout to Tilquata. He was upwind from me — smart man — back at the campsite, but I didn't dare do anything more than creep backward toward camp, moving like I was riddled with rheumatism. Still, them eyes stayed on me. Like a fool, I was armed with nothing more than my skinning knife. I'd rather have had my revolver, or better yet Ol' Dragon, my Hawken.

You got to kill a thing before you can skin it, and most often, killing a thing's a whole lot easier with a gun than a knife — and not so close-up.

I'd backed a good six feet when that thing in the bushes shifted, grew taller, and I realized it had been crouching down. Up and up it stood, right out of the saplings and brush. And by the time it stopped, danged if I wasn't looking at a fully haired man, brownish and shaggy, half again taller than me and wider at the shoulder than a rifle is long. There was something else, too — a godawful stink had dropped on me like a wool blanket dipped in a gut pile. I realized then that it wasn't me, but the creature that smelled so bad.

I spun, reaching out to run, and grabbed me a handful of hair. Slammed straight into a solid, muscled wall of it, in fact. I backed up, frantic, thinking that Old Ephraim was finally on me, and that I was about to end my days as a grizzly mauled carcass.

Pushing away from that mass of hair, the first thing I noticed was the stink, worse than before — a godawful rankness that was equal parts boiled dog and festering canker, with a goodly amount of sour sweat poured over the top of it.

A face stared down at me, more confused than angry, looking like nothing I'd ever seen before — more man than grizzly and more grizzly than man is the only way I can describe it. And if it was possible, this hairy man was bigger than the first.

Now I'm not a small man, and I will admit

to a gut I have acquired in my dotage. But back then, when I was green, I fancy I was leaner than I am now, and a bit taller than your average trapper. But this big brute was easy near twice my height.

It stared at me, all haired up in that full-body beard. It had yellow teeth as long as my small finger, and some of them were pointed, like a wolf's, but that's where that similarity ended. This thing breathed down on me, and a growl like a low, deep moan squeezed out with its rank breath.

I nearly fell to my knees, so weak had this experience made me. Then I heard branches snapping and knew the first one was coming up behind me — I was caught between two of the creatures! The sound behind me was not the alternating, crushing gallop of a bull grizzly, but the two-legged run of a man, and drawing closer with each stride.

I turned my head in time to see that creature plow right into me, and my bean hit the ground hard on what must have been a rock. When I came to, I was fuzzy headed and couldn't seem to make my legs or arms do what I told them to. That brute had pinned me, and was closer than most men get to their wives' faces each day.

It panted, pushing hot clouds of foul breath deep into my mouth and nose, its tongue a quivering, slick, pink thing cupped just behind those curved yellow teeth. A thick sound worked upward from deep within the beast's gut, and I knew I was about to be its next meal.

But then it just sniffed at me.

Now, I've never been accused of smelling like a flower, but this thing seemed mighty interested in what I smelled like — my hair, beard, ears, the works.

The big one stood looking down at me, squinting like it was trying to remember something important. Then its eyes widened and bulged a bit. I saw it stagger and I thought as sure as the day is long that it was going to drop on top of me, too. That's when I saw bare arms close around its neck and I knew Tilquata had come to my rescue.

That big creature turned on my friend, raging full bore, and grabbed at the Indian swinging on his back. As they spun, I saw Tilquata's short axe, half the head driven between the beast's shoulders, red blood steaming in the chill morning air.

Tilquata dropped off and scampered a few feet away, taunting and luring the wounded creature. But that creature wasn't done, not by a long shot. It bellowed and ran straight into my warrior friend, knocking him down.

Now I'd known Tilquata for years, and let

me tell you, he was as muscled a man as you'll find. Like most of the men of his tribe, he was lean and hard as wood and not accustomed to backing down from a scuffle, nor afraid to start one. But in this instance, I feared Tilquata had met his match.

The beast continued to bellow in a roar equal parts bull-grizz and raw, crazy-man howl. It picked up Tilquata with his two giant hands and whomped him all over that little clearing, flinging him in the air, into trees, against the earth.

Within seconds the brave was a crushed, broken man, with bones poking through one arm's skin like shiny decorations. One of his legs was bent wrong, and dark purple welts covered his arms, neck, and bread basket where the thing had grabbed him. Even his buckskins had been ripped away like paper off a parcel.

As I watched that thing batter Tilquata around the camp, overpowering him in every way, and me nearly useless to help him, addlepated and lolling as I was like a little girl's dolly, I realized that the stories were true — the Skoocooms lived.

Folks of Tilquata's tribe had mentioned the creature at night, at times when the fire was low and tobacco had been enjoyed.

Then they would say that one word — skoocoom.

And as I watched that thing lean low over Tilquata's nearly still body, I recalled what little the Chinook had said about skoocooms.

Called 'em angry spirits who were neither man nor beast, said they walked upright on two legs and had toes and fingers instead of claws. At the time I remember thinking that Indians were just like whites — always looking for reasons behind things rather than just taking things as they are. But seeing that thing savage my friend, I knew that at least part of the story had been true — this was neither man nor beast. And it was damn angry.

My friend landed hard on the ground less than ten feet from me, his head bouncing on a spongy matte of pine needles. High on his shaved forehead, I saw the white glisten of bone beneath where the skin had ripped away when he'd been smacked against the rough bark of the pine, and blood pumped from a raw crater beside his eye.

Then I saw Tilquata smile at me. I kid you not, even as the light of life dulled in his eyes, he smiled.

The skoocoom bent low, grunting and chuffing, and grabbed Tilquata by the shoulder. As his near-limp body flipped over, the warrior's long, fine-steel skinning knife flashed upward and found purchase to the hilt in the beast's gut.

It howled a ragged cry that shook the very trees around us, and I knew then why Tilquata had smiled. Gouts of hot, steaming blood pulsed outward, dousing my friend, and still he smiled, though by then Tilquata was dead.

And there I was, so useless from that knock on the bean that I could do nothing for the man, my best friend, but watch as he died. I couldn't even figure out how to raise a limb.

Oh, I tried, and I must have raised some sort of noise, for that creature that had been sniffing at me, turned his attention back to me. His dark eyes widened and he commenced to whomp on me like you might on a friend, just to show how strappy you were.

It had all happened so fast that I was confused, and guessed I was near death myself. I watched Tilquata's foe, that murderous haired brute, lurch about the clearing, spraying his blood all over our strewn gear, the smoking remains of the campfire, the rabbits we'd intended for supper.

For a moment, as his big, blood-slick hands wrestled with that knife, which must have been wedged hard in bone, that skoocoom's eyes settled on me. His nose worked hard at the cool morning air, blood threading out of his open mouth, and we looked at each other, eye-to-eye, man-to-man. I tell you what, that massive beast looked as scared as any creature that knew it was breathing its last. Despite what he did to me, to my friend, I felt a sting of sadness for that skoocoom.

His eyes bore no anger, no vengeance like you'll often see on a dying man. Just sadness and maybe a little confusion. He dropped to his knees, then the other, smaller skoocoom rushed over and grabbed him by the shoulders.

They yammered in grunts and barking noises I couldn't make out, then that big one wobbled, and the smaller one eased him down on his side. The last thing I heard was a groaning, sobbing sound. Then I, too, faded. Never suspecting I'd wake up again. But I did.

Something like a fist rapped me hard enough on the head to revive me. I forced an eye open. It was a tree trunk and my head had rapped against it. And then another one. God almighty, didn't that throb. It took me a few minutes before I remembered what had happened to me, to Til-quata. And then a few more until I came around to the possibility that I wasn't dead. And if I wasn't dead, I reasoned, then where was I?

The landscape kept changing, rising and falling. At some point, while my world swirled like water eddying in a mountain stream, I realized I was being carried. There was some sort of stink, and hair, lots of hair. I don't know how long it went on, I was that addled. Then I was dropped. Hard. I moaned, I know because I heard it. And whoever carried me heard it, too.

The smell seemed worse than ever and I worked hard to open my eyes. They fluttered and finally cracked. Dabs of dark and light worked through what must have been crusted blood on my eyes. I squeezed them shut and opened them wider. The dark bits took shape, like when you twist a spyglass, until I saw what must have been a dozen skoocoom faces staring at me. I closed my eyes again and wished to god I'd died back at the campsite with Tilquata.

Her touch surprised me with its gentleness. I never expected those massive, callused hands could convey any manner of kindness. In truth, she didn't seem to know much doctoring, but she did apply a poultice of sorts to my chest. She'd made it of leaves and mosses and something that smelled an awful lot like camphorated dung. This matted affair was wetted down, though I hate to say by what, and I was forced to lay there naked under that dripping mess. At some point, those beasts had stripped me of my buckskins.

All of them, too, were naked, but they had the advantage of being covered in hair. I may be a bit of a hairy man, but I ain't no skoocoom. They must have seen I was hairy enough, though, what with my beard and chest and whatnots, and that the buckskins weren't attached to my own hide.

I guess that must have shocked them to see that they could peel off my skin and I'd still be alive, all them days and weeks later. I kept trying to gander about the cave, see where it was they kept my clothes and possibles bag and such. But it was no use. They'd probably tossed it away or eaten it, for all I know.

So I was sprawled right out there in the middle of a cave, them skoocooms gawping at me all hours of the day and night. It was a family of them. Girls and boys and fathers and mothers. Old ones, too — I could tell 'cause they were slow and frail looking, and a bit gray around the edges.

The little ones would come over and point at me and poke me. If I could have moved anything more than my mouth, I would have showed 'em where the bear went through the buckwheat. But I was crippled up and still addled in my head. And my voice seemed to have no effect on them.

At first they'd stare when I spoke, then they ignored my yammering. That same she-skoocoom wouldn't hardly ever leave my side, and I'd wake up with her drizzling water into my mouth from handfuls of wet leaves and pine needles.

For all their stink and grunts and odd noises, they were not much different than any human family you'd find. Seemed like half the time the males and the females argued, waving their arms, hitting at each other, jabbering and pushing.

The young were the same as human children, playing and what sounded like singing and bothering the old ones and getting hit for it. They cried, too, and sounded just like people.

I tell you what, you want to learn all about something, you just lay back and look and listen and keep your yap shut, and you'll do some learning, by god. I know what I'm saying. I lay there for what must have been a couple of weeks. Early on, the cave, a damp, cool place of rock and earth, would start to move and get fuzzy on me and I'd pass out for a spell. As time wore on, though, such episodes grew less frequent.

After a few weeks, the she-skoocoom started feeding me wriggling grubs and the soft bits of pine cones and roots that tasted as awful as a handful of sand. Then one day, I felt a throbbing in my hands. Pretty soon, I felt like I fell onto a giant mound crawling with them angry red ants, like I was on fire and being chewed alive at the same time.

I kept from whimpering for as long as I could, but soon there wasn't nothing for it and I howled and screamed like a birthing woman. As I did, I saw my own hands come slapping up at me and claw at my face, my chest. I whipped off them rank poultices and soon I was up on my knees and wobbling in circles, barking and drooling and screaming to get the fire off of me. The entire time this was happening, that skoocoom family made its own noises, pointing and covering their mouths and generally keeping clear of me.

For all that bother, the feeling only lasted a day or so. Then I came out of it all right.

Well, sir, I saw seasons come and go, and I

reckon what few friends I had must have long since given Tilquata and me up for dead. I had given up on ever seeing a human again.

But do you know, if you live with something long enough, after a while you sort of get used to it. That's the way it was with me and the skoocooms. I guess I even got used to the smell, though in truth I did breathe a lot through my mouth.

My time with them gave me plenty of opportunity to think about things. Like, for instance, why that young male skoocoom dragged me home I'll never know. Nor will I know if he was the son of the big one who got ambushed by Tilquata.

I am convinced they had been curious and only wanted to sniff us, inspect us, you might say. But I reckon Tilquata figured they were fixing to eat me, so he had attacked. And that was a most valiant thing for him to do. One of the kindest things anyone ever did for me, in fact.

But that young skoocoom who lugged me, I saw him now and again. He was one of the males who always seemed to keep an eye on me when I was well enough to wander on my own outside. They never tried to get me to help gather food — they ate everything but meat, which I found odd.

I had reckoned those creatures would need piles of meat to keep their bodies that big.

They did eat with gusto, but it was all day long, and lots of everything, from moss and bark to grass and leaves, nuts, roots. And in berry season of late summer, they looked to be in heaven. All big-bellied and smeared with paste. Yessir, I survived in decent order.

What I did miss, though, was my clothes and a warm fire. And as the seasons grew colder, it was that lack of fire that changed my life forever. One night in late fall, it was colder than a gravedigger's backside. Them skoocooms, being covered in thick hair, were sprawled out all over the cave, flopped and snoring like full dogs. But that chill air was making me tremble as if gripped with the ague.

I huddled up as best I could, but I had nothing to cover myself with. Every time I'd tried to gather up strips of bark or pine boughs for just such a purpose, they'd up and eat them on me. I reckon they figured it was like I was hoarding a feast, when all I was looking for was a bit of warmth.

This one night, the she-skoocoom saw me shivering up a storm. She eased over to me and gathered me up in them big long arms and hugged me close like she was happy to see me, as if I'd been gone away a long time.

Well sir, she warmed me up. That's all I'm saying on the matter. But there were an awful lot of cold nights that came and went, and I doubt I would have survived had she not taken pity on this poorly haired fellow.

One day in early spring, I found I wasn't being watched that closely by the young male who'd saved me in the first place. More to the point, I reckon, now that I've had years to think back on it, he might have been sweet on the she-skoocoom who'd been keeping me warm all winter. Whatever the reason, I found myself unguarded and in solid health. It was early in the day and the melt was on, so I kept wandering, heading east, looking back over my shoulder every so often to see if I was being trailed.

I'd been kept a near-recluse for the better part of a year in or near that cave, and yet when I was away from it, I admit I missed it a bit. But I kept walking. I walked for days with little rest, just long enough for a smidge of shut eye, and then I was up and at it again. Come to find out, I'd been in a little valley, hidden and protected by happenstance, so as to look like nothing more than an impossible tangle of trees and rock.

Once I had climbed up and out of it, which took me most of a morning, I looked back and couldn't tell just where it was, so thick were the trees and so oddly angled were the boulders. I gave a grunt and a wave and turned my back on that little valley forever.

I knew I'd never see that big, hairy girl again. But I like to think that somewhere out there, running around in that strange little lost valley, is a creature I'm proud to call my own.

I hope it's a boy, gone on to raise sons of his own, but mostly I hope it's happy. Happier than I've been since then. What I thought I was looking for, what I left the valley for, is something I never found in all these years.

Don't look so shocked. There's love and then there's other types of love. And then there's affection and there's survival and there's instinct. I reckon what I had with that she-skoocoom was a knotted up tangle of all them things. Just don't you judge me, lest you want me to judge you, too. I know what people get up to. I know. And no, I ain't trying to change the topic, neither.

If I thought I could make the journey back there, I'd lay in a request right now and have someone help me find that little valley. But even if I was up to it, I don't know where that valley is or how to get there. I tried, oh how I tried.

I spent what amounts to years of my life going back to where I thought it was. But I never could find it. Not to say that it was some magical place or something I only imagined, because it wasn't.

Why, even today I'll be off in the woods alone and I'll get a whiff of something rank. I'll sit there for a longish spell, until, Ol' Mossback, my mule, decides he's had enough.

I'll have been thinking back on the sweetness of memory. Something I doubt you're believing, even though, I'm here to tell you, Maple Jack ain't never told a lie in his life.

Now fetch me my jug before I have cause to jump up from this bed and take a round or two out of you for being an insolent pup.

TROUBLE AT TALL PINE
A ROAMER STORY

I lifted my beer mug and drained it. Over the foamy rim I kept my eyes fixed on the barkeep's jowly face. The big man stared back for a moment, then looked away, folding his drying rag.

It was the same rag, I noted, he had used to wipe the tobacco drooling from his pudgy mouth and pooling on the shelf of his chin. And it was the same rag he had wiped each glass with since I entered. No wonder the beer had an extra tang to it. I decided to nip that thought in the bud while I still had an appetite.

"So, where can I get a hot meal?"

The barkeep, his back to me now, wiped at his bottles with more vigor than he had in years, judging from the layer of greasy dust over everything back there. The only spots that gleamed were on the bar where elbows rested.

" 'Bout anywheres," he finally said, turning and folding the rag again.

"Try a campfire," another voice said. "About twenty miles in any direction but here."

I didn't know the voice behind me, but from the tone and the comment I just knew it had to be someone wearing a tin star.

I sighed and closed my eyes for a moment, trying to savor the already fading flavor of the beer on my tongue. It had been a long, hot day and all I wanted was to follow it up with a hot meal. Preferably with potatoes. I am partial to a big plate of well-buttered potatoes, a goodly helping of beef gravy over the top of it all. Follow it up with a shot of rye and a cup of real coffee, and I would sleep fine.

But it was happening again. And it would keep happening. Again and again in each little town, no matter where I go. And all because I had the great good fortune to be born hard looking. I've never committed a crime in my life of which I am aware, but this face leaves me a marked man.

In every town I hear the same things — vagrancy, impeding justice, trespassing. I still don't know how they made that last charge stick, the signs in most bars say public drinking house. The so-called offenses I'd committed over the past few years were remarkably similar to each other, somewhat creative, and tiring as hell.

If there is a specific look to outlaws and ne'er-do-wells, I must have it. I'm on the large side, above six feet tall. I'm well muscled and I have a big, block head topped with short, curly black hair. I also have a couple of scars on my face that I earned in close skirmish in the war, though no one wants to hear that.

I would have to agree with people if they were basing the outlaw look on my eyes alone. They're dark, no getting around it. I've been told they're merciless, but I'd prefer thoughtful. Out of necessity, you can imagine, I'm a fair hand with a gun. I've been alone enough in my life to get in a good bit of practice.

I opened my eyes and looked at the bartender. He'd backed down to the far end and was busy rearranging rows of upended glasses on a towel. He must have said something earlier, motioned to one of those fellas at the table off in the corner. And all because I bore a remarkable likeness to no one in particular and yet to every criminal in general.

I don't even bother with banks anymore. The last one I entered emptied of the other patrons in short order. All I wanted was to cash a pay chit from my former trail boss for services rendered and employment cut short — I'd been accused of raiding the cook's emergency stores of ready cash. It didn't matter that I was on watch amidst the longhorns when the theft took place.

I've been told it's a case of mistaken identity more times than 1 can remember. And I had my fill of it before I rode into Tall Pine. And then that marshal, in his roundabout way, asked me to mosey on out of there when I'd just ridden in, and was so close to a hot meal.

I turned around and looked at him, careful to not rest my elbows on the bar, careful to keep Fatso polishing his dirty glasses just to my right at the edge of my sight line.

The marshal looked at me hard. "Don't I know you?"

I sighed inside and wondered, not for the last time, if I would ever not hear that. "I doubt it, marshal. I've never been here before."

He tilted his head to the side and smirked. "I've not spent all my time in Tall Pine, you know."

Great. Next it'll be how I look an awful lot like most of the people on his little stack of dog-eared Wanted sheets. I could see his mind working, adding up all those reward figures.

Which sported the highest amount? Whichever it was, you can bet that would be me. Or I'd be him. It didn't matter anymore. Part of me had almost become a bit of each of those bad men. Almost, but not yet.

"Now look, marshal. I came in here looking for a cool glass of beer." I flicked the empty mug with my fingertip. "And I'm still looking. And I could use a hot meal, maybe a bath and a real bed to sleep in. Nothing more. Well, maybe a cup of real coffee. But that's it. I'll be on my way tomorrow. Last time I checked, these things are still well within a man's legal right and grasp, even out here on the frontier."

He stood up straighter, pulled arms back and rested his gun hand high on his waist. He poked a finger up under his hat brim to clear his line of sight, and said, "Are you trying to tell me the law? And in my own town?"

"No, I'm telling you that I'm thirsty and hungry and tired, though not necessarily in that order."

His mouth smiled but his eyes didn't make it a matched set. He didn't have anything in his mouth save for his tongue, but I could tell he was chewing on something. He looked at me, through me, and saw something he wanted to see. An idea forming. And then he came back to himself. "How long you say you been in town, fella?"

He knew something I didn't know. "I didn't say. But now that you're asking, I just rode in. Ask at the livery if you want proof. I'm sure my horse is still dusty."

"Nah, I don't think so." He chewed some more on something. "You been here a day, I just bet, all right?"

Right then, I counted two things that were wrong — aside from the usual. The afternoon sun had slanted up over the tallest building across the street and it glowed through that window directly behind the marshal and into my eyes.

The other wrong thing was Fatso. With all this talking I forgot about him. He wasn't off to my right anymore. The marshal's eyelids twitched and I knew either Fatso was going to hit me hard with something even harder or . . .

Ah, there it was, the unmistakable throaty clicks of shotgun hammers cocking back all the way. I hoped he didn't have too much chicken grease on his fingers.

The marshal smiled and pulled his pistol. "Now ease that gun belt to the floor slow.

353

All right?"

I did, managing a half step forward at the same time. My cleverness did not go unnoticed.

"Far enough," said a fat voice behind me. I was confused. Apparently so was Fatso.

"Slim, shut your mouth. Last time I looked I wore the badge in Tall Pine, all right?"

"Do you always do that?" I asked, raising my hands slowly.

The marshal narrowed his eyes. "What?"

I shook my head, didn't say anymore. My mouth will be the death of me. Prove my father right. The floorboards popped and groaned. Fatso came around the bar.

"Pick that up," the marshal wagged his pistol at my belt.

Fatso stood by my side. We both looked at the marshal. Fatso hoped he meant me. I went with it and reached down.

"Not you." He wagged the pistol again. "Slim, get that gun belt, all right?"

The big man grunted and fumbled. He tried to hold the cocked shotgun and keep an eye on me and bend a body that had been carefully conditioned to not bend any lower than a chair. I have no idea how he pulled on his boots in the morning. Maybe he slept in them. He tried to slip the shotgun barrels through the belt but it kept slipping off. He finally shifted his eyes from me and laid down the shotgun. He got all the way down on his hands and knees, looking like a great sweating bear, and picked up the belt.

I waited until he was halfway up and said, "Slim?"

He paused and looked at me, eyebrows raised.

"Just checking," I said.

He growled and pulled himself up by the edge of the bar. Part bear, I knew it.

I misjudged Slim. Most fat men are of an even temperament, and go out of their way to be cordial. But every once in a while life will surprise you with exceptions to every rule. I haven't yet found a way to see them coming. That's why they're called exceptions, I guess. Slim was one of the biggest I'd come across in a long time.

Something that felt a lot like the butt end of a shotgun stock slammed into the side of my head, pinching the tip of my ear and sending a warm feeling down the side of my face. I think I lost my hat.

As that glowing sun dimmed I heard someone say, "Well, all right all right."

". . . ought to give some thought to waking up, y'hear?"

It was the voice of God. Or a freight train. An awful clanging joined the voice that was saying, "Hey! Hey you!" God on a train.

I opened my eyes and that took all my strength. There was that same sun staring down on me. No matter where I went, it seemed he was always following. I took it as a good sign and turned my head to find out just what God riding a freight train looked like. I have to say I was disappointed.

An old man with no teeth, a chaw-stained beard, and a flop-brim hat smiled down through steel bars at me. He dragged a tin cup across the bars and said, "Mornin'," still smiling.

What was God doing behind bars?

I answered, but no one told me that I could speak Latin so fluently.

"Come again?" said God.

I pushed myself up to a sitting position and the earth swayed and lifted before settling down to a more reasonable version of itself. I touched my head and wished I hadn't. That side was swollen and there was something split and rubbery stuck to it that once could have been my ear.

"You took a wallopin'. 'Course, you mighta deserved it." God shuffled off and it occurred to me that he wasn't behind the bars. He was in front of them.

I tried English again. "What . . ." I swallowed. "What do you mean?"

He turned back and the tin cup was full of something hot and steaming. He held it toward me. "You're gonna have to get up and take this. I wouldn't wait on ya even if I had keys."

As much as I wanted to sit still I could smell that was real coffee and I figured that only a dead man would ignore that heavenly scent, so I pushed to my feet. A lifetime later I had that cup in my hands, so hot it burned my fingers. I let it. It helped clear the cotton batting from my head. I even let it burn my mouth. Never had a mouthful of coffee tasted so good.

"You look pretty bad." He was staring at me.

"Thanks."

"I'll get you some water. Clean yourself up."

While he was gone I drank my coffee and tried not to think of what I didn't do to deserve these accommodations. He returned with a shallow pan slopping full of steaming hot water. An old piece of shirt floated in it. He slid it under the door through the wide space in the bars meant for food trays. I am familiar with this feature.

"What did you mean when you said I

deserved this?" I said as I dabbed at my swollen head.

He carved a thick, black curl of tobacco off a lint-covered block. If I had eaten the day before I would have had that to deal with as well. There's always an upside to not eating.

"Well now, I could get myself in trouble for sayin' too much. But I ain't never found trouble by keeping my mouth shut." He looked at me as if waiting for a response.

"Fair enough," I finally said.

By now the water in the pan was a deep red, almost black. I looked out the window and found I was on the second floor overlooking the main street of Tall Pine. Something plinked off the wall to the left of the window.

I looked straight down at the street and saw a handful of men, a couple of women, and some children staring up at me. They were shouting and a few of them arched their arms. A rock made it in through the barred window and pinged off the cell door. The old man, who by now I was pretty sure wasn't God, stepped back and kept chewing.

He laughed. "You're not popular here, mister."

"I wonder why that is," I said, and I meant it.

He stopped chewing, his cheek bulging with the chaw. "If you really don't know then you're either mighty forgetful or a liar."

"Or innocent," I said, assuming the worst. "This has something to do with that marshal, doesn't it?"

"Doesn't everything in this town?" He mumbled it, but I heard him.

He turned back to his table and held up the coffeepot. I passed him my cup. As he filled it he said, "The child died in the night."

He wasn't making sense. In fact, none of this made sense, but I was curious now. "What child are you talking about?"

He moved close to the bars and held the cup through. As I took it he held it and stared into my face. "Young James Dougal was beat pretty bad and strangled two days back. Whoever did it left him for dead."

"He lived then. For a while?"

The old man let go of the cup but still stared at me. "Yep. He didn't come around, though. Too bad he couldn't have told us anything."

"But surely people saw me ride in yesterday. It was yesterday when they brought me in here, right?"

"Yep, it was yesterday."

Boots clunked on the stairwell off to the left and out of my sight line, but from the tightening of the old man's features, I guessed his boss had arrived even before I heard that nasally voice from yesterday's saloon get together.

"What are you doin', Muley?"

The old man turned to the table and gathered up the coffeepot. "Bringing the prisoner coffee is all. Like I always do."

The marshal walked into view, smiling and not looking at me yet. The general surveying his troops, reasserting his authority. Muley edged by the lawman, who didn't move out of his way, arms still spread, hands on hips.

As Muley shuffled out of view I heard him say, "She'll have breakfast ready shortly."

The marshal turned to face me, still smiling, and said, "Not for this one."

If I thought I had a chance of getting away with it I would have reached through the bars and choked him. That put the dead boy in my mind. It hadn't been me who killed him, but how easy it could be to kill a person.

I hadn't had to kill in a long time. Not since the war, but that doesn't mean that I hadn't felt like dealing the final blow to a few folks over the intervening years. And this fellow came as close as anyone to receiving my full hate at that very moment. I was in here because of him, I hadn't eaten in more than a day, and my head was twice the size it should have been.

"You ain't gonna let him eat?"

The marshal turned to Muley. "I think you heard what I said, all right." He turned back to me. "How's that sit with you, child killer?"

"I didn't kill anybody, let alone a child. But then, you knew that."

I let my words hang in the air between us. He stared at me with no expression on his face, but suddenly he looked old and haggard. I had struck a nerve. Somehow, somewhere I got to him. But only for a moment.

That smile crept back onto his mouth and he said, "You got a visitor, killer man."

He walked to the door. I heard it creak open and he shouted down the stairs, "Come on up, sweetheart."

A softer step sounded on the stairs, then I heard a woman's voice say, "Get away from me."

The door squeaked and the marshal stepped back into my view, still wearing that self-confident smile.

She walked into sight before she saw, pulling away from the marshal's grip on her arm. She hugged her arms close but didn't look at him. Loose strands of hair hung in her face.

He stared at her, his smile fading.

They walked to my cell door and she still didn't look up. He stood with his arms crossed, then winked at me and said, "I'll leave you to it, all right."

He turned and brushed against her enough to push her closer to the cell. All I could see was her unkempt hair, gray streaking a dark brown, her arms folded tight across her belly. Her dress was dirty, hadn't been changed in days.

The door squeaked, boots clunked slowly down the stairs, and then she lifted her head and looked at me.

I am not a skittish man by nature. I've been surprised any number of times by loudmouth drunks with guns who thought I was looking for a scuffle, and I've always stood my ground.

I've been bushwhacked by a down-on-his-luck miner who, it turned out, had the same name as my best childhood friend, though it was not the same person. But nothing prepared me for this woman.

As soon as I saw her face I knew who she was. Those aged eyes rimmed red and cried out, her nose as red, the mouth set straight across like a rail fence blocking entrance. This was the dead boy's mother. Even though there were bars between us I took a step backward. I couldn't help it.

Now that she was no longer in shadow, I noted that one eye wore a violet smudge beneath, high on her cheekbone, as if she were overtired much of the time.

"Why did you kill my boy?"

I expected the question, or worse, but it still felt as though I had been caught smiling and gut-punched hard. Of all the questions a man could be on the receiving end of, that has to be the most difficult. How does a man go about answering that?

I gained back my step and she stood still, inches from the bars, inches from my hands. I looked her in the eye and said, "Someone had to have a reason to do something like that, I would think. I am truly sorry to hear of your terrible loss, but I had nothing to do with it. I don't even know anybody in this town. I rode in yesterday afternoon looking for a hot meal."

She stared back at me for a few moments more, then exhaled quickly, a shuddering sound, as if she was reluctant to let go of each precious second of breath.

Then her eyes told me she had decided something. I think she knew before she came to see me, but she was a woman who no longer trusted her instincts.

The shouts of the crowd in the street below rose and fell according to the amount of hot air available. Right now it sounded like they had a steady supply.

"I know who did it," she said in a voice little more than a whisper, as if she had known all along. "But I don't know why."

"Ma'am," I said, grabbing the bars. She didn't move. "If you're convinced I didn't do it, would you please tell the marshal so I don't hang?"

Even as I said it, I saw the change in her eyes. It was a subtle shift. In less time than it takes to blink, the fear and look of defeat replaced the brief flare of conviction.

And at that moment I, too, knew who killed her son. And I knew that I would probably hang for the crime anyway.

But I was a long way from dead. Another rock whanged against the iron bars of the window. "Ma'am, who hit your face?"

But she cut me off. "I know what to do now." She turned toward the door.

"Be careful," I told her.

She stopped and I thought she might turn around, but she continued on through the door and down the stairs.

I leaned against the wall by the window and peeked through. For the moment the crowd had lost interest in my second-floor window. They grew silent, and a few seconds later the rabble parted ranks and the woman walked right through the middle of them. She disappeared between two buildings down the street and they stared after her. So did I.

It should have been dark, but since it was summertime, I knew it was late in the day. I still hadn't eaten anything.

Several times during the day when I thought I heard footsteps in the marshal's office below, I yelled toward the stairwell for water, food, anything. But when I raised my voice my head throbbed like a cannon volley.

I thought of yelling out the window but I reasoned that a food request made to an angry mob from someone who was considered prime lynching material might not be wise.

I was too tired, hungry, and sore to give much thought to the problem at hand, but when my thoughts drifted to food and sleep and pain-free living, I forced myself to think of the consequences of not doing anything and that scared me enough to think harder.

I didn't have much to work with, but I knew somehow that the marshal was guilty of murder. Why? I had no idea. But I saw how he treated her and I saw how she took it — not very well. I also saw the look of pain and defeat in her eyes, and that would probably cloud out everything else in the end.

No matter what the dime novels tell us, good folks don't always get the upper hand. It's the powerful who win out. It works that way in nature. Who is man to think it's any different than wolves in a pack or elk in a herd or crows in a flock?

If the marshal killed the boy and she knows it, then he has some sort of power over her. Something sinister and unspoken.

I thought back on her eyes. For a moment I had seen something there that might get me freed or might get her in trouble. The worst kind. The kind you don't recover from. But with her son dead, did she care anymore what might happen to her?

I finally gave up and laid back on the roughest cot I have ever been acquainted with. I must have been bone tired because the next thing I knew it was dark and I woke up in heaven. The smell of coffee and chicken and rolls and butter and berry pie lifted me up off that cot as if I had angel wings.

"Hope you're hungry, big fella, cause Mother's outdone herself tonight. I already et, so I know."

Muley's back was to me as he stood over his little hall table. An oil lantern glowed enough to let me see the golden skin of chicken, steam from a cup of coffee, and I fancy I saw a pat of butter losing the fight with that warm browned roll.

He handed the coffee through to me and I set it on the edge of the bunk. He turned back to the table. He lifted the tin plate by the edges and I was already opening my mouth like a baby bird. A shadow moved between the cell door and Muley and crossed the glow of the lamp. Then I heard a dull thunking sound.

Muley fell forward, hit the little table, and slipped to the floor, the table's contents landing all over him. It seemed like a joke or a dream.

A voice said, "If I told him once, it was a hundred times. He was not to feed this prisoner. That old man will never learn."

The marshal stepped into the lamp glow and said, "You know what, drifter? We ain't gonna wait for the marshal. We're gonna do this by my rules. I'm a fair man, just ask anybody in this town, all right, and they'll tell you true."

He smiled and pulled a ring of keys from his back pocket. He jangled them in front of his face and unlocked the cell door, then tossed the keys on the floor by Muley's sprawled body and stepped back from the door.

"Come on," he said.

"No." I stood still in the center of the cell. "You're up to something and I don't want any part of it. There's still someone who knows I'm innocent, besides you. I'm better off waiting right here." I was bluffing far beyond the value of anything I had and my stomach knew it.

"So sure of yourself, smart mouth. Well don't be." He pulled his pistol and cocked the hammer. "Let's go." He gestured with the pistol.

Despite a man's convictions, there are certain things he'd better not disobey, and number one on that list is a heartless man with a gun. I swung open the door.

As I stepped into the hallway in the dim, fluttering light of the oil lantern I saw welts on the marshal's lips, and what looked like a scratch on his chin.

"Been kissing an alley cat, marshal?"

He came up behind me fast. I could smell his rank sweat. He kicked me behind the knees and I fell forward, tripping over Muley's legs. I was weak and my arms didn't prevent my face from hitting the wood floor. This time the other side of my head was ringing. Perfect, a matched set.

I opened my eyes and a big, juicy chicken leg was so close I could have licked it. I know because I tried. As I stood, I grabbed it and raised it to my mouth. Of course, he knocked it from my hand.

"No, no, no," he said. "How many times do I have to tell you, all right?"

I stood swaying, too weak to argue, my head hanging down, my arms limp.

"Keep walking, drifter. Straight ahead."

I looked into the dark ahead of me. "Stairs are over there," I said.

"This is the back way. Now move."

I walked down the stairs, feeling my way in the near black. At the first floor the barest of light from the moon angled in through a window.

"To your right," he said and pushed me into a door that swung open as I touched it. We were in the back alley. A horse nickered ahead of me in the dark.

"Get on that horse and run, drifter. Be a

few hours before the posse catches up with you. But it will."

I pulled myself into the saddle. It wasn't my horse but it was a good horse and saddle. I felt for a sheathed rifle, knife, anything, but no luck.

"Now git," he said, "before I change my mind and kill you right now." He laughed and I urged the horse into a trot with my heels. I laid low over the pommel, trying to reduce myself as a target. I expected a bullet in the back any second.

I didn't have much idea what was going on, but pieces were coming together. The cool air of the evening felt good after the stale smells of the jail cell.

Except for the food smells, that is. I was still imagining what that chicken would have tasted like as I broke that horse into a gallop and we pounded hard westward out of town.

I have tracked men before and I have been tracked before and neither is a pleasant experience, I can tell you. When you're on someone's trail, you're afraid they might pop up behind every boulder and catch you dead to rights.

If you're being followed, you imagine every boulder hides someone hoping to claim their share of the bounty, be it glory or revenge or money. Before I spotted the morning's first light, I slowed and looked for a place to hole up.

The hills in these parts are gradual and rolling and only sparsely treed. If I could find a place well into the undergrowth, I might be able to wait out the posse.

As I picked my way among a tumbledown of boulders at the base of a ragged little peak, I went over in my mind for the fiftieth time that night what the marshal's motives might be in letting me go.

He was covering up something, that much was certain. The welting and scratching on his face told a part of the story, but which part was anybody's guess.

I was so tired I could barely keep my eyes open. Any surge of power I may have gained from being freed in such a bizarre manner was long gone. Even the momentum of it had long abated.

The horse, a fine bay with a good set of legs under him and a tooled saddle on top of him, felt the same. He was flagging. We both needed water, and the best source for that would be deeper into these treed slopes to the north.

The big bay found water. Always trust a

horse's nose. I let him follow it and soon we were drinking from a small, clear stream that bubbled its way through the thickening forest.

We chose a path deeper into the foothills where spruce and poplar grew tall and a breeze played the leaves, offering a sound like ocean waves washing over sand.

For a few minutes I was carefree again, breathing in crisp morning air, and feeling the random shafts of warming, restorative sun fingering through the treetops. The bay's steps were lighter. He snorted and sniffed at the breeze and shook his head from time to time.

I found a low, hollowed spot thick with trees, save for a patch of wispy grass large enough to keep the horse busy, if not satisfied, for a few hours.

I hobbled him with a length of rein leather and hoped it would keep him close by. Keeping him quiet was another matter. If he heard other horses, he would be inclined to nicker and that would reveal my position. I had taken pains to backtrail and wipe out what traces I could of our presence, especially closer to our hiding place.

Though the water went a long way in restoring my strength, hunger gnawed at my insides like it would soon break through to my outsides. After I took care of the horse I flopped to my knees in the grass and rooted for anything that might give sustenance. I couldn't find any berries, and I didn't dare venture beyond our hiding place.

I pulled up a stringy white root that tasted so bitter I spat it out and wiped my mouth on my grimy shirt. I finally settled for lichen that I scraped off a boulder. Then I forced myself to chew a handful of short grass.

It was sweeter close to the root, which explained the bay's continued interest in it. And though it was hardly satisfying, it was something in my gut. I ended up chewing on some bark for the sheer pleasure of using my mouth for something more than mumbling complaints. Then I found a spot in undergrowth against the slope and piled more deadfall branches and leaves into what I hoped was a natural-looking little shelter. I settled in for a little rest while I could get it.

A normal man in the spot of trouble I was in might have been inclined to run that horse ragged in any direction but back to Tall Pine. But I guess I'm not normal, because while I lay there I was thinking of what I might do to get things righted.

Go back to that town? Certain death. Wait until dark and head out on the run? Greater possibility of survival, but it meant a life on the run. I was undecided about what to do when I dozed off.

The bay nickered low and I awoke, curled up behind my brush pile. I heard something clumping the earth, then the sound doubled. Two horses? And close enough for me to hear. I cursed myself for using old leaves. They rustled with every move I made.

The sound faded and as it did I fancy I heard a man's voice, though I couldn't make out the words. I listened a moment more and, as quietly as I could I slid myself, pulling with my elbows, out of my resting spot. Then I low-walked over to the horse.

"Good old boy," I whispered, rubbing under his neck and jaw. I was surprised that the two horses that passed hadn't indicated to their riders there was a strange horse nearby. They probably tried, but a man must be sensitive to his horse.

As I untied the hobble and rerigged the reins I kept a sharp ear. Sure enough, those two riders retraced their steps, but this time they came down the other side of our hidden glade.

And this time I did hear a voice, then another. The bay lifted his head and perked his ears. I scratched between his eyes and whispered low, soothing sounds to him.

". . . too much. I'm all for headin' back," said the first voice.

A second voice, deeper, broke in. "We can't just give up and you know it. That man killed a boy and the boy's mother and stole a horse. We can't let that stand."

"Don't forget Muley," said the first voice, a younger man.

"Yeah, he took quite a knock. But that old dog is tough as nails."

"Yeah. Marshal's taking all this pretty hard, though."

"Well, she was his girl. Or at least he wanted it that way. Not so sure she felt the same way."

"We'll never know."

Then the horses stopped and one of them dismounted.

"What are you doing?"

There was a pause, then a sound like rain on leaves. "What's it look like?"

"Hurry up, then."

The bay jerked his head up and down and I had to rub his throat hard to distract him. The man remounted but they didn't ride on.

There were small sounds, shiftings in the saddle, something crinkled. Then I heard a match flare and it wasn't long after that I recognized the pinched odor of tobacco smoke. It always smells out of place outdoors. Nothing I could ever get used to. I'd tried but it wasn't for me. Not for the bay, either. He nickered low and I had a time to keep him from moving his feet.

"You hear that?" It was the deeper voice.

A pause, then, "Nope."

"Okay, well we better find the others. If you're done, that is. My word, you're worse than a woman with all your fussin'."

"That'll be enough from you," said the younger man, then they both laughed and soon all that was left of their presence was the fading smell of cigarette smoke. That and the information they'd given me.

Oh, that poor woman who had already been through so much. Much more, I guessed, than the murder of her son. I remembered her tired eyes and all that gray in her pretty brown hair.

Call their information a lucky break, call it divine intervention, I don't care what label it carried, but as they rode off I knew what I had to do. I was not about to let that marshal get away with his killings and saddle me with the blame.

It was my thinnest remaining sliver of prudence that kept me from mounting up and riding as fast as that horse would carry me back to town. But a hasty act like that would only serve to get me killed without ever seeing the marshal. I had no weapons, but I did have a tired horse and fifteen miles to travel in full daylight.

No, it would be smarter to bide my time. I would ride back to Tall Pine after dark. I'd need every advantage I could give myself. I vowed I would make that marshal talk, or I would die trying. Before tomorrow morning, I would either be free or be dead.

The rest of the day passed slowly. I spent the time trying to cobble together a plan, but it was a waste of effort. I knew precious little about the town. What I needed was the urge that anger and instinct will lend a desperate man. These, I had aplenty.

I needed a weapon and I knew where to get one. It would require a break-in. Beyond that, I had no idea what to do. The marshal might be at the jailhouse, considering he'd clubbed his overnight help in the head. That was my plan, then. Ride into town, steal a gun, and knock on the jailhouse door. So be it.

I scraped more lichen and waited for dark.

Cutting a wide arc and sticking close to the tree line as I rode, I returned to town from the north. It took me less time than I expected to see the few dim lights of Tall Pine, glowing dull and small at the base of the hills. It occurred to me then that any pines the town may have been named for were at best a few miles to the north, up where I sat in the trees.

Odd how things get named. A town with no trees named after a tree and no one thinks anything of it. An innocent man labeled a killer and no one thinks anything of it. This town was packed full of people who thought me a double-murderer, a horse thief, and a clubber of old men. I hoped I could get them to change their mind. I dug in my heels and guided the bay toward town.

Within a stone's toss from the backs of the buildings, I dismounted and let the bay loose to graze in the sparse meadow. No need to tie him to a rail on main street. That would only tip off someone to my presence. I rubbed his neck and whispered, "Thanks, fella," and slipped through a gap between two darkened buildings.

I wish I had my hat to pull down over my face. My still-swollen head and cut ear would draw attention faster than a sign around my neck saying KILLER RETURNS. I stuck to the shadows. It was easy. Most of the town was asleep. My bootheels echoed off the wooden walkways, even though I stepped easy.

I was almost to the front of the saloon when I heard a tearing sound across the street. I froze. A match flared and the glow framed a hat tipped forward. Someone lighting a smoke. Could be a person who doesn't sleep well. Could be someone waiting for a killer to return to town.

I backed up and squeezed between the saloon and another building. Just enough room for my shoulders. How did they manage to swing hammers when they built? My mystification at mankind knows no bounds.

The back door to the saloon was unlocked. I opened it enough to slip inside and felt my way along a wall. From the piled empty crates and rags I guessed I was in a storeroom. Not two feet away, in the dark, I heard the unmistakable sound of a man snoring. A drunk sleeping it off. Not for the last time that night did I wonder what I was doing. That bay was a good horse and could have carried me far away come morning.

I held my breath and deliberated. In too deep now, I thought, as I stepped toward where I hoped the door to the saloon might be.

I reached out a hand and touched a wooden slide latch. In no time I was behind the bar and feeling with the flat of my hands everything but what I wanted. I nearly gave up when my fingertips brushed the cold, rounded steel of a gun barrel.

I traced it down and it was the same double-barrel shotgun that fat Slim had used to knock some sense out of me. My crabbing fingers were doubly rewarded with three shells next to it on the shelf. I pocketed one, cracked open the gun — sure enough it wasn't loaded. I slid two shells home, clicked the gun closed, and straightened my back.

There is nothing so different from its daytime self as a saloon at night. Whatever else he might be, from what I could see Slim at least tried to keep the place tidy. Chairs were upended on tabletops, a sure sign the floor was swept, but the dead smells of stale beer and smoke, when not being added to, flowered in the dark.

I imagined this room just a few hours before, full of men wearing guns and swearing oaths to haul that killer up the nearest gallows.

As I turned back to the storeroom I spied the pickled-eggs jar on the back of the bar. I didn't even hesitate. The wood bung lifted with no noise, but I made a fair amount as I plunged my hand in and crammed an egg whole into my mouth.

I was on my second when I remembered the sleeping man in the other room. I tried to keep my grunting and slurping to a minimum. I reached in and my hand splashed in a couple of inches of vinegar and nothing else. All the eggs were gone. I cursed the fat bartender again and set the bung back on the jar.

Just inside the storeroom I heard the steady, heavy breathing of a man in the full throes of deep sleep. I envied him. Then my toes nudged a bottle. It clinked against another and I reached down to steady them and succeeded in knocking them over. Never have I heard a sound as loud. Thousands of bottles must have toppled into each other before they stopped rolling and clanking.

The sleeping man was now awake and saying, "Uh? Uh?"

I backed toward the bar but I had already closed the storeroom door behind myself. Too tidy, that's me. I crouched low, the shotgun held in front of me. What little moonglow there was from the open outside door was blocked out as a massive mountain of a man rose from the shadows.

"Who's there?" said a deep voice, not sounding drunk in the least. I hesitated, then said, "That you, Slim?"

"Yeah? Who's there?"

I aimed for the top of the mountain and, as I felt the gun butt meet resistance I said, "I owe you one."

The mountain crumpled in a loud mess of bottles and boxes and many other unseen items that also made a heck of a lot of noise. I tripped over other bottles and added to the din. Once outside, I didn't hear any more noise and figured Slim really would be asleep for a while now.

Unfortunately, all that noise alerted a few folks around town. It seemed that the windows of every building I ran behind lit up as I passed, the warm glow of oil lamps casting squares of light on the otherwise black ground below. I did my best to avoid them and made for the marshal's office.

As I ran across the street I noted with relief this end of town was still in darkness. Smack ahead of me the marshal's office windows cast a light that wasn't there before. Good. Someone was home. Odds that it was the marshal were pretty good. What was I going to do with him? I didn't know.

Hold him prisoner and fend off the entire town until he confessed? Would he? Probably not. Could I force his guilt out of him?

Maybe, but I'd need a witness to verify the confession.

Could I hold the town off long enough? That all depended on how much they liked him. I did not believe he was popular. But a town will rally around its least-liked member if only because he's one of them. And I suspected that would be the case in Tall Pine.

As I left the street I had to run through the light cast by the marshal's office lamp. It was just for a moment, but as I passed through it I heard someone shout, "I seen 'im!"

Great. I jumped into the dark, narrow alley between the marshal's office and a little warehouse with the livery out back where the bay had been waiting for me just a day before.

I faced the back stairwell of the lawman's office, wondering if that was the best way to enter. Behind me, a hammer clicked back into the deadliest position of all. I turned slowly, arms up.

A match scratched and bloomed, a lamp glowed, and the marshal said, "Well, all right all right. Welcome back to Tall Pine."

He held his pistol on me and backed into the little stable. Hay was more strewn than stacked, and full sacks of feed leaned in piles.

"Come on in," he said. "And rest that scattergun by the door, will ya?"

I did as he said and, for a quick moment, I thought of bolting into the night, but I felt sure he had someone waiting in the shadows behind me, waiting to lay me low. I wouldn't get far.

I stepped into the stable. He waved me around to where he was standing and he backed himself toward the door.

Now that I faced the cause of this mess, I wasted no time. "What did you do to her, marshal?"

He answered my question with one of his own. "What did you tell her, drifter? Way I figure it you said something to make her think I killed her damned bawling brat boy. She come at me swingin' a knife. Wasn't nothing could be done but defend myself."

I asked my question again. "What did you do to her?"

He kept the revolve pointed at my chest, sighed, and wagged his jaw back and forth, thinking, weighing his response. Finally, he said, "Same thing I done to the boy. Just pinched it off right there," he tweezered his Adam's apple with his thumb and forefinger. "Ain't no more blathering that

384

way, all right."

He was still smiling, even after admitting murder to me.

"Why? What did they do to you?"

"Funny," he said. "That's what she asked me. I told her they ain't done nothing yet, but they would have. Give them enough time, they always do."

"That bruise on her cheek," I said, trying to keep him talking. The more I knew, even if no one else heard, the more I might be able to use later to convince someone I was innocent. If later ever came.

The more distracted I kept him, the more chance I had of outmaneuvering him. I didn't believe it, but it felt better than to admit to myself I was already a dead man.

"Oh, that wasn't nothing. She struggled a little at first. That's what you do with a woman like that. Take the starch out, then you got something you can use. Otherwise she's always trying to get the better of you."

I wanted to beat him to pieces right there. I'm not a small man and I don't use my fists all that often, but I wanted to attack him like I had never wanted to beat a man before. It was his pistol that kept me still.

"And then?" I asked, my jaw set so tight I could barely squeeze the words between my teeth.

"For a dead man, you are a curious sort of fella." He worked his mouth again, as if chewing on something. I'd seen him do this before, in the saloon, and I knew he was weighing what to tell me. The prideful man in him won out. "I give it to her." He smiled at the memory. "Was a long time comin' and I finally give it to her. Right where you are now, matter of fact. On them grain sacks."

I glanced down as if the scene was still visible. I could only imagine the fear she felt.

"And the boy?" I asked. "He knew, didn't he?"

"Pretty smart for a dead man." He chewed some more, then said, "Saw the whole thing, that nosey kid did. Nothing a kid should be watching. It's a man and a woman's private time. He needed a lesson anyway. Too long without a daddy was his problem."

"What's yours?" I said.

"You."

I saw the hand squeeze the revolver's handle and then he fired. I had enough time to almost get shot in the chest. When I saw his hand contract on that six-gun, I turned my body from him, duel style.

It was enough to avoid dying, but not

enough to avoid getting skinned. The bullet tore across my chest, taking a little of me with it and leaving a trail that would no doubt make people in public bath houses step away from me in future.

He had enough time to thumb back his hammer again and that's when we heard the unmistakable clicks of the shotgun hammers. Muley stepped into view behind the marshal.

"Marshal's problem is he talks too much." Muley poked the lawman in the back with the business end of the shotgun. "Drop it away, marshal."

I watched the marshal's eyes, hoping to see a change, some indication as he pulled that trigger again.

He stared at me and smiled, then said, "All right, all right," and spun around, dropping to his back on the floor at the same time. He fired up at Muley but Muley's not as tall as the marshal figured.

I dove to the side as Muley triggered both barrels. The shotgun emptied itself into the marshal's chest.

As the sound and smoke fought for escape from the tiny storeroom, I climbed out from behind the grain sacks and looked down on the marshal. He'd lost that smile — and a whole lot more.

"I give him both barrels. One for the mother, one for her boy," said Muley, looking at the marshal as if at a mangled snake.

"All right, all right," I said.

Muley, his head bandaged in white muslin like a struck thumb, slapped my shoulder and said, "You got the last word . . . all right." He winked at me.

It took endless hours, but explanations were made and everyone heard everything in every possible way. Finally, the townsfolk acted as if they were convinced of my innocence.

It helped that a few members of the posse had overheard a snatch of what the marshal told me in the stable. They concluded, without too much work on my part, that the marshal had been the killer. In fact, when I finished speaking, they seemed to agree to a person that the marshal always was a no-account sort of fellow.

That bothered me not a little, but I wasn't about to rile this crowd any further by pointing out that they could easily have lynched an innocent man and kept a murderer in office. I let it go, glad to know I wouldn't be dogged all my days. At least not because of the dead man's deeds.

As the hubbub eased and people drifted

home for a few more hours of sleep, Muley invited me back to his house. As we walked down the town's one side street, I asked him about the shotgun he was still carrying.

"Belongs to my boy," he said. "They call him Slim. For some reason that damn marshal broke into the saloon tonight and fought him for it. It's how I come to be at the marshal's office. That, and I wondered how it was that the jail cell keys ended up on the floor next to me when I come to. But mostly I wanted a word with him about mistreating my baby boy."

"Is Slim going to make it?" I slowed my pace.

"Oh, Slim's okay. His mother's tendin' his head."

My sigh of relief was no act, but I changed the subject just the same. "What would you have done if the shotgun hadn't been there?"

"Huh," he said, rubbing his own sore head. "I reckon I would have muckled onto that rascal barefisted."

I didn't say anything, but thanked my stars for the shotgun.

"You look doubtful," said Muley, glancing at me. "Mister, I can still get my licks in." He puffed up all of his five-and-a-half feet.

"After tonight, Muley," I said. "I have no

doubts about you whatsoever."

Soon, we stopped in front of a little shack situated away from the town proper. "Here's home," he said, pushing open a clunky little door.

Inside the well-lit abode, an enormous woman smiled at us from a cookstove laden with bubbling pots and the most luscious food smells I have ever come across. I was a little hesitant to enter, unsure if Slim was still there, and what he might do to me if he was.

I didn't have long to wait.

Slim was seated in front of a little stove in a small wooden chair that squeaked in relief as he hefted himself up. His head was bandaged the same as Muley's, with a shocking amount of muslin wrapped and tapering to a point at the top. He crossed into the kitchen and stood looking down on me.

"I want to tell you how sorry I am, about your head an' all," he said as he stuck out a massive hand. We shook, my own sizable hand all but hidden in his.

"And yours," I managed. "Took a nasty knock, I see."

"Yep," said Muley, slapping the big brute on the back. "But Mother set him right. She'll tend your head, too, and that grazin' you took to the chest, of course. Can't sit down to the table without that being taken care of."

The enormous woman, still smiling, patted Slim's chair and picked up her scissors and a roll of muslin.

I looked to the stove, where a coffeepot steamed and thick stew bubbled, and to the countertops, where loaves of bread and mounds of biscuits and pies — I lost count after the fourth — all waited to be eaten. What was in the oven I couldn't be sure, but I think it may have been a chicken or two. Maybe a roast. With potatoes and thick gravy.

I turned back to the family, all three of them smiling at me. I sat down and Mother wrapped my head in muslin.

The things I do for a hot meal.

CATCH AS CATCH CAN
A MAPLE JACK TALE

I knew that leaving Mildred Tenterholden was the best thing to do. It was messy, what with all her crying and yelling and bouncing that two-dollar china cup off my head, but it had to be done. I grunt, even now, when I think of that dainty cup. The lump from it's mostly gone, though if I probe the back of my pate, I can locate the sore spot.

I'm not sure what she was thinking, but as my eyes teared up from the pain, I watched that cup wobble then come to a standstill, upright and unhurt, on the polished floor beside my boots. I was ruminating on the fact that this woman wanted more than I was willing to part with. Like . . . my life, in a manner of speaking.

I plucked up my boots and took a last look at the woman who, for some crazy reason, had her flowered hat set on being my wife. I gave her a brief nod, slipped on out that door, and clunked it shut behind me. She didn't follow.

I let out a long breath and started legging it. Little did I know I may have been better off staying put in that fancy, powdery house. Well, maybe not. But before long, I had cause to reconsider my hasty departure.

Let me back up a bit and fill you in on who I am and what I do. It might help. My name is . . . well, never mind that. Folks call me Maple Jack. Have for as long as I can recall, on account of me coming out West from Vermont, the land of sugar maples, when I was no taller than a tree stump.

Back then I was long on possibilities and short on experience. I reckon I've tightened the distance between those two notions a good bit since.

I have few talents, though I have acquired a good many skills in my time. I've been a fair hand at roundup, branding, castrating, the whole works, and I can still put my shoulder to that wheel when I really need to.

There was a time I preferred to keep a horse under me whenever possible, but it's been a long while since I've ridden anything but the aforementioned Miss Tenterholden. Come to think on it, she is a might long in the face.

Oh, I've also trapped beaver, skinned buffalo, and prospected some, and though the work was fine, the financial reward for each task was paltry. But I can, by God, catch a fish. Always could, and it's been a good talent to have through the years. Feels like money in the bank to me, though I'd never had enough cash at any one time to justify a bank account.

Heck, I've only ever been in a bank twice in my life, once to cash a check at the end of a short trail drive from Dios to San Juabel, and the last had been not long after I was "resurrected," as Miss Tenterholden called her rescue of me.

She made a withdrawal to fund what she called my "requirements." Right about then I got the twitches deep down. Anyone other than me thinking they knew what I required was sorely mistaken or just plain wrong.

Not too long after the teacup incident, there I was, pretty near right back where she'd found me two weeks before — only this time I was awake and sober as a schoolmarm, though only because I was penniless. And fishing in the river instead of lying half in it, passed out and in danger of drowning, as she'd found me.

Under a gray rock by the riverbank, I found a fat, white grub, legs still raking the air, and speared him on one of the store-bought hooks I keep in my possibles bag. I swung and tossed my hand line. Fishing's something anyone can do, though most people don't do it well.

As I hauled the line back in, then tossed it out again, I watched the little stick float. I'd tied two feet above the hook to keep it off the stony bottom, free from snags.

I thought back on this and that, nothing and everything, looked at the days as if I were seeing them through a stereopticon. Some visions were clear as the water at the edge of the river, some were murky and full of motes, as if a detail I hadn't noticed before got startled and clouded the view as it left.

I wasn't even sure why — and I meant exactly pinprick why — I stayed any longer than was necessary at Mildred's fancy little mansion. I'd recovered within a day or two, well enough for shuffling back to the road. Could be the kindness she showed me. I guess I felt obliged to linger around the place for a spell, though there wasn't much for me to do. She had servants for near everything.

She'd found me on one of her Sunday buggy rides. Dragged me into her barouche and off we went. Course, this is what I've been told. I only remember waking up in a four-poster with clean duds and thick quilts. But do you know what? There was not a drop of Who-Bit-Sam in the place. Dry as a landlocked boat. For two whole weeks. Twitchy? I guess to hell I was twitchy.

Everything I own is on my person or in my coat, so when I left, there were no concerns about toting baggage. My possibles sack was looped about my neck on a leather thong and cinched at the mouth. In it I keep my money — when I have it — plus matches, flint and steel, fish hooks, and two small carvings, once richly colored in orange and blue and red.

The first is of a burro with full panniers looking down as if weighted by its flopped ears, and the second is a man, made to stand beside the beast, one hand out and looking up. He even has tiny notches like whiskers on his face. Just like me.

Whenever I shake them out of that old leather pouch to look them over, the colors are not like new and so, always a bit of a disappointment — as with most things from the past, except maybe memories. But the memory of where they came from remains heartening.

They were given to me by the small,

homely Mexican woman who carved them. I don't recall her name. Haven't in years. But I remember her hands — like worn leather, but always with a dusted look to them. From keeping them so often in water, she'd told me, they were always chapped and dry.

She cleaned in the kitchens of three cookhouses and cafés in Santa Calla, where I had met her. In her spare time, since all of her money went to keeping her parents and nieces and nephews fed, she carved little figures out of soft woods, and painted them with dyes she made herself from berries.

Santa Calla was one heck of a town back then. Within an hour of arriving that late April day, fresh down out of the Sierra, leaving my claim and chipping at rocks behind me forever, I'd gone to the back of the café that looked most promising for a bit of scrap on the cuff.

Later that day, much to my surprise, I sold that worthless claim. It had been an arid gulch of choking dust and well-sifted gravel before I ever came to it. The man and his son who bought it were strangers, it seemed, to anywhere but a beloved plot of Southern land they kept on and on about, how they would take their mining riches and return one fine day to buy that land.

Once I realized I'd hooked them, I was impatient and hurried them along in the transaction. They balked and hemmed and hawed and finally agreed, paying the assayer his witness fee, then peeling their worn, folding notes and clinking gold and silver into my palm.

In the time it took for me to walk from the back-room office, out the front door, and unhitch Florence, my burro, from the rail, I felt the clean rush of relief, like a dunk in a sunny patch of water on a coolish day. Then, just as quick, shame like a heavy blanket dropped on me.

I knew what I'd just sold those men was less than a pig in a poke. At least with that you get a pig. The claim offered nothing but a leaning old shack, a hole in a bare rock face, and an old sluiceway that hadn't ever worked right for want of more wood. And even if it did, the creek had been diverted long before I bought the land.

I recall searching that day for a thought to help me feel less guilty about taking their life savings in exchange for a worthless claim. But as the man says, "You pay your money, you take your chances."

Only I didn't count on feeling so low, and I reminded myself for days afterward that they were grown men. Just because the last three owners of that mine failed to have a single scratching worth their time, the temptation of possibility is what drove them to the purchase. If not my plot, then someone else's.

Still, in the grand scheme, I suppose until we do what we know is right by our fellows, there will always be a long line of bitter men looking to pass their anger and shame on to other, more innocent but desperate, hopeful men.

While I fished, I sat and thought about that for a while on the riverbank. As I located the float and twitched the line, her name popped into my head as quick as a twig snapping.

Lucenza, the little carving woman.

I wondered if she was still alive. Not any older than me, but she'd had a more difficult life, filled to brimming with worries and promises and disappointments. All from men who'd left plenty of seed but no roots. I supposed I'd been another of those to her. As a whelp, I never set out to let anyone down, but over the years it always seemed to happen, just the same.

She carved all manner of little figures each night, working away at them so you could even see features like noses and cheekbones and little pokes for eyes. When I asked her why she did them, she'd shrug and dig at the little wooden creation, knife and figure each lost in the palms of her thick hands. I recall leaving her early one morning.

It always happened the same way. I'd get to thinking of how I'd been rambling for years and had next to nothing to show for it, and so in a fit of agitation, I'd light out before sunrise, without a word. It seemed best that way. A cleaner, less painful way of departing. Sometimes they'd see me, sometimes not. It was better for me if they didn't.

Then there was the young woman who had convinced her little boy I would be a good father. They had not been that difficult to leave. Truth be told, I had regretted the entire stretch of time with them. The boy was unpleasant, the mother afraid and skittish, like a much-beaten dog. I didn't think of them often. I wished them well, but was happier to spare them no further thoughts than that. Says something about me, I am sure.

I tell you what, other than a different feeling I know of, a tight trembling on the fishing line has to be the best one going. That distinctive tug, like no other on earth, dragged me out of my musty old mind and told me I had a fish on.

All right, I feel like a preacher whose congregation is sprawled out snoring in front of him. Bear with me as I'm getting to the meat of the matter — to the point, I've heard it called. And trust me, it's a sticker.

I yarned that fish on in, steady and true. I had him hooked good, and he fought like he should, given that his life was on the line — which it was. Then there he was, twisting and flopping on the mud, a rainbow trout, thick in its sagging middle as my forearm used to be, back when I a mite taller. I rapped him on the bean. No need for him to suffer because I wanted to admire his beauty.

I always regret taking the most valuable thing a creature has, its life, so I can fill my belly and not have to give up my own most valuable thing. It's a rough swap, but you pay your money. . . .

I admit I was more than a little played out myself, not that it was hard work, but because I hadn't had a proper feed yet that day, nor the day before. I find doing regular things takes something out of me now where it didn't used to.

So I worked my way back to the edge of the mud, onto the grass, where I'd probably get a little wet but not sopping, and was about to sit on down when I saw that log in the tall green grass, a little above me on the bank. I crawled up and over it, and laid down on the dry, shady side.

Just a quick wink, I told myself, and before I knew it, I was cutting wood. My fine fish was laid out waiting on the cool bank mud, line trailing from its mouth up to my hand, looped a few times around my wrist and forefinger, and tied in a light knot for safety's sake, the rest of it tucked in my breast pocket.

Well, sir, I've done a wagonload of fool things in my life, I'm here to tell you (which only shows how lucky I am), but grabbing winks behind that log tops that pile of foolishness.

Some time later — how long I had no notion — I awoke, groggy and confused about why my arm was flopping and jerking like a fish itself. Then my arm whipped even harder, as if it had a mind to leave me behind and go off on its own.

It takes me longer than it ought to get my eyes open and clear the fuzziness from my brain. I sat up, pulling back on my arm, and heard a queer noise like gravel sliding or maybe drunkards belching. Or both. As I said, I was a little groggy from sleep.

I peeked through that tall grass and over the log, and what I saw made me want to close my eyes tight again and wait for the fever dream to pass.

But it was no dream. It was a mountain lion, one of the biggest I have ever seen, and it had my trout all but eaten. The only thing left was the head and I saw that disappointed, downturned mouth of the fish poking from the big cat's whiskered chops.

I stared at that cat's head, mighty big when you're fifteen or twenty feet from it. Those eyes, oh I've never seen the like. A brown-gold with flecks of something even brighter in there, like seeing true gold glinting in the sun at the bottom of a shallow streambed. And they were fixed dead on me. I could not move. Look such a beast in the eye and tell me you ran from it — I won't believe you.

Its whiskers were as thick as that steel fishhook, and sticking straight out like porcupine quills. But the two things I noticed most of all were the yellow teeth that kept right on working that fish, even while that cat watched me, and the noises that bubbled up like coffee percolating from deep inside that animal, on up through its gizzard, and right out its mouth and at me. And all the while I heard my fish snapping and cracking.

One of the cat's big bottom corner teeth

403

was broken and jagged. I remember thinking a bone might have caused it, and immediately had thoughts of my own limbs snapping and cracking in that great maw.

I finally remembered to breathe. It was then I noticed my arm, half-extended over the log, wagging in time with that cat's chewing. My fool limb was trying to conduct the cat like a bandmaster at a Sunday afternoon park concert. And then it occurred to me why — I was still attached to that fish. And if that fish went the rest of the way inside that lion's chops like it was about to do, then I would be attached to a mountain lion, too.

I reached with my free hand to loosen up the fish line and that lion's mouth, still gripping the fish, opened wide around my fish and shot a growl at me, warning like, and that free hand of mine slapped right back out of sight of its own accord.

I don't think the cat could see all of me, but it doesn't matter. By then that light knot I'd tied on my hand to keep it safe had somehow ratcheted down on itself and welded into a hard knob. I felt it, but I couldn't quite see it, and I definitely couldn't reach for it. What a fix.

I figured at the rate that cat was dining on my fish I had a good half minute left before it was satisfied enough to leave. And then it would drag me with it. And it would also be in pain because of a certain fish hook it had just swallowed. And it would see that a man was following it. A man who it might associate with that pain it was feeling in its gut. Wouldn't take me long if I were in his shoes to turn on me and give me what for. Then it came to me — my trusty Barlow folding knife.

And as fast as that thought came to me, I remembered that the knife was in my coat pocket, along with my possibles bag, which I had taken off in case I had to go in after a fish.

I'd laid the coat away from the water, it being a hot day and the coat being the vessel to carry my worldly goods. It was too far from my grasp. I could inch forward and nibble on that line. But it was newfangled and, truth be told, not at all for fishing but more suited for cinching loads, it was that thick.

I wished for a gun. And wishing didn't do any good. Several years before, I'd lost my sidearm to the threat of hunger. My old Texas Paterson had been with me since the war — I'd taken it off a deceased reb. He didn't need it and I did.

I had to snap the fingers of that cold

corpse to get it from his blue-skin grip —
the holster slid out from under him easier. I
offered a whispered prayer of thanks and
low-walked out of that thicket.

In the end, after all those years, it bought
more than a week's worth of tinned beef,
peaches, and coffee. Kept body and soul
together. And all to end up as a mountain
lion's dinner. Strange world.

I lay behind that log, my arm twitching
with each bite, and it occurred to me: Pull
on it. I told you I was fuzzy when I first
woke up. So I gave it a bit more tension.

The chewing stopped and that cat made a
sound I hope I never hear again in all my
days: It sort of barked and coughed all at
once. And then it growled.

I gulped, but didn't let up on the pressure
I had on the string. Not that it would have
mattered, because right about then it went
slack. I peeked over the log and that beast
was crouched down, shuffling toward me,
in full kill pose, I'm certain of it.

I lowered my head and tried to flatten my
tied hand down as close to the log as
possible.

I'll always be grateful that sound carries in
that little river valley. Far off, from the narrow trail a quarter-mile away, I heard the

squeak and clatter of wheels on gravel — a work wagon, maybe. And so did the mountain lion. He spun and took off.

My flopping arm nearly left me as that thing dug into the riverbank mud. The line connecting us zinged tight and the brute stopped short, confused and yowling again.

I couldn't take another wrenching like that so, keeping low, I skinned over that log. As soon as that cat felt slack in that line it cut loose again. Seconds passed before it winced and spun. I gave it slack once more and it took off. And this time, so did I.

We made it well into the woods like that, stopping and staring at each other, then bolting. In my prime I couldn't keep up with a mountain lion, let alone now. But between that fetched-up hook nagging him and being that they are ambush killers, I don't think he knew quite what to do with the man who trailed him so boldly. If he only knew how harmless I was to him, I feel certain I would have followed that fish in short order.

Finally, that cat made it past a big old oak and I happened to stumble 'round it the other way. Don't ask me how — to this day I cannot recall in much detail how we did it — but me and that cat whipped right around that tree, passing each other at least once as we ran. I think by that time we were both cinched tighter than stink on a gut pile and twice as crazed, and were looking to get away from each other.

I am forever grateful that the tree that chose to come between me and that mountain lion was thicker around than a fat man. We ended up on either side of it, me whining like a babe with colic, and that cat alternating between wincing at the sting of that hook in its jowl and swatting at me with paws the size of stove lids tipped with claws the like I've only seen hanging around the necks of Comanche braves who earned them in a way I wasn't prepared for at that moment.

At some point we both stopped and stood panting and staring at each other. I tugged at that damnable knot on my wrist. By then my hand was swelled up and throbbing like a bag of bees. But I did know that if I didn't do something soon, that cat would grow weary of this game and figure out a way around that tree and commence to tear me up. I did the only thing I could think to do: I muckled onto that knot with my teeth and keeping my eyes on that cat I chewed at it like I was hungry and it was a two-dollar steak.

I may not have much in this world, but I

do have a decent set of choppers — mostly still with me. I've taken care of them all these years. Always had a natural inclination to shy away from sweet foods — I'll take a cup of coffee and a wedge of cheddar over a slab of pie most days. If I've a hankering for a sweet flavor I'll tuck into a nice, crisp fall apple. Or maybe a can of peaches. But right then all I wanted was for my teeth to work double-time on that blamed fishing string.

By then, we'd closed to within a man-length of each other. I felt a couple of those strands pop, and I kept right on gnawing like a beaver in a brushfire. We made another turn around that tree, because the cat was too smart to stop, and I knew if I didn't keep on moving, it would run into me from behind.

I don't know about you, but I'd rather face my end than have it sneak up on me all coward-like. Three feet now and that cat was yowling like his backside and his head were both on fire. There was another noise and I don't know but what it might have been me. It was a sort of high-pitched, girl-ish squeal. That's the last I'll speak of that.

As tough as that string was, it wasn't near tough enough to keep that cat from figuring out a different way around the tree in short order. I didn't waste any time in churning up sticks and leaves as soon as the last of that string snapped. I was halfway to China when something occurred to me that caught me up short.

Call it an attack of the guilties, call it humanity, call it what you will, but I stopped right there in that forest. I was headed back the way we'd come, back toward my coat and the road. But that growling, coughing, barking, crying cougar pacing on a short tether, tight to that big old oak tree was pitiful, and I knew I couldn't leave him there.

What if he was too bothered by the pain that hook caused to ever free itself? What if it just stayed right there, whipped tight around that tree, getting more sore every day until that hook wound brought on a full-blowed body fever? What then? Why, I knew the answer — that big, beautiful brute of a cat would die. And all because of my store-bought fish hook.

I swallowed and gulped, I tell you, as I turned back toward that mewling, yowling beast. But I knew what I had to do. Figured I was old anyway, and not much use to anyone anymore but maybe myself. Is that enough reason to keep on with it all? I still don't know the answer.

But I do know that a man, when hit hard

enough just above the ear — heck, it don't even have to be all that hard — will drop like a sack of wet sand right where he stands, unconscious to the world.

I reasoned that since the cat had ears and a head roughly the size of man's, a few stout raps on the bean, just like I did with that fish, would soon render it near unconscious. Enough for me to work that hook out of its jowl, anyhow.

Didn't take me long to find a short, thick club of an old branch. I snapped off the pokey bits and licked my lips a few times as I quivered my way closer to that beast, which of course had turned to face me.

I made sure I came up to it from the near-wrap side. Should the thing lunge at me, I'd have an extra heartbeat of time to scamper backward before it mauled me.

The cat stood there, looking ready to pounce. It had stopped growling and whining and stared at me with those vivid gold eyes, its ears flat back.

I commenced to whomping on that cat's head. Figured I wouldn't kill it, at least not with a stick, but it kept jerking its head back and forth. I can tell you for a few brief moments there I was having myself a fine time. Been many a long year since I had the upper hand in a tense situation.

I could at one time hold my own in a saloon brawl, and I've tossed my share of men — some my friends — over poker tables. One even went through a front window. Spent half a year's wages paying that one off. I had the dumb fortune to fall asleep in the alley beside the saloon shortly after the incident. Woke up to someone toeing my boot and a voice saying, "Yep, that's him all right."

As I would with a man, I was trying to land a quick, clean blow to just above the cat's ear. The problem is that a cat's ears are already pretty near the top of its head. So I tried to wheedle my way to where I could whap him just behind the ear — figured that was where I might have the most luck.

"Stand still and take it!" I yelled at that great beast cowering before me, that fishing line tensed right out like piano wire. I tell you I was feeling more like a man than I had in a long time. And I liked the feeling.

The cougar was confused more than anything, now that I think back on it. Sure, he kept on lashing out at me, but I kept right on handling him with the stick, up one side and down the other, working his head like a surly rock that won't pop loose from the middle of a prize corn patch.

I was beginning to think that maybe man is the only beast who will succumb to such a beating when I heard a noise behind me. It was a snort and a bawling, low and rough. I knew what it was before I turned my head. The cat did, too.

For the time it takes to blink, that cat and me shared a look, right into each others' eyes, like we did before back at the log, only this time it was more like shared pity.

I spun my head and yep, big as a small horse and twice as fat and hairy, was a silvertip grizzly bear. He dropped to all fours and started swinging his head back and forth like he was saying "no" in a big way, his head a hairy pendulum. And that killer clock was telling me one thing: Time to run. But I knew enough to not turn my back on such a beast. I backed away, talking to it like it could understand English. If it did, it didn't let on.

Meanwhile, the mountain lion had backed away as much as the string allowed and had also quieted down considerably. He was just showing his teeth and laying them ears back. I noticed I'd bumped his noggin up a bit. I felt bad about that. I only wanted to cold-conk it to get the hook out. Then I planned on skedaddling before it came to.

Add a bear to the batter and I wasn't so

413

sure I wanted anything to do with that batch of biscuits. I backed away, keeping one eye on the bear, one eye on the lion — no simple trick, since they were about forty yards apart. But such a distance means little to a full-grown grizz on the gallop.

He came on, slow and steady, swinging his great shaggy head, his ears perked in curiosity, his front feet almost facing each other at the instep. But it was those curved claws I was more concerned with.

Every time he set a foot down those gleaming black knives shook, his shoulder hump wagged, and his head swung. And he bawled like an old range boss I once worked for.

I was the only one of the three of us to keep my peace. At one point I backed into a tree, then scooted around it right quick. Good thing to have between me and a bear. The club I'd used to button up that cat's head was still in my hand and I gripped it tighter.

Then, when the bear had to make a choice between me and the mountain lion, when the bear was two loping horse strides from either of us, the cat growled and shrieked like a surprised woman and — *ping!* — went the fishing line back against the tree.

The lion let out a long, trailing sound like

a cross between a curse and a growl and it wasted no time in turning tail. All I saw was a golden blur heading away. He was eating up the ground, stretching his big muscular body full out, weaving through those trees like they weren't even there. It was enough to grab the bear's attention.

I tell you what, that bear was no idle loafer. He hit the trail no more than a few bounds behind the cat. I watched, peeking around my tree, as the bear's rolling, wagging rump wobbled in a full-bore run on out of sight and into the forest, the pair of them bawling and mewling.

Then I slipped on over to that string-wrapped tree, keeping an eye on the woods just in case, and what do you think I found? If you guessed a fish hook, you're only partly right.

I also found a fingertip-size chunk of pink meat that could be but one thing — the inside of that lion's cheek. No wonder it howled like a knife was being twisted straight into it. And it was speared neat as you please on the hook. I was about to wipe it off on the oak's bark, when I stopped myself and pondered, keeping an eye toward the trail.

That hunk of meat was still wet with the cat's spittle and I said to myself, "Now,

Maple Jack, doesn't that mountain lion owe you a fish supper after all?"

I unwrapped the line from the tree, quick like, and stuffed it in my breast pocket. I held up the hook with my strange new bait and started back toward the river — keeping an eye behind me all the way. In my other hand I held my club, just in case. I guess I had enough surprises for one day, thank you.

As I approached the river, my mouth commenced to water. Yes sir, I most definitely wanted to catch the fish that would be tempted by lion flesh. A big hog of a trout, to be sure, tucked under the bank, just waiting. As I thought on this, I admit I felt closer than ever to that mountain lion. I fancy we were both masters of escape. Tired as I was, I had to smile.

Then I heard a god-awful roaring from deep in the woods — no telling which beast it was. And I'll be danged if it didn't sound like they'd turned around.

I hurried my pace and as I broke through the riverbank brush I saw, just above me, a gleaming black barouche piloted by a scowling woman in a flowery hat.

O Unholy Night

A ROAMER AND MAPLE JACK STORY

Now I've been called a lot of things in my day — and I ain't claiming that some of 'em ain't true nor deserved (except when that shined-up fella in Reno called me a "flibbertigibbet." I ain't met a soul who can tell me what that means, but I reckon that dandy's sniffer is still smarting from our encounter). But I ain't never been called a liar, leastwise not to my face, though this here story might tempt you. But you best be careful — I'm quicker than I look.

Oh, but this is dry work. Pass me that handsome decanter off the mantel, will you? That's it, the one with the stopper carved like an enraged bear. That was a gift from a Blackfoot war chief. I helped his kin out of a tight spot with a big boar grizz one time. He claimed — the chief, not the grizz — that I was a god among men, and that not even bullets could stop me. I ain't in no hurry to put that to the test, but I appreciate the sentiment — and the whiskey.

Anyways, along about late November one year not long ago, right in the midst of a squall, I got a knock on the cabin door. Seems it was my chum, Roamer, dragging himself on in for a warm-up and to eat most of my winter-stored victuals, as usual.

I swear, the man is twice as wide as a bull bison and half as friendly looking. Big galoot don't talk much, don't say much when he does, but as the old saw goes, "Still waters run deep." And he's a deep pool, no mistake. But to look at him, you'd think he'd as soon peel your ears off, broil you over open flames, and chomp your crackled hide.

I could tell something was gnawing at him, so I waited until he had finished most of a mule-deer haunch and belched up a couple rounds of holiday cheer. Then I asked him what it was he was trying to figure out how to tell me, and he finally come out with it.

Seems that as the winter was shaping up to be a corker-and-a-half, a ranching acquaintance of his down in the lowlands of southern Wyoming had need of two line riders to lend a hand for the winter.

"Not a snowball's chance in hell," says I, all puffed up a like a holiday bird.

Now I've done my fair share of line riding — nursemaiding a bunch of shivering dogies, all the while living in a tiny shack with no heat and a whole lot of mice. It's lonely, low-paying work, the sort young, green cowpokes are best suited to. But I suspect Roamer, who picks up strays and causes and obligations like a hangdog hound draws flies and fleas, had not so much offered a helping hand as volunteered us both for the task.

Next thing I knew, he'd all but notched-and-nailed the deal: "You'd be doing pretty much what you do here anyway. I'm told the line cabin is decent, all done up to accommodate a half-dozen men in high custom. Rancher's wife comes from money back east."

"Hmm," says I, pulling on the jug and considering, pipe in my mouth and a blaze crackling by my feet. Truth be told, I had a notion such a distraction might be a good thing for me. Beat the feathers out of staying holed up in my cabin. Part that I didn't like was spending Christmas out on some strange range. But if Roamer was along, and a jug or three of the cheer, I reckoned it might not be so bad.

Oh, but I had no idea how wrong I would be. . . .

419

■ ■ ■ ■

Our traveling weather coming on down from my place high in the Beartooths of Montana Territory was decent for so late in the year. We stopped off at Punkin Weeder's place — he runs a dugout mercantile along the banks of the Snake.

Every spring, when the water's up, he's bobbing and swimming and cursing and blaming everybody and everything under and above heaven for his misfortunes and woes.

But once the waters drain, he's right back at it, drying out his wares and bubbling up the best popskull this side of hell. I also needed a sackful of tobacco twists. I'm partial to the riverboat rope — it's black as sin and smells like Methuselah's armpits, but it will keep lit in a stiff wind.

Roamer, he don't require much. He'll sample a pipe now and again. And drizzle whiskey into his gullet and he'll go on for hours in all manner of foreign tongue — he says they're real ones, too. But as often, he'll wedge his big, hard face in a book when he's not working. I read a bit now and again myself, but it mystifies me how that man can end up wandering lost inside a big old book like *The Odyssey*. He's forever rummaging in that one. Says it speaks to him.

I told him you want something that'll speak to you, ladle up a bowl full of Maple Jack's Midnight Special Double-Barrel Whistle Berries. Hell, they're good for a full-blown conversation that'll stretch right into next week.

Another day or so and we made it to the ranch and commenced to pack up what we'd need for a few months wet-nursing a bunch of homesick beeves. We didn't dally, much as I'd have liked to — they got themselves a decent cook and I am partial to well-prepared food. But it was already late in the season, and the ranch owner kept on and on about the hard winter coming, so we headed out.

Wasn't but a week after we settled in that the snow commenced. There was still plenty of grazing ground for them, especially on the flats where the wind whistled through hard enough at times to peel the hair off a horse's hide. (You laugh, but I've seen it happen.) But it went on and on, and before we knew it we had a couple of feet of snow on the ground. And then we were staring dead ahead at Christmas.

I am used to snow and lots of it, living as I do higher than most mortal men can stand, but the big weather we were getting, and without letup, caused us no little concern for the cattle. Somehow, we were coping with it.

Then, before we knew it, we got hit with another brute of a storm. Started falling early on the day before Christmas Eve and kept right on. Christmas Eve morning, we saddled up our heartiest mounts — me on my ornery mule, Ol' Mossback, and Roamer on his massive Percheron cross, Tiny Boy — and figured that we'd be back to the cabin by that night.

If only we had known what was about to happen, we would have dug a path for the home ranch, gathered what few pennies we were owed, then skedaddled for parts unknown — anywhere but on that wind-stripped, barren plain.

But we are nothing if not men of our words, so we kept on with the task at hand. We fortified ourselves with the knowledge that a bubbling venison stew, thick dumplings, a few jugs of shine and twists of tobacco, and a warm fire were all waiting for us back at the cabin.

As the day progressed, however, so did the snowfall. And with it, gusting winds and sinking temperatures the likes of which I'd not seen in years. We got ourselves turned around, righted our course, got turned around again, and managed to do so a few more times during the afternoon.

It wasn't good. Not good at all. For the past few hours, we'd roped and dragged countless dead or nearly dead animals out of drifts. But really, there was nowhere for the live ones to go except back in another drift, which, being cows, they promptly did.

We tried to get a tally on just how many beeves we lost to the blizzard that had no end, as I'd come to think of it. But all we managed to do was get more and more lost.

Throughout the day the wind and snow, incredible as it seemed, increased. We'd taken to the ground, leading our mounts, reins wrapped around mittened hands, trying to break through the thigh-deep, stiff-topped drifts that swelled before us.

Each new gust of icy wind peeled another layer of skin off Ol' Mossy's hide, and left me breathless. I couldn't recall ever having breathed, in fact.

"Roamer!" I bellowed my friend's name into the maw of the storm. It was sometime in the afternoon, still light, but that was about all I could tell through the scrim of ice beading my eyelashes, and stiffening my beard and moustache into a rock-hard mass on my face. Felt like my head was twice its normal weight.

I was about to bellow his name again when something slapped me on the bean. I looked around — or tried to — and there was my big friend, not a foot from me. He'd tossed the end of his lariat to me.

"Tie it off to your saddle horn!"

"What?"

"So we don't lose each other!"

I nodded and dallied it — not an easy task with hands number than clubs of wood in my snow-clogged mittens.

Too late, we considered turning back. But when we tried to orient ourselves on this wide, flat valley between ranges, we found ourselves not knowing which direction to head.

I tried to get a leg up and over on my raggedy breathing whilst I chewed the icicles on my moustache and saw Roamer doing the same — a trait we share when we're ruminating on a thing. 'Course, there wasn't much use in thinking, since the world around us had turned white and cold with snow and ice crystals and one hell of a stiff wind.

Both me and Roamer knew what it was we were facing, we just didn't want to admit it. A night out in this, with no idea where the cabin might be, would all but cook our goose.

I looked behind us again, but even the tracks we'd just made had nearly filled in with the blowing white stuff. The animals were beyond exhaustion and I wasn't too far behind.

Roamer, he's a big boy, and a damn sight younger than me, too. I expected he'd hang on a good while longer, outlast us all, me and the beasts. But I knew, too, that he'd spend his last breath trying to save us all. Fool kid.

Ol' Mossback shuddered and pitched forward, wedging himself into the drift before us. His backside stayed upright and his ribcage worked like a smithy's bellows. It seemed the final nail in the coffin lid.

"Sure as hell hate to end it all like this!" I shouted as much for myself as for Mossy, unsure if Roamer was within earshot.

Now, the wind was blowing at a pretty good clip, for sure, but when Roamer wants to empty his lungs, by God, the man will be heard.

"You quitting on me, old man? You wanna end up as wolf grub in a snowdrift, you be my guest."

I've been called a load of things in my day, most of them not safe for print (even if they were, I'd not know how to spell them), but "old man" ain't something I like to hear. I didn't return fire, but I did double my efforts and fairly dragged Mossy through that biggest of drifts facing us. And then I stopped flat dead.

Or rather I was stopped by something — a wall. My knee hit first, then my forehead hit with a *whump!* I thought maybe the drift had thickened into an ice wall. I dropped back, wagged my head, and Ol' Mossback did the same.

I squinted at it, bent forward, and saw no ice wall. It was dark in color, and hard, but giving, too, like wood. I pounded on it, then shouted to Roamer and yanked on the rope connecting us.

"Line camp!" I shouted. "I found the camp!"

Roamer reached out and touched it as gentle as a kitten, then harder until he punched it with the back of his hand.

"It's not possible. We're nowhere near camp!" His shouts barely reached me.

When you're as stumble-blind lost as we were, does it really matter if you think you're one place then find you are someplace else? "Stop complaining and help me find the door!"

While we scrabbled around the building

trying to find some way in, I had to admit old Roamer was right — even though we were good and lost, there was no way we had made it back around to the camp. We'd been out on the flats when the wind picked up, and there had been no gullies in sight that looked as if they would keep a building hid.

Side by side, we slowly worked our way around the building's wall, just inches from our sniffers. It was too long to be a line camp, and I hadn't felt a window yet. From the long, low shape of it, I guessed it was an old abandoned homestead. I reached up and felt the jutting overhand of a roof's edge. At least it had a roof. Now we just needed to figure out a way to get in the thing.

"Any luck?" said Roamer.

Same thing I was about to ask him. "Naw, not yet." And if I had known what was in store for us, I would have gladly kept right on clawing my way through the snowdrifts until I seized up tighter'n a sun-shrunk pelt.

But I didn't, and I'll regret it past the moment of my last drawn breath.

Roamer found an open doorway. We crowded to it and pushed on through a last stiff-peaked drift. Once we were in, we found it was a lean-to that cut much of the wind, wide enough for two mounts, and deep enough that we could all crowd in there.

We tied the beasts to what had once been an old hayrack, and that still contained dusty hay unfit for eating, but would prove useful in building a fire.

Bad as the weather was, the animals took a bit of coaxing to wedge in there. Once in, they weren't keen on staying. Mossback looked agitated, so I gave him a talking to. "You want to go back out there, Mossy, you be my guest. But don't come crying to me when you end up froze solid upside down in a drift." I don't know as my talk did much good, but then again he didn't head for the door, neither.

Tiny Boy stood nickering and blowing, nerved up to beat the band. We figured it was all that work we'd put them through. Ha, I say.

After a minute of slowing our own hard breathing, Roamer said, "This can't be all of it. There has to be a way inside."

We re-rigged the lariat and, leaving the beasts, we groped our way back into the blowing, freezing storm. Icy pellets drove at us, blinded us, and forced us to fumble along, noses pressed to the wall while we scrabbled for sign of entry.

"Door!" yelled Roamer, but his voice gasped, his teeth knocking together like rocks in a spring freshet.

"Dig, boy. We got to get in there."

We went at it, but it was slow going, pawing as we did with arms so stiff we couldn't do much more than use them to push at the drifted snow. Finally we managed to move enough that Roamer wedged one of his sizable pins into the gap. Soon, we were both inside.

It was cold and dark and still, and it smelled like dust. But at least it was out of the wind. I heard our breathing, still hard but slowing. It took a full minute before my eyeballs thawed enough to let me see just what it was we'd climbed into.

"Jack, look . . ." Roamer's voice was a chattery thing and I knew he had to get warm soon. I wasn't much better, but I leaned toward what he was rapping on. It was a table beside the door. "A lamp."

And by God, if he wasn't right. Roamer fumbled with the glass globe until he managed to raise it.

"Crank the wick," I said between teeth chatters. "Matches in my pocket . . ." I worked like the devil himself was chasing me, but once I tugged the mitten off my right hand, I could not get my fingers to do my bidding.

I must have dropped a half-dozen matches on the floor before I was able to hold onto one. It took forever to light the thing, then it went out. I snapped two more when a small flame finally danced into being right before our begging eyes.

With both hands trembling, I managed to hold the burning match to the stub of wick Roamer had coaxed upward. It sparked, danced, nearly went out, then with sudden hunger, burst into brilliance as it met the ancient oil seeping up the wick from the reservoir.

Never have two men been so pleased with their efforts as we were with that warming circle of lamp glow. For long, long minutes all we could do was stand before it, raw hands extended, shaking with bone-deep cold, our breath still pluming out like smoke from locomotives churning up steep grades.

"We have to get ourselves a real blaze going," I said, not wanting to leave the meager giver of warmth, "or we're sunk before we float."

Roamer nodded and lifted the lamp. We made our way, one step at a time, into the dark room. To our left, against what we took to be the back wall, sat a stone fireplace, but no stacked wood. We turned from the fireplace and Roamer held up the lamp. What we saw was one of the most confusing things I have ever seen.

Laid out before us was what looked at first glance to have been a home. It was filled with furniture, and as we slowly walked forward, we marveled at the inexplicable nature of what it was we'd found. It could not be a stage stop as it was in the midst of a barren place between ranges — ain't no way a body had reason to be there with intention.

I have been in a fair number of odd situations in my life, and maybe one day I'll get around to telling of all of them, but until then, you stay satisfied with this one, you insolent pup, and pass me the jug.

But I'll tell you, this one sits atop the heap, no questions asked. Because in short order we found out what that building was — and it wasn't some old sodbuster's home nor a stage stop, but a full-bore gambling parlor and saloon. In the middle of a place it had no right to be. I kid you not.

Our little lamp revealed several round, dust-covered, baize-top gambling tables all laid out with stacks of chips and cards fanned and strewn, as if in the midst of being used. And there were bottles of whiskey and glasses, too.

For some reason, not me nor Roamer had the urge to test the strength of what promised to be an aged and fiery liquid. And if I ain't tryin' it, you know something's not setting right with me.

We poked around the long room. The far back wall gave us another shock. Running the entire width of the building was a fine looking bar, an old brass rail down low for a drinking man's boots to rest on.

Behind the bar stood the expected assortment of bottles, a clouded mirror, and a pair of nearly lifesize paintings of women of ill repute. It is possible we held the lamp up and inspected them a bit longer than was necessary, given our situation, though purely for curiosity's sake. Might be they could provide us with clues as to what the place was.

Roamer's big, low voice, less chattery than before, cut into the gloom. "You've been around this country for a long time, right, Maple Jack?"

I could have been offended by his question, but I knew what he was driving at. "Yep," I said. "I have. Beginning to think it's been too long."

"You ever recall hearing of a saloon anywhere near here?"

I didn't need to mull that over, the answer was no, plain and simple. But how do you admit such a thing when you are standing in the very middle of the thing you know should not exist?

"Naw, I can't recall such a thing. But we got bigger fish to fry, boy. It's time to put that fireplace to use, elsewise we're going to be in sorrier shape than we already are."

In short order we had a fine pile of wood, especially with Roamer on the go. By God, but that boy can smash things apart when the mood takes him. In truth, the activity felt good, getting our blood pumping as we reduced a couple of chairs and a table down to short chunks of wood. Given the amount of dust and lack of sign of anybody about the place, I doubted anyone would object to the destruction.

It wasn't long before flames hopped and that old dry wood popped and sparks shot up and outward from the stone fireplace. We crowded the fire so close our clothes started stinking and smoking. With the heat, we gained back some of our own temperaments. I looked over at Roamer and his homely head was as red as mine felt. We smiled, nodded, not needing to say any more than the heat could offer, our faces bent to the flames.

I was about to suggest we bring the animals in when someone behind us shouted, "Hey! Hey there!"

We both spun and stood, our backsides to the fire, our stuttering breathing and the snapping of the greedy flames the only sounds.

Finally, in a whisper, Roamer said, "You . . . you heard something, too."

It wasn't a question so much as it was his way of making sure he wasn't as buggy as I felt.

"Yeh." It was the only word I could muster.

From where the bar stood at the far end of the room, we heard a sliding sound, then a clinking, and an unseen man laughed. But it was an echo of a laugh, the sound something makes when you drop it down a long mine shaft or a deep well, and it clips against things all the way down.

Roamer checked his sidearm and I followed suit. He hoisted the little oil lamp again and we moved side by side toward the back of the room. Our little light parted the dark ahead, and we gained a pinch of confidence and warmth from the blazing fire at our backs.

We reached the bar and Roamer nodded to the left. "I heard it from this way."

"No," I said. "Definitely from over there." I nodded toward the right. And so we each ended up looking in opposite directions. And I saw more than I expected. I am willing to admit that I may have yelped.

Roamer grabbed my arm. "Jack?"

"Over there," I nodded once again toward the far back right corner. "I . . . I seen a barkeep. I swear it! Had sleeve garters, bald head, moustaches." I looked at Roamer, "And he stared right at me and smiled. Then he wasn't there."

"What do you mean, 'wasn't there'?"

I rasped a trembling hand across my face. "I mean what I say and I say what I mean — he just up and disappeared."

"You want to know what I think?"

"Don't I always, boy?"

"I think somebody's playing games with us, Jack." Only his voice didn't sound half as funny as he meant it to.

We backed toward the fireplace and its still-crackling blaze.

"Throw more wood on that thing."

"We're nearly out."

"Then let's bust up some more chairs. I don't like much of what's going on here, nor can I explain it. But I'll be jiggered if we ain't going to have light to see what it is we're dealing with."

Roamer reached out and dragged a table back toward us. "What if we aren't able to see just what it is we are dealing with?"

"I swear, if you weren't so big, I'd consider taking a round or two out of you. Just for being insolent." I stirred the flames, keeping as much of me angled toward the fire as possible while still looking toward the shadowy room. "How anyone as big as you can be as annoying as you are is beyond me."

For the first time in what seemed days, Roamer laughed his low rumbly sound, like river rocks clunking together underwater. Hearing him almost made me want to laugh, too. Almost.

And then, from beyond our fire's glow, sounds began to mingle with the popping and snapping of the dry wood burning. The sounds grew louder until they paused us both. We looked at each other, drew our sidearms, and butted up to the fire once again, our sniffers facing the gloom.

Seemed like, as the room warmed, the sounds got louder, almost like the place was coming alive around us. I heard poker chips tumbling and plinking against each other, bottles clinking against glasses, murmuring voices rising and falling, laughing and talking.

It was as if we'd walked into a busy saloon in any old busted-down cow town all over the West. Only difference was we weren't in any old cow town, we were stuck out in the middle of a blizzard in the middle of nowhere, Wyoming Territory.

"Oh Lord," I whispered, and a woman giggled just behind us.

We spun, close as ever to firing our guns, but there was nothing there. Just our fireplace, blazing away. I looked at Roamer and he was sweating, too.

"You smell that?" he whispered.

"Well excuse me, mister. But a man can't help how he reacts in a situation such as this."

"No, I'm talking about cigars. I smell them. Maybe a pipe, too."

And by God if he wasn't right. But neither of us saw smoke hanging in the air.

Another laugh bubbled up, off to the side, with more voices raised. We spun, saw nothing. The laughter, as if at our expense, came at us again, but from a different dark corner. We backed to the fire, the shadows acting tetchy, jumping and drawing out like wet wool wherever we looked.

We made it to the fireplace and managed to drag more chairs and tables with us. It seemed the warmer we made the room the more noises and smells came at us. But what else could we do?

"I have to go for Mossback and Tiny Boy," said Roamer. And he crept back to the door we'd come in through — the only one we'd found in the place. But it was wedged shut.

Try as he might, the big man couldn't budge it. And considering his size and power, that's saying something. He looked at me with anger and frustration in his eyes. I didn't want to leave the fire, but I made my way over to the door, the sounds and smells of the room louder than ever.

We both heaved and hoed on that door, but she was stuck fast. I like to believe it was the storm that froze it shut, but given everything happening inside that strange place, I knew I was wrong.

We hoped the animals were faring better than we were. At least they were in a lean-to out of the wind.

We finally gave up on the door and made our way back to the fireplace. I tossed on more wood while Roamer busted up another chair and piled the rest of the gathered furniture in front of us, like a berm to keep away whatever it was that shared the place with us.

Roamer glanced at me. "You don't look so good, Jack."

If I looked as rough as he did, we were both in a world of hurt. His cheeks were frostbit, his eyes wide as teacups, and that smile he'd pasted on looked like something an undertaker had worked up.

All night long we stayed that way, moving as little as possible except to bust up more furniture. Every time we tried to speak, the noises in the room grew louder, drowned us out to the point where we ended up silent and staring, and got less than a wink of sleep between us.

When it seemed like forever came and went, we saw fingers of gray light poke through the gaps in the door's boards. And what's more, as the wood supply ran low, so did the room's sounds grow quieter.

The poker chips stopped plinking, the glasses and bottles no longer met with a clink, the voices began to fade, first to whisper levels, then they pinched off altogether. Soon, even the last whiff of cigar smoke drifted away.

The biggest relief was that we no longer heard the howling of the wind outside. We didn't say a thing to each other as we headed for the door. Roamer gave her a tug, both of us knowing she'd be stuck fast and we'd have to bust our way out. But imagine our surprise when the flimsy old thing gave way and swung inward to reveal a wall of hard-packed snow.

We didn't care. We dug like prairie dogs and soon we were out, breathing hard and looking all about us.

It was as we expected — the storm had gone elsewhere. And though we were surrounded by a sea of stiff peaks of snow, drifted like sand dunes or frozen ocean waves, we were at least free and alive.

As we stood pulling in deep draughts of chill winter air, Roamer turned to me and said, "A happy Christmas to you, Jack."

I was confused, not sure what it was he was driving at. Then it occurred to me that yes, sir, it was indeed Christmas Day.

I closed my eyes and smiled. "And to you, too, boy. Many happy returns."

There we were, two fools atop a snow drift on Christmas morning, smiling and liking the warmth of the rising sun on our faces.

"Let's get our beasts and bust a trail out of here," I said, suddenly filled with an urge to make tracks. "Now that I can see where we're at, I believe that if we head due northwest for a couple of hours, we should make it back to camp. The stew'll be cold, but if there's one thing we know how to do it's make a fire."

I meant it to be a little joke, but it fell flat.

We made our way around the outside of the building to the lean-to and dug our way in. The space was cold, but mostly free of snow. It had drifted across the opening but not far into the makeshift stable.

I was about to call out to Ol' Mossback and Tiny Boy when we saw they weren't there. From behind us more sunlight slanted into the space, and lit it well. There at our feet, sprawled in the old, dusty hay, were the rib, hip, and skull bones of two animals, a horse and a mule, likely.

But not freshly killed.

They were the racks of animals long dead, beasts neglected and forgotten. The bones, pitted and pocked with age, bore the discoloration only long, dry years can bring. Patches of dusty hair clung to the skulls, dried and shrunken into the eye sockets. Harness buckles were still visible, attached to withered strands of what had once been leather.

Near the rib cage of each beast lay curled, puckered wings — the remnants of saddles. Tarnished conchos told me I was looking at my own saddle, and so, at Ol' Mossback beneath. Beside me, Roamer was silent as he stared at what had been his big and trusted friend, Tiny Boy. His eyes shone with silent tears. Roamer takes a beast's death hard, as we all should.

It was me who broke the spell. "Mossy? Tiny? Roamer, how long were we — ?"

But I couldn't finish the thought. None of it made a lick of sense. What we were seeing just could not be.

Roamer only shook his head. Finally, in a cracking voice he said, "Jack, we better go — anywhere but here."

I expect he felt the same creeping feeling I did, like when you wake up in the desert to see a rattler flicking its tongue a couple of inches from your face. Leaving quick was the smartest thing we could do. We legged it as hard and as fast as we could from that foul place.

We stopped once, and looked back as we gathered our wind. Though the snow-covered land all around was flat, and the two lines of holes we'd punched with our feet were visible from where we'd started to where we then stood, we saw no sign of the phantom saloon. It just plain wasn't there.

"Let's move, Jack."

For once I had nothing more to add.

We tramped for three hours more, pretty near steady, before we ended up at that line camp. And when we got in there, we fed the stove 'til she glowed cherry red, then we bubbled that stew, and tugged the jug. And do you know, tired as we were, it still took us most of that day to give in to a slumber neither of us particularly wanted.

I'll wager we were each thinking of Ol' Mossback and Tiny Boy, wondering how long their sleep had been.

A few years have passed since all that happened to us, and to this day I cannot explain it. I will say that since then, I feel older somehow, as if I'd been hoodwinked and missed out on a whole bunch of living. Like there's some long fog of time in my memory. I ain't asked yet if Roamer feels the same.

I had occasion a few seasons back to pass back down into that country, and I tell you what — I chose not to. I traveled a route through the mountains that skirted that hellish place by a good hundred miles. Even though it was high summer, the very last thing on God's green earth I wanted to see was an old saloon where there shouldn't be anything but grass and sage.

But that Roamer, as I said, he's a bookish man, and he can't let go of a thing as easy as me. It's in his nature to poke and prod until whatever it is he's annoying rears up and sinks a couple of fangs into him. That curious sniffer of his will get him into a world of hurt one day, mark my words.

On his most recent visit up here, in between bites of venison steak and mountain
onions, he told me he went back out there
and tried to find that saloon. Can you
imagine?

I got so worked up at the thought of it, I
left off the rest of my grub (which he
finished for me . . . how thoughtful of him),
and I had to tug on the jug a time or three,
just to settle my jumping nerves.

I finally worked up the courage to ask him
what he found. And do you know what the
old bookmaster said? That there wasn't
nothing there. That it was "one of those rare
things in life with no explanation."

But Roamer's wrong. There is an explanation, and I know exactly who has the answer:
Old Scratch himself. But until I'm ready to
stump off into the sunset, I ain't in no rush
to meet that evil bastard.

It's coming up on Christmas again, and
while it's still one of my favorite times of
the year, it has been forever tainted for me
by that long-ago long night. Even extra pulls
on the Christmas jug don't seem to help all
that much — but that don't stop Ol' Maple
Jack from trying.

ACKNOWLEDGEMENTS

"Trouble at Tall Pine" appears here for the first time.

"Snows of Montana" first appeared in *Where Legends Ride,* Express Westerns, 2007.

"Half a Pig" first appeared in *A Fistful of Legends,* Express Westerns, 2009.

"Been a Long Time" first appeared in *Time-shares,* DAW Books, 2010.

"Scourge of the Spoils" first appeared in *Steampunk'd,* DAW Books, 2010.

"The Witch Hole" first appeared in *How the West Was Weird, Volume II,* PulpWork Press, 2011.

"Maple Jack and the Christmas Kid" first

appeared in *Christmas Campfire Companion,* Port Yonder Press, 2011.

"Catch as Catch Can" first appeared in *The Traditional West,* Western Fictioneers, 2011.

"Just Once" first appeared in *Cactus Country, Volume 1,* High Hill Press, 2011.

"Lost Valley of the Skoocoom" first appeared in *Beat to a Pulp: Round 2,* Beat to a Pulp Books, 2012.

"O Unholy Night" first appeared in *Six-Guns and Slay Bells,* Western Fictioneers, 2012.

"Pay the Ferryman" first appeared in *Livin' on Jacks and Queens,* Piccadilly Publishing, 2013.

"A Small Thing" first appeared in *The Trading Post,* Five Star Publishing, 2018.

"Snake Farm" first appeared in *The Untamed West,* Western Fictioneers, 2018.

"Lucky Tam" first appeared in *Moving Foreword,* BenBella Books, 2019.

"Peaches" first appeared in *The Spoilt Quilt,*

Five Star Publishing, 2019.

"The Last Drop" first appeared in *Why Cows Need Cowboys,* TwoDot, 2021.

"Bloodline" first appeared in *Fire Mountain,* Five Star Publishing, 2021.

ABOUT THE AUTHOR

Matthew P. Mayo is an award-winning author of novels, short stories, and poetry. He roves the byways of the world with his wife, photographer Jennifer Smith-Mayo, and their trusty pup, Miss Tess, in search of hot coffee and high adventure. For more information, drop by Matthew's website at MatthewMayo.com.

Printed in the USA
CPSIA information can be obtained
at www.ICGtesting.com
JSHW020436040324
58327JS00003B/3

9 781432 898106